RICK

LIGHTHOUSE SECURITY INVESTIGATION WEST COAST

MARYANN JORDAN

Author's Note

Please remember that this is a work of fiction. I have lived in numerous states as well as overseas, but for the last thirty years have called Virginia my home. I often choose to use fictional city names with some geographical accuracies.

These fictionally named cities allow me to use my creativity and not feel constricted by attempting to accurately portray the areas.

It is my hope that my readers will allow me this creative license and understand my fictional world.

I also do quite a bit of research on my books and try to write on subjects with accuracy. There will always be points where creative license will be used in order to create scenes or plots.

Rick (Lighthouse Security Investigation West Coast) Copyright 2022

All rights reserved. No part of this book may be reproduced or transmitted in any form or by any means, electronic or mechanical, including photocopying, recording, or by any information storage and retrieval system without the written permission of the author, except where permitted by law.

If you are reading this book and did not purchase it, then you are reading an illegal pirated copy. If you would be concerned about working for no pay, then please respect the author's work! Make sure that you are only reading a copy that has been officially released by the author.

This book is a work of fiction. Names, characters, places, and incidents are either products of the author's imagination or are used fictitiously. Any resemblance to actual persons, living or dead, events, or locales is entirely coincidental.

Cover: Graphics by Stacy

ISBN ebook: 978-1-956588-14-9

ISBN print: 978-1-956588-28-6

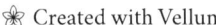 Created with Vellum

1

CAIRO, EGYPT

Abbie Blake opened her eyes, blinking as the hazy dawn's light started to streak through the lacy cotton sheers that hung over her windows. She stretched, climbing from the bed as the Fajr prayer calls sounded out from the nearby mosque.

Walking over to the window, she gently pulled the sheers to the side, her gaze falling onto Mustafa, her gardener, wearing his cream-colored galabeya, as he knelt on his prayer rug in the middle of her villa's garden.

Smiling, she lifted her face and breathed in deeply, the familiar scents wafting past. Baking bread. Flowers curling up the trellises. The rich coffee coming from her kitchen, which she knew would be accompanied by eggs and ful, the stewed seasoned fava beans.

Padding into her bathroom, she quickly showered and dressed for the day. She kept her makeup light but dried her long hair before pulling the dark tresses into a low ponytail.

Walking down the tiled stairs, she appreciated her housing, knowing it was small by American standards but huge to many locals. The two bedrooms upstairs shared a bathroom, and downstairs was a small living room, a nook with room for a dining table, and an open kitchen. Like many of the villas in Ma'adi, she had a small but beautiful garden filled with lush grass, palms, shrubs, and an abundance of flowers, all behind a tall wall. *My very own oasis.*

Offering her a good morning greeting, she called out, "As-salaam, Sabah," while smiling at the petite woman standing in her kitchen. Her housekeeper was at the stove, stirring a pot.

Wearing a long blue skirt with a white blouse and her dark hair pulled up in a bun and covered in a hijab, Sabah looked over her shoulder and smiled. "As-salaam." She dipped the beans onto a plate, then loaded it with bread and eggs before setting it on the table. "Here, eat. Eat. I'll get coffee."

It didn't take long to finish her breakfast, and the plates were whisked away before she had a chance to take them to the sink. Sabah and Mustafa had been with her for several years, essentially coming with the villa. Offering her thanks for the meal, she hurried back upstairs to finish getting ready for her workday.

As she stepped out into the garden, Mustafa stopped raking and turned to greet her. The lines emanating from his eyes could have come from years of working in the sun, making it impossible to guess his age. His hair and beard were lightly streaked with gray, and his spine was slightly bent as he leaned on his rake. His galabeya was stained with dirt, and she could see he'd already spent time weeding this morning. With his own version of good morning, he dipped his chin and called out, "Naharak saa'id, Ms. Blake."

"Good morning," she returned, meeting his smile with one of her own while tossing her hand upward in a wave as she walked through the wrought-iron gate and onto the residential street. Heaving a sigh, she was ready for her least favorite part of the day. Getting to work was sometimes a logistical nightmare.

Fighting to board the crowded, hot train that broke down as often as it worked, she accepted that she'd never get a seat and always had to stand while the masses packed in around her. Catching a cab was sometimes impossible, but when necessary, it often involved placing her life in the hands of someone who drove in any direction necessary to get to the destination, even if that included wrong ways and on sidewalks. And if the pedestrians didn't get out of the way, they could become collateral damage. It wouldn't be the first time she'd seen that happen.

Finally, alighting from the train, she joined the masses that swept through the open doors and onto the sidewalks. Walking briskly down the block to where she worked, she entered the next crowd, making her way to the security checkpoint of the American Embassy. It didn't matter if the guards knew who she was. Protocol and identification were always followed and needed.

Finally, her heels clicked along the tile floor in a rapid staccato as she hurried toward her office buried deep amongst a labyrinth of other offices. She hated being late for work. Glancing at the clock on the painted concrete wall in the hall, she knew she wasn't technically late. But she was a believer in being early.

Careful not to slosh the cup of strong coffee in her hand, she had to concede that the wait at the coffee station was necessary, even if it added a few minutes.

Unlocking her door, she stepped inside her small, windowless office. She placed her cup on her desk before hanging her scarf onto the back of the door. Firing up her computer, she sat at her desk, logged in, and began going through the security steps necessary to start her day's work.

Footsteps were heard just outside her office, and she looked up to see her boss. Smiling, she greeted, "Good morning, Michael."

Michael Hawn was a civilian contractor with the US Army at the embassy, and she was his gopher— basic office work and running errands. He had a military assistant to handle the secure information, so her tasks for Michael were more mundane.

"Good morning, Abbie." With a nod, he headed into his office, and she started on the tasks that would fill her day. One of the perks of her office being so buried meant she was never interrupted by others just stopping by to chat. But that was fine with her… she preferred solitude while working.

The morning hours passed quickly, and soon, she was ready for lunch. After securing her computer and locking her office door, she made her way to the first floor, across the stone courtyard made more attractive by large potted palm trees. Entering the cafeteria, she slogged through the line, then turned and headed to a table where several women she knew had gathered.

They were all pleasant to spend time with, but only one was a real friend. Abbie never enjoyed the small talk that others seemed to live for. But soft-spoken Mary Hayes was easy to spend time with. She worked as an entry-level data analyst for the State Department.

Lunch passed quickly enough, and she and Mary were walking back across the courtyard. "Have you got any plans this weekend?" Mary asked.

"No, not really. I'll probably do my usual. Stay in, read a book, and go shopping."

Mary chuckled, shaking her head. "We should go on a tour. Anything to get out and do something."

"That's true. Although, the office you work in is really nice. You even have a window," she joked.

"Working as a data analyst is so much better than my last job where I was just a gopher—" Mary winced, scrunching her nose. "Oops. Sorry."

Abbie laughed and shook her head. "No worries. There are a lot worse jobs I could do."

With plans to get together over the weekend, Abbie took the elevator back up to the sixth floor. Once again settled into her office, she rebooted her computers and got back to work.

A knock on her door had her look up to see the smiling face of the young Army lieutenant assigned to assist Michael. "Hey, Sam."

"Hey, Abbie. How's it going?"

"I'm good. What do you need?"

Laughing, he shrugged. "Can't I just pop in for your company?"

Lifting a brow, she pretend-glared. "I hardly think you need a distraction from your work."

"Hey, working with you is the best distraction. Anyway, I needed to let you know that you've got a meeting with Michael at fifteen hundred hours."

"Thank you." She waited until he left and then stood quickly, having just enough time to race to the ladies' room before walking directly into Michael's utilitarian office that only Sam currently occupied. He nodded toward her, then stood and walked to a panel behind Michael's desk. Sliding it open, she slipped through, hearing it close behind her. Quickly going up one floor, she knocked once and then opened the door, walking into the well-appointed office.

A heavy desk in front of bookcases and a credenza, all made of heavy wood, centered on one side of the office. A polished wooden table surrounded by padded leather chairs was on the other side of the room. Michael sat in one of the chairs and nodded toward her as she moved to another chair in the office of the CIA station chief operational officer.

Tom Olsen. In his fifties, he was trim and fit with thick silver hair and blue eyes she knew didn't miss anything. He worked on the seventh floor. The floor where the elevators would open to a military guard that only gave passage to step off the elevator if the person wanting access was allowed. She had that access but not to take the elevator. Not for a lowly State Department assistant.

At least, that was what almost everyone thought was her job. That was her cover.

The truth was she'd been a military intelligence captain in the US Army, having served in Afghanistan. Her specialty was geospatial and photogrammetry. Not a particularly romantic career, and she used to find that she could cause a conversation to come to a complete halt when she'd mentioned what she did for a living. And that was with others in the military who knew what the hell was going on.

Now, she'd been out of the military for a couple of years, having been recruited by the CIA. So to everyone else at the embassy, she was simply one of the State Department employees at the embassy and her assignment was with Michael. In truth, Tom Olsen was her boss. And Michael was his second in command, also CIA. And while Sam was actually an Army lieutenant, he was in military intelligence, assisting with the cover for Michael and Abbie.

"Good afternoon, Michael. Tom."

Tom nodded as well and indicated she should take a seat at the table. She sat in a chair opposite them at the table, her attention focused on the folder in front of him. Wasting no time, he flipped it open and slid it in front of her.

Eager to see the contents, she pulled out the papers of maps and blueprints. She scanned them, instantly analyzing the graphics. Pressing her lips together, she darted her gaze up to Tom. His face was impassive, and she fought to keep from rolling her eyes. She'd worked with him enough to know that his poker face would give away nothing.

"Is there any information you can give me?" she asked.

"Only that we obtained it as a record of interest. I want to know everything you can tell me about the location indicated."

If he had any more information, he would have given it to her. Tom didn't waste time when he wanted information. He'd give her what he could and then turn it over to her expertise.

"Yes, sir. I'll get right on it, but please remember, my month of leave is coming up soon," she said, standing.

"You're the best, Ms. Blake. That's why I stole you away from the Army," he quipped, also standing. "Do what you can before you take your leave, and then be ready to begin again when you return."

Leaving through the doorway she came through, she descended the stairs, entering the room where Sam grinned at her. He inclined his head toward the folder. "New assignment?"

"You know it." She was anxious to begin her analysis and didn't stop to elucidate. Sam was easygoing and never took offense, for which she was glad, hoping to keep their working relationship congenial. He'd once asked her out, but she'd politely turned down his invitation for a date. He was five years younger, and at times, it seemed more like ten. He definitely didn't lack female companionship.

Something about the brash young lieutenant occasionally got on her nerves. Maybe it was how he always seemed envious of her job duties and her relationship with Michael and Tom. He was one of the few who knew her cover and occasionally bristled at the reminder that she'd outranked him when she was on active duty and then courted by the CIA.

Settling back in her office, she turned on her computers, then scanned the images into her geo-imagery comparison software. This was her reality… a covert CIA career while pretending she was nothing more than an assistant's assistant. She snorted and shook her head. Her cover didn't matter to her—it was her true job that she loved even though others would consider it boring. *But here in Cairo?* She was beginning to long for the chance to return to the States.

Glancing at her clock, she'd barely started on the project when it was the end of the day, so she locked the folder into her office safe. With her scarf in her hand, she descended the elevator and walked out of the embassy along with many of the other staff members.

The city was teeming with masses of people, cars driving along the roads amongst buses, trams, and donkey carts, all seeming to move at the same time but not necessarily in the same direction. The old, monochromatic buildings around the embassy were all concrete high-rises, resembling many large downtown metropolises. Windows were small in the buildings to help keep them cool.

Abbie didn't cover her head when she left the embassy, not feeling the need in downtown Cairo as she moved along with the others heading to the train station. By the time she made her way to the train, she draped her scarf over her hair and wrapped the ends around her neck, tying it in the back. With her crossbody purse pressed against the front of her, she maneuvered into the subway car, squishing past others as she headed toward a group of Egyptian women, preferring to stand near them. She'd never had a problem while on public transportation but always played it smart. For a woman traveling alone, it made more sense to be with other women. Several of the Egyptian women smiled and nodded, murmuring their greetings, and she replied in kind, receiving more smiles.

What should have been a twenty-minute train ride stretched almost fifty minutes with multiple stops and unscheduled halts. The heat was oppressive, something she could never quite get used to. The smells of cologne, groceries carried in cloth bags, and unwashed bodies in the heat were familiar, although not welcome.

Finally getting off at her stop, she breathed easier as she made her way toward the tree-lined streets of Ma'adi. The suburban district south of Cairo was located on the east bank of the Nile. With a population of nearly one hundred thousand people, it was where many international expatriates and well-to-do Egyptians lived. It also served as the location of some smaller embassies, international schools, sporting clubs, and museums. Many of the US Embassy employees lived in apartments and villas throughout Ma'adi.

She walked along streets lined with two- and three-story shops, the scent of spices and cooked meat filling the air, making her stomach rumble. She came to a bridge overhead that was actually a flyover road.

Several Egyptian families lived in corrugated metal shacks underneath the bridge. It was a common cut-through, and as she walked along, she smiled and greeted the small children playing in the dirt path before greeting the mothers squatting near open fires, tending their food. She dug into her purse and pulled out a few coins, buying several loaves of naan, the traditional bread. The women would not have wanted a handout, but selling their loaves preserved their dignity, and in truth, Abbie loved the bread.

Arriving at her villa, she smiled as she walked through the gate. While the garden was lush with the colors of cornflowers, daisies, and myrtle, the floral scent of the jasmine made her feel as though she had a corner of paradise. Mustafa and Sabah were finished with their work and had already left for the evening. She enjoyed their company but preferred her solitude. Entering the house, she pulled off her scarf and relished the cool interior. The concrete villa had small windows that kept out the oppressive direct sunlight, a few with window air conditioners, and tall palms that offered shade.

She dropped her bag onto the wooden table and moved directly to the refrigerator. Filling a glass with the bottled water, she noted it was time to order more. The bottles were the safest way to ensure her drinking water was clean. She relished the cool liquid as it flowed down her throat, washing away the dust and grime she breathed in during her commute home.

She lifted the lid on the pot that Sabah had left on her counter, discovering the stuffed grape leaves. Sabah always filled a huge pot, saying it was easier to spend one day making them and then Abbie could have them for several days. She'd use lamb and lots of rice, knowing Abbie liked the fatter rolls. Dishing several onto a plate, she added the naan and sat at the table. Her meal was quickly finished, and while Sabah told her to leave the dishes for her to wash the next morning, Abbie never did.

Grabbing a bottle of wine and a glass, she walked out into the small garden and sat in the shade of a eucalyptus tree hidden behind the tall concrete wall. The sounds from the road outside began to fade, and as she sipped her wine, she relaxed.

In the peace of the evening, her mind drifted to the assignment she'd been given at work, then sighed. *Is this it for me? Work and then come home alone and spend my evenings thinking about work?* Before she had time to fall down that rabbit hole, her phone vibrated, jerking her away from her musings. Looking down, she grinned.

"William! How are you? Is everything okay with Sara?" Her brother was several years older, now living in Maine with his wife. He'd also served in the Army as a Delta but had gotten out several years ago and now worked for Lighthouse Security Investigations, an elite, private security firm. He'd met Sara in French Guiana when he'd rescued her after her kidnapping.

"Whoa, slow down, sis." He laughed. "Everything's okay. Sara's fine. We listened to the fetal heartbeat the other day, and the baby is fine."

"Oh, I'm so excited for you two!" With the time

difference, she knew it was the middle of the day for her brother and could hear voices in the background.

"Hey, Blake! Tell your sister she needs to come visit us!"

Everyone at LSI called him by his last name. "Yeah, *Blake*"—she laughed—"I think I do need to visit. Who is that, anyway?"

"Ignore him! That's Rank's brother, Rick."

She'd met Rank the last time she'd visited Maine. She now remembered that William had told her that Rick was a former SEAL who had joined LSI.

"I want to talk about your upcoming leave. Mom and Dad will fly out from California whenever you can manage to get a trip in. That way, you can see them and us at the same time."

"Oh God, that would be fabulous. What about Todd? Have you heard from him lately?" She was the baby of the family, William was the middle child, and Todd was her older brother, a career Marine.

"Not recently. We got a call off to him when we found out we were expecting, but we haven't talked to him since. I think Dad talked to him a few weeks ago."

"Well, if he could come home at the same time, that would be perfect. But I know the odds are pretty slim," she admitted.

"Yeah, you're probably right. I hate to call and run, but we're back at the compound. When you're here, you can talk to Mace some more—maybe lock down the chance to work here for LSI. Stay in touch, stay safe, and I'll talk to you soon."

"Love you, bro. Give Sara a hug from me," she said before they disconnected. Tossing her phone onto the small table next to her, she snagged her wineglass and drained the contents. She closed her eyes for a moment, letting a faint breeze blow over her. Her parents were still in California, although they had downsized from the large house where she and her brothers had been raised. William and Sara were in Maine. And Todd was still in Afghanistan, or at least that's where they thought he was. *And here I am in the Middle East, in the land of the pharaohs.*

She loved her job, loved to travel, and loved visiting new places and doing new things. But setting her wineglass back down on the table, her heart gave a little squeeze, and she wondered if something else was out there for her. Home. Family. Waking up next to someone who she loved, and they loved her. Maybe even having kids one day.

The last time she'd visited her brother, she'd met his boss, Mace Hanover. He'd been inquiring about her skills and wondered about her plans after her tour in Cairo ended. She'd been flattered and was interested in a possible job at LSI, but she had time on her CIA contract to make up her mind.

As the sun disappeared, she stood and grabbed her phone, empty wineglass, and the almost empty bottle of wine and headed inside her villa. *The future is out there, but right now, all I have is me. And that'll have to be good enough.*

Yet as she locked up her house and headed upstairs, she couldn't help but wonder how long it would be good enough.

A few evenings later, she and Mary sat under the

same shade tree in her garden. They dined on the stuffed grape leaves, chicken kebabs, naan, and salad until they were full, then moved to two cushioned chaise lounges near the jasmine and sipped wine as they relaxed.

"You look like a woman with a lot on your mind," Mary said.

She smiled, knowing it wasn't hard for Mary to see through her moods. Abbie had never surrounded herself with girlfriends. Her brothers' friends were always over, and then with ROTC in college, she was once again in a smaller female pool of people. And while female officers are in demand, she always felt the need to be better, smarter, harder, and tougher to succeed in a male-dominated environment. Now, she found working covert for the CIA equally demanding. After all, she could say very little to even a friend like Mary about what she did, having to pretend she was nothing more than a personal assistant.

She offered a vague yet truthful reply. "I guess I'm wondering how long I want to stay here."

"Tired of Cairo already?"

She shrugged. "I suppose."

"Well, you snagged this beautiful villa, so at least your downtime can be nice. You know what my apartment looks like. Sure, it's big, but I have two roommates!"

"That would drive me crazy. I love having my private time."

"When was the last time you went on a date? A real date?"

"Hey, I date," she protested, then scrunched her nose. Sighing, she shook her head. "Okay, I suppose it's been a while."

"Not since Chuck," Mary quipped.

"Well, cheating bastards hardly count," she retorted, refusing to give her last disastrous relationship more than a passing remembrance. "It's so hard to find someone and make it work."

Mary sighed and sipped more wine. "Yeah… I get it. It's hard. I get lonely. It seems like the guys I meet are interested in sex only. Or maybe dinner, dancing, and then sex. But I'd like to find someone special."

"Anyone at the university?"

Mary was taking a couple of classes at the local American university. Laughing, she sat up straight, cleared her throat, and spoke in a professorial voice. "Early archaeological sites discovered there was a town underneath Ma'adi, found in 3500 B.C., and that this lovely area we live in is an example of building activity that has destroyed some of the archaeologically significant sites." Mary looked over and grinned.

Abbie chuckled at the abrupt change in subject, shaking her head. "So you have been paying attention in your class."

"Oh yes. Believe it or not, Professor Adamson keeps my attention and not just because he's cute." Settling back in the chaise lounge, Mary sighed as she finished her wine. "But alas, he's married. It's so hard to really meet someone here."

Abbie nodded. She'd begun thinking more often about what she wanted out of life. The military and now the CIA offered her adventure, travel, and opportunities she wouldn't get elsewhere. *But is that enough?* It no longer felt that way. *Is it so terrible to wish for a happy ending? And can I find that working for LSI?* She'd only met a couple of her brother's coworkers but imagined that she would be happier in that environment and closer to family than she was now.

"Maybe I just miss my family," she finally said.

"You're going home for a visit soon, aren't you?"

A smile spread across her face as she nodded. Just the thought of being back in the United States and seeing her family made her feel lighter.

"Yes, and it might work out where I can see everyone without traveling so much. I talked to William, and he said that my parents would fly from California to Maine so I could see all of them at one time. And Todd may even be able to swing some leave to meet us there."

"How long will you be gone?"

"I've got almost a month, and I'm gonna take it all in Maine. My brother and his wife are expecting a baby, and they've invited me to stay with them. I can still travel and see other friends and do things, but I can use their place as my home base while there."

"Well, here's to happy trips home," Mary said, leaning over while holding up her wineglass.

Abbie clinked their glasses together, then settled back, letting the cool breeze and the scent of jasmine float over her.

Abbie sat on the plane a few weeks later, looking out the window. Just like every time she flew in and out of Cairo, she couldn't help but look down, first seeing the mass of buildings that she knew were crammed full of humanity. The buildings were the same color as the sandy desert that spread out on either side of Cairo, with a strip of the Nile running through the middle. The great pyramids and Sphinx were visible for only a moment, then everything fell away to a beige nothingness that filled the horizon as far as she could see.

She leaned back in her seat and popped in her earbuds for the soft music that would drown out the conversations around her. She'd given her findings on the images to Michael and Tom and received no feedback from either of them. Not that she'd expected it, but after spending days on an assignment, she couldn't help but wonder if she'd had any success.

She thought about her upcoming trip to Maine and smiled. Her parents and Todd were going to be there when she arrived. She decided for the first four or five days, she would just enjoy time with family and not leave her brother's house. Once her parents flew back to California, and Todd flew back to wherever he was stationed, her plans were fluid. Closing her eyes, she imagined walking through the woods. Hiking along the rocky coast. Maybe even taking a few days and going to Canada.

She'd vacillated about what to do with her career but finally decided to talk to Mace. She had no idea if Lighthouse Security Investigations still had a place for her and her skill set, but it would be foolish not to find out if it was a possibility while she was Stateside. *Maybe, just maybe, something new is out there for me.*

She looked out the window, the tan-colored horizon all she could see. And then, the world disappeared as the plane rose into the clouds. *And when I come back? Will it be to pack up or to stay?*

2

MAINE

The sunrise from the top of the lighthouse cast a glow over the waves crashing onto the rocky coast below. The three men stood leaning against the railing, steam from their coffee mugs rising into the early morning air.

"You won't get sunrises like this in California," Carson said, lifting his cup to his lips.

"No, but I'll get the sunsets," Rick replied, thinking that the West Coast sunsets he'd seen while serving in the Navy were the best anywhere. He darted a glance to the side to see Mace observing him with the same intensity he'd had in the military. Wishing the enigmatic boss at LSI would speak, he knew he had to be patient.

Mace had partnered with Carson Dyer, a former Special Forces and CIA operator, to set up LSI West Coast. Carson had come to Maine to have another meeting with Mace and had been open to talking to any Keepers who might want to transfer. Rick was the only one who'd approached them about the change. He loved his job but felt the need to start on the ground floor of something new. And helping to start a new LSI chapter out in California would give him the same opportunity that his brother had when Rank joined up with Mace here in Maine.

He held his breath, wondering what Mace would say. His boss was a big man with dark hair and scruff and could pin anyone with an intense eagle eye that would make a former SEAL squirm. And Rick respected the hell out of him.

Finally, Mace nodded. "Gonna miss you on my team, but I understand, Rick. Just like your brother helped me start LSI, you can do the same with Carson and LSI West Coast. There's something special about being at the beginning of a new and undoubtedly successful business. Carson's lucky as fuck to have you."

Rick breathed a sigh of relief while trying not to make a sound. Mace chuckled, and Rick figured he hadn't been successful. "Means a lot to me, Mace, that you understand. Being here with you at the helm and working with Rank, getting to know Helena and now my niece has been really good. But the idea of starting somewhere new has a lot of pull for me."

"I didn't come here to recruit from Mace, but he's right. I'm damn lucky to have you join me," Carson added. Carson's persona appeared more casual next to Mace's intensity, but underneath was a steel core of duty, honor, and determination. Rick felt camaraderie the moment they'd met. "Starting a new team of Keepers will be easier with someone with your experience."

RICK

"Have you talked to Rank yet?" Mace asked.

Nodding, he replied, "Yeah. To be honest, I did before ever talking to either of you. He was good with it—understands the reasons for needing to strike out on my own, forge my own path, all that shit. He said he hated to lose me being here all the time, but he gets it. Helena, on the other hand—"

Mace chuckled. "I figure her reaction was about like Sylvie's. My wife hates change."

Mace's wife worked for LSI as their administrative manager, and Rick knew she mother-henned the Keepers. "My parents had just gotten used to having Rank and me in the same place. I'm sure I'll hear about this from my mom."

"Well, it's a good move," Mace said, clapping him on the back.

"I agree," Carson added. "As soon as you get things finished here and move out, LSI-WC will be ready for you to help me build."

With that, the three men finished their coffee and headed down the curved concrete stairs to the bottom of the lighthouse. Rick grinned as he climbed into his SUV, ready for new adventures. But first, a day spent kayaking on the water was just what he wanted.

Rick parked outside Blake's house, then jogged around toward the back where he knew the kayaks were stored. He'd meant to come the previous week but knew Blake and Sara were playing host while his family visited.

Rick met Blake's brother, Todd, at the local bar the other night while Sara entertained the rest of her in-laws. With Sara now expecting, he figured they were baby planning. God knows that was what happened when his brother, Rank, and wife, Helena, had a baby. His parents went on a crazy baby-buying spree.

When he called last night, Blake told him that he was taking everyone to the airport in Portland today, so he could come any time, and the shed would be open.

Blake's house was built on the edge of the water, and as he made his way around the back, he decided to step up onto the deck for a better view of the ocean. As he got to the top of the steps, he halted, looking toward the sun glistening on the waves. *Fuckin' amazing.* He'd thought about buying a house for himself but now was glad that he hadn't, considering he was moving. *All the way from Maine to California.* It wasn't without some drawbacks, but what decision in life was all on the pro side? Cons also had to be taken into consideration. He'd learned that from his dad growing up. *"Line up the pros and cons, son. Write them down. Study them. And then make the best decision you can."* He had, and California and LSI-WC made sense.

A slight noise had him turn around, his body jerking back when he realized he wasn't alone. There, in one of the loungers, was a woman. Long black hair flowed over her shoulders, the ends barely lifting in the breeze. Wearing stretchy pants that fit her long legs and an oversized sweater, her outfit was topped off with blue fuzzy socks on her feet. Her head was turned, and she faced the side, but her eyes were closed, and as he stood watching the unmoving beauty, he realized she was asleep.

Not a man to hesitate, he was struck with uncertainty. If he tried to go back down the steps, he might frighten her if she woke up suddenly. On the other hand, he could barely remain standing where he was, looking like a creeper. Turning away slowly, he reached his hand out for the rail, sure of his stealth as a SEAL. A squeak came from behind him, and he jerked around, seeing the woman sitting up, her grayish-green eyes wide as they stared at him. Then her eyes narrowed, and he quickly threw his hands up.

"I'm sorry! I'm sorry! I didn't mean to wake you. Actually, I didn't think you'd be here. Not that I know who you are, but I'm assuming you're Blake's sister." In truth, as soon as he'd seen her unusually colored eyes, he knew she must be Blake's sister.

She stood, her assessing gaze moving over him, and he couldn't decide if it felt like a visual interrogation or caress. Her gaze held him captive as though time halted in place. He wanted to be worthy, hoping whatever decision she made about him meant that he could stay and continue basking in her perusal.

All he knew was that he liked her eyes on him. A lot.

She walked closer, her movements smooth, almost gliding. If he didn't know about her career, he would have sworn she might have been a ballerina. Her head tilted back as she neared. Even though her legs looked amazingly long in her pants, it was obvious she was almost a foot shorter than him. But hell, at six feet, five inches, he towered over most people. "I'm no threat... promise."

She cocked her head to the side. "I know. Believe me, I can take care of myself. But besides being a possible stalker, peeping Tom, or thief, who are you?"

Unable to hold back his grin, he replied, "I'm Rick. I'm a friend of Blake's. He said I could borrow a kayak, and I knew they were kept back here."

Her gaze settled on his face, her eyes narrowing slightly. "A Keeper."

She obviously knew who he was, but hearing the word *keeper* leave her lips gave him a jolt. The image of her wanting to keep him raced through his mind, and for the first time, the image of a woman wanting to *keep* him seemed like a fuckin' good idea. He cleared his throat, blinking out of his stupor. "Uh... yeah."

Her intense gaze was still moving over his face. "You must be Rank's brother?"

Nodding, he wasn't surprised at the question, considering he assumed she'd met a few of the Keepers before. "Yeah." He ran his hand over his chin. "Guess it's not hard to tell."

"Twins?" she asked, brows lifted, a smile playing about her lips.

"No, but we get that a lot." He chuckled. "He's older, but we're pretty close in age." Now it was his turn to cock his head to the side. "And am I right in assuming you're Blake's sister?"

The woman scrunched her nose, chagrin crossing her face. "Sorry, yes. I'm Abbie." She reached her hand out, and he wrapped his fingers around hers.

Her grip was sure. A handshake that was a firm greeting. No limp daintiness that was usually accompanied by a giggle. No hard squeeze that some men and women used to assert dominance. His mind raced to remember what he'd heard about Blake's sister. *Army? CIA? Stationed somewhere overseas?*

The feel of her slender fingers in his created a warm, strange desire to pull her close and hold her tight. Her gaze held his, and he had the sensation he could drown in the murky depths of her eyes.

"Did you come here for a particular reason, or was holding my hand your intent?"

He jumped, loosening his fingers, and laughed. "Sorry about that. I got a little lost in your eyes." He dropped his head back and stared up at the blue sky. "Jesus, that sounded like a really bad line." Lowering his chin, he watched as her lips quirked upward before they spread into a wide grin. Chuckling, he added, "I feel like we need to start over."

"I don't know." She shrugged with a wink. "I think we're doing just fine the way we are."

He barked out a laugh. "Well, all right."

She turned and walked toward the sliding glass door, and his heart dropped at the idea that he'd read her wrong and was being dismissed so easily. She looked over her shoulder and said, "Can I get you something to drink?"

His breath hitched, and he wouldn't have cared if he was a drowning man who didn't need a drop of water, he would've taken her up on her invitation for anything. It didn't matter what she was drinking, he'd agree just to prolong their interaction. "Absolutely. Whatever you're having, I'll have the same."

She inclined her head toward one of the deck chairs. "I'll be right back."

He walked over and settled onto the thick-cushioned, sturdy chair. He heard the slide of the door open behind him and took to his feet, twisting to see if he could help.

She stepped out with two long-neck bottles of beer in her hand, walking soundlessly on her fuzzy-socked feet, and handed one to him.

"Thank you." He stood for a second, wishing he could think of something witty to say, but that was more Rank's forte. He waited until she'd settled into the chair next to him before sitting again. Her presence knocked all rational thought out of his mind, but with the manners his mom had drilled into him and Rank, he was determined to be a gentleman.

As she shifted in her chair, pinning him with her intense focus again, the ability to make small talk seemed to flee. "Um... so, you're stationed in Cairo?"

"Yeah. I've been there for a few years. Before that, I was in Afghanistan for a while."

"Army, right?"

"I see William has been talking about me."

A chuckle rumbled. "It's hard to imagine Blake being called William."

"It's hard for me, Abbie *Blake*, to think of my brother stealing our last name as his own." She laughed. "But then, I think you'd know a little bit about that, wouldn't you?"

This time, a rueful grunt slipped out. "Hell yeah. Rank's name is John. My whole fuckin' life, he's just been my brother, John. With the last name Rankin, he had a drill instructor on the first day shorten it to Rank. Me? I'm just Rick. Same name I've always had. Sometimes being a younger sibling can suck when the older one is so fuckin' great at everything."

"Tell me about it." She nodded emphatically. "I've got two older brothers to try to live up to. But didn't you have your own call sign when you were a SEAL?"

"How'd you know I was a SEAL?"

"Puh-lease! I'm used to my brother being cocky as a Delta, and I've met Rank. I remember hearing that both of you served as SEALs. He's definitely got the demeanor of a SEAL."

Throwing his hand over his heart, he fake-pouted. "Rank is cocky. But me? I'm just confident."

She laughed again, and he loved the sound. Her whole face lit, and he could swear her eyes actually sparkled. There was a realness to her that had been lacking in the women who just wanted a piece of him as a notch on their frog-hog belt.

"Nothing wrong with a confident man."

His brain jump-started at her comment, but she wasn't finished, and her next comment showed she was just as sharp as she was beautiful.

"But, Rick, you deflected away from telling me your call sign."

Dropping his chin, he shook his head slowly. "Well… it was Jolly."

She opened her mouth, but no sound came out.

Then her mouth snapped closed, and her brows lifted. "Uh… okay. Uh… Jolly?"

He dropped his chin and shook his head slowly, a long sigh leaving his lips. "Had an older instructor who said I was as large as the Jolly Green Giant. Hell, I didn't know what he was talking about. I thought maybe the Hulk and figured that'd be a cool name, but no… he meant some cartoon character that was in commercials for a brand of vegetables. I had to look it up and then couldn't believe that it stuck." He sighed heavily again. "So yeah… I became Jolly."

Laughter burst out of her, and once more, he was mesmerized by her beauty. And for the first time in years, he was glad he had a call sign that made someone so happy.

As her mirth slowed, he turned the conversation back to her, wanting to know everything he could. "If I remember what Blake bragged about, you were a captain. Military intelligence."

"That's right."

"And now, CIA."

He almost withered under her intense gaze before she finally nodded. "Yes, but over there, everyone just thinks I'm State Department."

"What was your specialty?"

"Geospatial and photogrammetry."

He blinked, but the words had slid out with no expression from her whatsoever. Suddenly, she burst out laughing, shaking her head. "The truth works every time."

"What do you mean?" He was confused, but her smile had him grinning.

"Whenever I tell people what my specialty is, I bring a conversation to a complete halt. Either they have no idea what it is and don't know how to ask or they do know what it is and know it's boring as hell to most people."

"Damn, Abbie, I was turned on just hearing the words come out of your mouth," he quipped.

She laughed again, this time snorting, which, in turn, led to both of them laughing harder. Finally, he added, "Anyway, fuck what other people think. If you do it, then it's amazing. People on our SEAL team who could analyze what the fuck we were looking for made sure we got in and out of our missions in one piece."

"Well"—she shrugged—"I didn't work on ongoing missions but did the up-front planning."

They sat for a minute, the breeze getting chillier as clouds rolled in from the ocean. Not wanting to leave, he asked, "Tell me about Cairo."

"You've never been?"

He shook his head and watched as a peaceful smile curved her lips as her slender fingers waved while she spoke. "It's beautiful. It's hot, but if you're standing next to the Nile under a palm tree, you feel as though you can breathe. You walk in downtown Cairo, and you feel like you're an ant in a massive anthill of humanity with everyone running around in different directions, and it seems like no one knows where they're going. You take a trip out beyond the tourist areas of the pyramids, and it's as though you can look into the past, imagining thousands of years ago. Go to the Citadel and some of the mosques, and you're looking back hundreds of years, thinking how modern that is. Cairo is a place where the centuries have each left their touch on the city, embedding themselves in everything you see."

"Damn, Abbie. That was a fucking good description."

She blushed and rolled her eyes. "Sorry, I guess I got carried away. In reality, it's all that, but mostly where I live, I sleep, eat, work, and then get up and do it all over again. When I stop and allow myself to think about the history I'm surrounded with, it's fuckin' amazing." Her gaze dropped to his beer, which was now empty, and she lowered her fuzzy socks to the deck and stood. Leaning forward to snag his bottle, she said, "I'll get us another one."

She shivered, and he jumped to his feet. He didn't want their time together to come to an end but hated to see her uncomfortable. "It's pretty chilly out here. I don't want you to get too cold."

She turned to walk toward the sliding glass door, then looked over her shoulder and tossed out a grin. "Then come inside with me."

At that moment, no force on earth or in heaven could have kept him from following her. Completely forgetting about the kayaks, he hustled after her, closing the door behind them. The entire time since he first laid eyes on her, he'd attempted to devour her with his eyes without being obvious. Fresh-faced, she looked younger than her age, which given her military and CIA career, made her at least twenty-eight years old. *Hell, if I'd met her at a bar, I would've wondered if they'd let someone underage come in!*

Everything about her was beautiful. The glossy shine of her black hair. Her slender legs were hugged by the fabric. The slouchy sweater hung below her hips, but he could imagine her ass was as delectable as the rest of her. And there was no hiding the curves when she'd walked toward him.

But what captured and held his attention were her eyes. Large, grayish-green, rimmed with dark lashes. She had pulled out two more bottles of beer from the refrigerator and turned to hand one to him, her gaze on his face. He wanted to kiss her but forced his hand to just reach out and take the bottle, not allowing his feet to carry him closer.

She hesitated, then smiled and led the way into the living room. He'd only been in Blake's house a few times, but each time was an experience. The deck led into the kitchen, which was complete with a brick fireplace. A wide doorway connected into the living room with another fireplace and full windows that overlooked the water. He followed her lead and sat on the sofa, making sure not to crowd her but remain close. He had no idea when Blake and Sara would get back from the airport but was more than happy to take advantage of the time that he had to get to know Abbie alone.

They talked easily—hell, he couldn't ever remember talking so long to a woman. Bar pickups usually involved a bit of flirting, drinks, and maybe a dance or two. Sometimes only the flirting did the trick. But sex was for a physical release, to destress after a mission, or out of boredom and a sense of expectation.

"So what was the deciding factor that made you want to leave the SEALs and work for LSI?" she asked, setting her empty beer bottle onto the end table and curling her legs up onto the cushions.

He started to offer the words that usually left his mouth when asked about leaving his SEAL team— the time was right, a new job opportunity, a chance to make more money. But with the sincere expression on her face and the way she gave him one hundred percent of her attention, he wanted to give her honesty. "I smashed my knee on a jump. A fuckin' training that should have been easy. Had surgery and PT. No problem, right? Hell, most of us have had knee surgeries before. But waking up from surgery, I just kept having the thought, *Is this all I'll do?* The answer to that should have been *hell yeah, the SEALs are the only thing I want to do.*"

Rick forced his gaze to stay on her face to witness her reaction. But she never flinched and instead, continued to nod slightly as though his words struck a chord with her.

He blew out a long breath and added, "By then, Rank had met up with Mace, and as soon as LSI was hiring, Rank was in. The first time I came here, I was impressed. Maine wasn't necessarily where I thought about settling, but I'm sold on the idea of this level of security and investigations business."

"And you've got family here."

He shrugged and nodded. "Yeah. Love my brother and never thought I'd see him settled with a great woman like Helena. And now with a baby? Damn, I'm happy for him."

"I sense a 'but' is coming."

Chuckling, he loved how she already understood him. "Yeah, you're right. I love this job. Love my fellow Keepers. Love my family. But… sometimes it's hard to prove myself when I always feel like I'm in Rank's shadow."

"Does he know you feel that way?"

"Hell, no! He never does anything to try to put me in his shadow. I just think…" He hesitated, knowing he was moving away, yet stumbled at saying he was headed to California.

"It's a younger sibling thing," she finished.

"Yeah," he mumbled, trying to find it in him to mention the move.

She reached out to place her hand on his arm, her understanding smile aimed directly at him. The feel of her hand on him was such a simple touch. Yet the warmth moved up his arm, and he placed his hand over hers, wanting to hold it in place to prolong the contact. A current zapped and crackled around them, like an approaching thunderstorm over the ocean that shattered the air as the jagged lightning bolted from dark clouds to the water below. So consumed by the atmosphere, he wondered if he was the only one who felt the change in the room.

Her eyes widened, and that was when he knew she felt it too. Want mixed with need. Desire swirled together with desperation. Caution gave way to potent lust.

He placed his empty bottle next to hers and leaned toward her slowly. Her hands gripped his biceps, and he wondered if she was pushing him away, so he halted, giving the power to her. But instead, her grip tightened, and she pulled him forward. He moved into her space, then slid his hands around her waist, lifting her easily until she straddled him. Now with her face closer, he closed the distance until they were a whisper apart. The last thing he wanted to do was make her uncomfortable or fuck up his relationship with Blake. He still hadn't mentioned he was leaving. He hesitated once again. "I don't want to read this wrong, Abbie. I don't wanna make a mistake here."

Time stood still.

She let out a shaky breath. "The only mistake you can make is by stopping."

Her breath whooshed against his lips, and feeling a weight eased off his chest, he lifted one hand and slid his fingers through her silky tresses. Gripping her firmly as he angled his head, he covered her mouth with his own.

He'd never planned on kissing her, but now that he'd had a taste, he never wanted it to end.

3

Abbie tangled her tongue against Rick's as she ground her core against the impressive bulge in his jeans. She was desperate for more.

From the second she'd opened her eyes from her impromptu nap on Blake and Sara's deck, her gaze had locked in on the large man standing near the steps. She'd only been on alert for an instant, but then she'd relaxed, feeling no alarm. Her brother's friends and fellow Keepers all exuded the same masculine presence. Then as her gaze moved over him, slowly dragging over each inch... and there were a lot of inches, her interest was piqued, and she quickly looked at his ring finger, relieved he wasn't married. *Of course, maybe he's involved, but at least I can look.*

And, hell, she enjoyed looking. Tall. Brown hair. Blue eyes. Scruffy, short beard. And muscles that appeared barely contained by the tight T-shirt. In fact, she would have been content to just keep looking. But then they started talking and the game changed.

He was part nervous and part cocky. Funny. Asked questions and appeared interested in the answers. He was self-aware, self-confident, yet self-deprecating. It was an intoxicating combination. And when she shivered from the chill, he noticed. She didn't hesitate to offer for him to come inside, thrilled when he agreed.

A shared military background brought an instant connection, but listening to him talk about his family reached deep inside her, loving how his family values were so similar to hers. And when she touched him, the air thickened with impending electricity as though a storm had moved through the room. The jolt she felt from their touch sent vibrations throughout her body, something she'd never experienced before.

And when he hesitated just before she thought he was going to kiss her, she wanted to weep with disappointment. The instant she gave him the go-ahead, his arms tightened around her, crushing her breasts to his chest.

Lost in the sensations that rocked her, she couldn't decide what she wanted to do first—run her hands over his thick muscles, clutch his face, trail her fingers through his short hair, or start removing clothing. The kiss short-circuited her brain, and she settled on just letting him direct their movements. That was a first... she had no problem taking the lead but something was so givingly-dominating or maybe dominatingly-giving about Rick that she was more than willing to follow his lead, instinctively knowing she'd benefit from whatever he wanted to do.

She was a woman who knew that sex could just be a

physical release and no more. No vows of forever... hell, no vows of tomorrow. She'd occasionally slept with men she'd worked with before, and as long as the expectations were the same, it was all good. But this kiss? *Damn!* She didn't want it to end.

One of his large hands slid to her ass and squeezed. Groaning, she gripped him tighter. His hand began to slide upward under the bottom of her shirt. Heated, she felt flushed all over, her clothes too restraining. Shrugging her shoulders, she managed to drop the oversized cardigan she'd worn outside to the floor without ending the kiss. She considered lifting her hands as a symbol of victory but wanted them back on his body quickly.

Now, his hand glided unfettered under the bottom of her shirt, the rough pads of his fingertips dragging over her sensitive skin. Every touch fired along her nerve endings, shooting sparks throughout her body. As his hand continued upward, the T-shirt dragged along with them until it snagged underneath her breasts.

She hated that her shirt was in their way, anxious for him to continue its removal. Desperation filled her as his hand lowered, leaving her shirt in place. Pressing against his shoulders, she separated slightly so her gaze could penetrate deeply into his, hoping to discern his thoughts. *Please tell me you're not going to stop!* Afraid to speak her thoughts out loud in the face of possible rejection, she remained quiet.

He dragged in a ragged breath as though the air was thick as he filled his lungs. Still waiting for him to speak, she tilted her head to the side. Patience had always been a virtue, but she was about to disprove that now. Thankfully, he finally spoke.

"I'm sorry, Abbie. I guess that sitting here on your brother's sofa isn't the place to do this. Especially since he could come back anytime—"

"He's not coming back tonight."

Rick startled, not hiding his surprise. Brows lifted, he repeated, "He's not coming back tonight?"

Heart lighter as it dawned on her that he'd stopped making out because of the possibility that her brother and sister-in-law could walk in on them and thrilled it wasn't because he wasn't interested, she shook her head and grinned. "No. After he and Sara dropped Todd and my parents at the airport, they're having a late dinner and staying the night at a hotel in Portland. They don't know how many of those they'll get to have before the baby comes." She shrugged and added, "I was perfectly happy to be alone."

A hesitation and ensuing silence stretched between them, each barely breathing. He tucked a strand of hair behind her ear. "And are you still happy to be alone?"

Her head slowly moved back and forth. "Right now, Rick, being alone is the last thing in the world I want."

His voice, rough like gravel, snapped back. "And what do you want?"

Her fingers dug into his shoulders. "Would you be shocked if I said I wanted you? In my bed? In me, in my bed?"

His smile started slowly, then laughter burst forth. *Gorgeous.* She squeaked as he laughed and stood quickly, one hand under her ass and the other around her back.

"I'm not shocked, but I sure as fuck would be disappointed if you didn't want the same thing I do. So which way is your bedroom, Abbie girl?"

"I've got the downstairs suite," she said, still grinning. With her legs wrapped around his waist and her arms encircling his neck, she held on. She loved the way he'd scooped her up and carried her as though she weighed nothing. It had been a long time since a man had picked her up, yet at that moment, it felt perfect. She spent her career and most of her time making decisions and being in charge. With the right man, she had no problem letting him cater to her needs when it came to sex, but it had been a long time since she'd been with the right man.

As soon as he got to the bottom of the steps, he moved into a small den and looked around. She inclined her head to the left and said, "The bedroom is in there."

He hesitated for only a second, but she clutched his face in her palms and said, "No doubts, Rick. No regrets. This can be for today only. Just to scratch an itch we both have."

"I know I should give a fuck what this might do to my relationship with your brother—"

"It's not going to fuck anything up, Rick. I'm not going to become some clingy, whiny, why-can't-you-fall-in-love-with-me person who's then gonna run to my brother with horror stories." She visibly shuddered. "I'm my own person. We do what we want when we want. If it's a one and done, that's good, too."

Laughing, he nodded, knowing it suited him, too. "Gotta love your attitude, Abbie."

With no other words, he stalked straight into her bedroom. Instead of letting her feet slide to the floor or tossing her onto the bed, he turned around and pressed her back against the wall. Settling her at the height where his cock pressed to her crotch, she felt the heat explode through her again.

He surrounded her. It was as though every inch of her was encased and protected by a wall of muscle. She knew beyond a shadow of a doubt that all she'd have to say was no or back up, and he would. But those were the last words she thought of saying. Instead, she wanted to crow for him to keep going and never stop. She settled for just hoping that sentiment came true.

She was held in his arms, her head directly in front of his, and they stared at each other for a second, their smiles indicating they had the same thought. Heads angled, their mouths slammed together in a devouring kiss. His tongue thrust against hers. He pressed forward, and she rubbed herself against his erection. His cock was cradled against her core, and her feet tightened around his ass.

He dragged his mouth away from her lips but stayed connected to her soft skin as he kissed his way along her jawline to her ear, then down her neck, sucking gently over her fluttering pulse. Hefting her slightly upward, he continued his assault as his mouth closed over her nipple, getting her shirt wet.

She threw her head back, banging it against the door. Not feeling the pain, she growled, "Too many clothes."

Without skipping a beat, he turned and walked

toward the bed. Once again, he didn't let her feet lower, nor did he toss her. Instead, he managed to keep their torsos pressed together as he placed one knee on the bed and laid her on her back, his body now on top of hers. She writhed underneath his weight, both loving the feel of him and desperately wanting the freedom to get her clothes off.

Her hands slid under his long-sleeve shirt, discovering the smooth skin of his thick muscles. She was no stranger to men's bodies, having seen her brothers and many of the men she'd worked with shirtless over the years. But there was something about these Keepers. Especially Rick. He was fuckin' huge, and as he moved over her, she wanted to trace each dip and swell of his body with her tongue.

He suddenly rolled, and he was on his back with her looming above. She scrambled to her knees and sat astride him, making sure to keep her core seated over his erection. With her arms crisscrossed and her hands holding the bottom of her shirt, she lifted her brow. "Sure you want this, sailor?"

"Hell yeah, babe. Show me what you've got."

With a laugh, she whipped her shirt over her head. Holding the material with one hand, she whirled it over her head and rocked on his hips like a cowgirl twirling a lasso while riding a horse.

His hands grabbed her waist, and it was his time to growl. "Goddamn, Abbie."

Still laughing, she threw the shirt to one side, not caring where it landed. His hands slid up to her bra and jerked the cups down, freeing her breasts. While he fingered her nipples, she unhooked the back and repeated the action, twirling it over her head before letting it sail in the other direction.

"At this rate, babe, you're going to have clothes all over the place."

"As long as they're off our bodies, I don't give a fuck," she quipped.

Her hands moved to the top of her yoga pants, and she lifted onto her knees so that she could shimmy them over her ass and hips, snagging her panties at the same time.

He flipped her again, and she was once again on her back. This time, he moved to his knees and assisted in sliding the rest of her clothes off, including her fuzzy socks.

"My feet might get cold," she argued half-heartedly.

"Abbie girl, I don't think any part of your body is going to be cold, but if your feet start to freeze, I'll let you put them under my ass to warm them up."

"I'll take you up on that." She laughed. Glancing down at her nudity, she speared him with another gaze. "Don't you think you're seriously overdressed? Or perhaps you think that I'm underdressed?"

"You are definitely not underdressed, girl. You are exactly the way you should be. But you're right, and I need to do something about leveling out the playing field."

He reached behind him and grabbed the back of his shirt, jerking it forward and pulling it over his head. He managed to toss it in a different direction than her clothes. She couldn't help but grin at the idea that their clothing would be found in every corner of the room. He moved away from her body, and she propped herself on her elbows to continue watching the show. Next came his belt buckle, the leather sliding through the metal with a rasp. Then the zipper as it lowered, the material spreading easily to give room to his erection. He bent to untie his boots, stepping out of them before shucking his jeans.

"Damn, sailor. Girls pay good money for that kind of show, and I get it for free!"

He barked out a laugh and dropped his boxers.

Staring at his nudity, she was no longer laughing as her mouth felt dry. He was big. All over big. Tall. Huge muscles. Thick thighs. Strong arms. Defined abs. A tight ass. And holy moly, what a cock. And with his fist around it, she blinked before looking up at him. "First of all, I've got to tell you, you've got a body to die for," she said. "And, second of all, anytime you want my mouth to replace your hand, you just say the word. It would be my pleasure."

"Christ, Abbie, you're a wet dream come alive. And I promise I'll let you have a go with your mouth and my cock, but first, I want to hear you scream my name."

She snorted. "If you want me to yell your name, then you'd better bring your A game."

His smile widened, and she was struck by how gorgeous he was. But not just beauty on the outside. He was fun. And it seemed like fun had been missing from her life for a long time.

He placed a knee onto the bed again. This time, his broad shoulders separated her legs, exposing her sex to his lust-filled eyes. He inhaled deeply through his nose, his eyes half closed. "The scent of you ready for me is like a drug. One I could get hooked on."

She had no response to that, but it didn't appear he expected one as he dove forward, his tongue lapping her folds before plunging inside. Her eyes rolled back in her head as her elbows flopped out from under her. Her fingers clutched the bedspread before moving to his shoulders and finally raking her short nails through his hair. With his talented mouth, she realized a part of her sex life had been sorely underused by partners more concerned with their satisfaction than hers. And that was the last coherent thought that crossed her mind as he moved up and sucked on her swollen nub. "Jesus," she groaned.

Lifting his face, he stared at her from between her legs and grinned. "Not Jesus, babe. You gotta yell *my* name." He lowered his head and sucked again as he inserted a finger, crooking it to hit the spot where she needed it.

Before she could think of a smart-ass response, her body exploded in fireworks, and she screamed, "Rick!"

She was barely aware that he crawled up over her body, kissing his way from her mound to her breasts, then up to her mouth, where she tasted herself on his lips.

Lifting his head, he grinned down at her with a cocky gleam in his eye. "Now that's what I like to hear."

"Oh, give me a break," she managed to huff as she caught her breath. "I can't begin to imagine the number of women who've cried out your name. I'd think you'd be bored of hearing it by now!" The smile dropped from his face, and she wondered if she'd offended him.

He shook his head slowly. "I may have heard it before, but there's no comparison to you, Abbie. Somebody saying my name when they are plotting what they can get out of me when it's over isn't the same. And someone putting on an act with fake noises just because they think that's what they're supposed to do doesn't come close to your realness."

She sucked in a small breath, holding his gaze. It sounded like there was a story there, but she wasn't about to ask him to unpack it now. Instead, she lifted her hand and let her fingers drift over his face. "Wow, sailor. You really know what to say."

"I promise it's the truth." He closed the distance and kissed her lightly, but it soon threatened to consume her as the feel of his cock pressed against her, and she wanted it cradled deep inside. Lifting her hips upward, she hoped her actions would communicate her need.

It must have worked because he shifted upward to his knees. Suddenly, the smile dropped from his face as he jerked his head around. "Where the fuck did I put my jeans?"

She raised her hand and pointed over the side of the bed. "I think you dropped them there."

He scrambled off the bed faster than a man his size should be able to move, and she was impressed. He snagged a condom from his wallet, and when he turned to roll it onto his cock, she stared at him, even more impressed.

He once again settled between her thighs and gently

entered with more finesse than she thought possible. But her body was ready, waiting, and more than willing, and soon completely filled, she wrapped her legs around his waist and groaned, "Please."

He lifted his weight off her with his forearms planted on either side of her head. The serious look on his face gentled as he nuzzled his nose alongside hers and whispered, "All you gotta do is ask, babe, but you never have to beg."

He began to thrust, his cock dragging along her inner walls, reaching areas she never thought possible. She had no idea if this was a one and done or if he might want a repeat performance while she was still in town. All she knew was, at this moment, her world only revolved around the two of them. And that was fine by her.

4

Rick meant every word he'd said to her. The few girlfriends he'd had in his past paled compared to his feelings for her. And every face from a one-night stand couldn't be remembered. After witnessing the raw honesty on her face when she'd cried out his name and fell apart in his arms, he'd wanted to roar with a primal possessiveness, hoping to give that pleasure to her again and again.

Her body was gorgeous. Not tall, her toned legs still seemed to go on forever and wrapped around his waist, encouraging him to keep pumping, making him appreciate every mile he knew she'd probably run. Her waist was small, and her rosy-tipped breasts were full. Her silky black hair spread across the bedspread made him ache to run his fingers through the thick tresses. And staring down at her face with those gray-green eyes looking back at him as he thrust in and out of her body made him want to see her fall apart in his arms.

He kissed her again, his tongue mimicking the movements of his cock, and listened to the little hitches in her breath, knowing she was close. Her body stiffened, and her fingernails dug into the muscles of his shoulders. Just as she began to quiver, he gritted his teeth, stifling his roar as his own release blasted into her. Lights flashed behind his eyelids, and for a few seconds, he wasn't sure he'd ever come so hard.

Their movements slowed until every drop was wrung from his body. The muscles in his arms, which had managed to carry fellow SEALs, now felt weak. As he tried to steady his breathing, he rolled to the side, pulling her with him.

Their bodies cooled with her head on his chest and their legs tangled. He didn't want to move. Didn't want to get up, get dressed, make idle conversation, then walk out the door. He wanted to fall asleep with her in his arms, but as rational thoughts slipped into his sex-induced feelings, he wondered if she wanted the same. Or if she expected him to do the things he didn't want to do.

"Hey," she said softly, leaning back to peer up at him. "What are you thinking?"

He tilted his chin down so he could see her face. A gentle smile curved her lips, and he had to taste her once again. The kiss was just as sweet as the first one they'd shared. Finally knowing she deserved an answer, he said, "Honestly?"

"Always," she replied.

"Don't want to leave." There. He'd given voice to his thoughts. Now that the words were out there, he waited, steeling himself for whatever she said.

Her lips curved even more as she shifted upward to lean over his chest, still holding his gaze. "Then don't."

A chuckle erupted from deep within his chest, moving her body along with his. "Just like that?"

She pressed her lips together for a few seconds, then nodded. "I'd like you to stay. I… had fun, and… well, I know we said no expectations, so I don't want you to feel any pressure. But if you'd like to stay, then I'd really like that, too."

"And Blake?"

"He won't be back until at least lunch or early afternoon tomorrow."

Feeling lighter at both the news that Blake wouldn't be home for a while and that Abbie wanted him to stay, he placed his hand on her head and gently settled her back against his side with her head tucked underneath his chin and her cheek resting on his chest. "Get some rest, babe."

"I hope that means I'm going to need it," she quipped.

"Hell yeah. As long as you agree, I plan on making the most of our time."

She simply nodded, her cheek moving against his chest, and he grinned. And thirty minutes later, he was still grinning as she straddled him, her long hair hanging in a curtain while she rode him, both of them coming at the same time again.

By the time they fell asleep in each other's arms, he had realized his mistake. They weren't just having fun because there was no way he'd be where he was if it was only casual. *She still doesn't know my future plans... but that's okay. We've got a while to get to know each other and have a good time first.*

"Last boyfriend?"

Abbie twisted around in his arms and grinned. "Oh, so after one week of great sex and fun, we're having the past dating conversation now?"

"Why not? I'm curious."

"About…?"

"How a woman as smart, gorgeous, and fun as you is still single. Which, by the way, is fine by me since that means I get to be with you." Rick sat on the large, flat rock with knees cocked, his legs surrounding Abbie as she sat with her back pressed tightly to his front. They'd finished the picnic and were now just enjoying the sunshine as they looked over the ocean below. Tall pine trees surrounded them, the green tops reaching up toward the blue sky, giving them a picturesque view as well as privacy.

For the past week, they'd snuck around to spend time together, getting to know each other as well as enjoying each other's bodies every chance they got. What started as just sex was now someone he wanted to know more about. And she loved being with him and looked forward to every moment they had together. *So much for my vow of being fine with just a one and done!* She enjoyed each conversation, finding it easier to talk to Rick than anyone she'd ever spent time with.

"I don't date a lot," she admitted. "Work... my cover... traveling. None of those things are very conducive to a relationship. Or rather a healthy relationship, I should say."

His arms tightened slightly. "Sounds like you were hurt."

She shook her head, her silky hair whispering against his cheek. "No. Not hurt. Just disappointed."

They sat in silence for a moment as he gave her a chance to share if she wanted. Finally, she twisted around and sighed.

"I hadn't been in Cairo long before I started dating an Air Force captain assigned to a different office. He wasn't the love of my life, but we dated for four months and had always promised to be honest with each other if one felt the desire to move on. I had an assignment that took me to Germany for two weeks. And while it sounds like a cliché from a romance novel, I returned a day early and went to his apartment to surprise him. It was a surprise from the moment I walked in to see him banging a woman on his sofa."

"What the fuck?"

Abbie snorted as she felt his body jerk. "It was as awkward as it sounds. What do you do? There's no protocol to follow! And it's awkward as hell to try to have a conversation with two naked people."

She covered her face with her hands, both at the memory and the bark of laughter coming from Rick at her ridiculous story. "The woman looked up and screamed, desperately trying to cover her body with her hands. He jumped up and grabbed a pillow to hold over his crotch."

Still laughing, Rick said, "I can imagine the scene just the way you described it. Please, tell me you nailed him."

"Nah. I saw his keys lying on the counter, so I walked over and pulled my villa key off his ring. Then I tossed his apartment key onto the counter and turned to walk out. The shit actually called out, 'This wasn't anything. She means nothing.' Christ, what a loser... as though that made it any better. How's that supposed to make the other woman feel?"

"What did you do?"

"I simply lifted my hand and flipped him off as I walked out the front door. He tried for several weeks afterward to talk to me, but when I'm done with someone, I'm done." She held his gaze, then lifted a brow. "Okay... your turn."

He opened his mouth, then snapped it closed.

"You don't have to if you don't want to," she assured at his hesitation.

"No, no," he rushed. Shaking his head, he added, "When I asked about your dating past, I hadn't thought about my own situation. But I don't want any secrets between us. I mean, it's only been a week, but I'd like you to know. I was almost engaged..."

She jerked slightly in his arms, and he quickly amended. "Okay, that's not entirely true. I was thinking about being almost engaged."

She pressed her lips together tightly as though to keep from speaking... or laughing.

"Christ, I know that sounds so stupid. It was about five years ago. I'd met her on base. She wasn't military but was civilian support personnel. We got along great, and for the first time, I thought maybe I'd found someone who could handle my life being a SEAL. I just didn't realize how much of myself I was letting her control, which sounds fuckin' ridiculous for someone who was a SEAL. She'd practically moved into my apartment, redecorated, moved things around the way she thought they should be, even planned what we'd do when I wasn't on a mission. Rank met her and thought she was a control freak who wanted to control me. At the time, I didn't see it."

"It probably felt good to have someone take some of the burden off you," Abbie said.

Nodding, he agreed. "Absolutely. Figured I didn't care what curtains were in the apartment, so if she wanted to pick them out, that was fine, even if I hadn't been consulted or didn't like them."

"So what happened?"

"I came home early, too."

"Oh my God… not you, too!" Abbie shifted again to face him fully. Her eyes shot sparks outward, her indignation palpable.

"Not like your situation," he hurried. "I got back early from my mission and couldn't wait to see her. I headed to her office and was just outside the door, ready to jump in to surprise her, when I realized she wasn't alone. There was a coworker with her, and she was talking about me. I know I shouldn't have eavesdropped, but—"

"Oh yes, you should! I certainly would have listened!"

Grinning, he tightened his arms around her. "Well, I can't change it now anyway. She was talking about how she couldn't wait until I was no longer a SEAL and I'd be able to get a better job. She talked about how our apartment was too small, I didn't make enough money to buy a house, and how she didn't get along with any of my friends. She kept going. It seemed that I had shit taste in furniture, shit taste in clothes, and shit taste in music. And then to top it off, she said the only thing good about me was the sex, but she really wasn't into sex anyway, so that wasn't truly a plus."

Abbie's eyes widened, and her mouth dropped open. The incredulous expression on her face was so adorable that he had to taste her and leaned in for a kiss. What he thought would be simple turned hot as she plastered herself to him, knocking him back on the blanket they'd laid on the smooth, warm rock. "The woman was obviously deranged."

He barked out a laugh, his arms tight around her as she lay full-body on top of him.

They held each other's gazes, and she finally said, "You know, our possible one and done has been obliterated."

"Fine by me. I want all your nights… days… minutes."

She laughed, leaning in to kiss him but stopped at the last second. "Good to see we're on the same page." She pressed her hips against his cock, glad to feel he was eager for her again.

RICK

Rick squinted through barely opened eyes as the hint of early morning sunlight streamed through the slats in his blinds. With no curtains to hinder the light's entrance into the room, he squeezed his eyes shut for a moment, then blinked again. A movement next to him sent a smile across his face at the feel of a warm body pressed tightly to his side. The warm body he'd spent the past two weeks getting to know intimately.

Having already memorized each curve, each line of muscle, each smile, the feel of long, silky hair, and the undeniable twinkle in the eyes of the woman sharing his bed, the slow grin that curved his lips widened.

Not wanting to disturb her sleep, he lay for a moment and stared at the bounty curled up next to him. He'd been around more than his fair share of women, many dressed and made up in the style of models, gorgeous enough to catch his eye at a bar, had moves that could send lust scoring through his blood on the dance floor, and could more than keep his attention in bed. But afterward, his attention waned. Flirty jokes from the nightclub fell flat in the light of day. Heavy makeup gave way to raccoon eyes and smeared lipstick. Cute moves gave way to possessive planning for their next time together.

On the other hand, he'd also had just as many women get up and walk out after the sex was over as the ones who'd wanted to cuddle. Honestly, he found the ones who left to be easier to deal with, considering that's all he wanted, as well. When he was a SEAL, the idea of a relationship took a back seat to his team.

Now, out of the clear blue, he'd met Abbie, and she checked all the boxes for a relationship and made him want to check the same boxes for her. *And the timing is shit.* He scrubbed his hand over his face, sighing heavily.

She wiggled slightly and began to blink her eyes open. Awake almost instantly, her smile spread across her face, and his breath caught in his lungs. His hand slid up her arm and squeezed her shoulder. "Christ, you're beautiful."

She laughed, snuggling in closer. "Even first thing in the morning?"

"Every moment of every day."

Her teeth landed on her bottom lip, and her eyes widened. She cupped his jaw, tracing over his stubble with her thumb. She didn't offer words but spoke with her eyes. He loved that about her. She never felt the need to fill in each moment with noise. Instead, she talked with her eyes, her expressions, and her body.

He leaned toward her, and they kissed. He settled between her thighs, cradled as though her body was made for him. He grinned, feeling she was as ready and eager as he. Once again, sparks flew through his body that he knew were much more than lust. Hell, it was more like fireworks that threatened to burst into the air, and he wanted to be buried deep inside her when they exploded.

He had no idea how she'd managed to come to mean so much to him so quickly, but in his heart, he knew that he wanted this woman in his life. Of that, he was sure. He held her gaze, seeing trust as she looked up at him and his gut clenched.

How was he supposed to let her know how much he wanted her and tell her that he was leaving, all at the same time?

5

"And then, honest to God, I started to slide off the back of the crazy camel!"

Rick doubled over with laughter, his sides hurting. He couldn't remember the last time he'd laughed so much or for so long. The smile on her face indicated she was pleased he liked her story.

Wiping tears from her eyes, she continued. "There were three men in galabeyes standing around, all trying to make sure I didn't break my neck while none of them wanted to actually have to touch me. The damn camel didn't listen to anything they were shouting or the fact that they had their guide sticks in their hands. All the beast wanted was to get me off his back!"

Still laughing, he shook his head. "Damn, Abbie, I can't remember the last time I laughed so hard."

They were lying on the bed in his tiny-ass efficiency apartment. They'd spent every moment possible together for the past three weeks. Of course, that didn't mean every moment of every day, but every moment they could slip away from work or family. Hiking, picnics, and meals out at restaurants far enough away so they wouldn't run into anyone they knew. And a lot of time spent here in his little apartment.

Neither had spoken of feelings or the future, but after that first night, it was evident she wanted to spend as much time with him as he did with her. And while they also hadn't talked about letting anyone else know what was going on, she'd indicated that her sister-in-law, Sara, knew something was up. Hopefully, their brothers were blissfully ignorant. Not because he was ashamed of what they had, but he didn't want to hear Rank's admonitions over not being up front with Abbie about leaving or for Blake to punch him out for being with his sister.

Rick went to work each day but was grateful he had no missions that took him away. Luckily, Blake had had two days the prior week where he was gone on a mission, and Abbie had spent both nights with him. He'd gone to work more than one day, trying not to fall asleep after having spent the night awake laughing, talking, and fucking. He inwardly winced. *It hasn't been fucking.* He didn't exactly know what to call it, but Abbie was not a fuck.

While his hands trailed over her body, he glanced toward the small bathroom and grinned. Somehow, they'd managed to have sex in a shower stall that barely held one person, much less the two of them. But they'd made it work, mostly due to the fact that his upper body strength could hold her in place as well as his lower body kept them from crashing to the floor.

Just hot, banging sex? That was what they'd started out doing, but that wasn't what was going on now. Not with all the cuddles, conversation, and kissing... all the things his usual one-night stands never included. *I wonder if a two-week stand is just like a one-night stand on steroids?* A snort erupted, and he tried to cover it with his hand.

"What the hell are you thinking?" she asked, twisting her head around with a twinkle in her eye. Her hair brushed over his chest, making him long to tangle his fingers through the silk again. "Oh, just thinking about your camel story," he lied. Even though she appeared to be as interested in him as he was in her, he didn't want to go down the road of defining what they might be. Especially considering he hadn't mentioned his future plans of moving to California. His head told him that it didn't matter, but the more time they spent together, the more it felt like a weight around his neck— something he should have mentioned as her feelings appeared to grow along with his. He loved being with her and figured the easiest way to fuck up the rest of her time with him was to bring up emotions, even though they were stirring.

She twisted her head and sighed before starting to stand. His arms tightened around her naked body. "Nope, I don't want you to leave."

She looked over her shoulder and held his gaze. "What incentive do you have for me to stay?"

"My quick wit? My conversational skills? The chance to spend more time in this luxury penthouse that's disguised as a piss-poor efficiency?"

Her body shook as she laughed. "What else have you got for me?"

He pressed his hips forward, his erection snuggling against her ass. "How about my big dick?"

Now it was her turn to snort as she laughed harder. "Okay, okay! You've got me. Now, show me what you can do!"

In a flash, he rolled on top of her, nestling his thighs between hers. He could already feel she was wet, but she confirmed. "Go for it, big boy. I'm ready."

He slid his cock in, not bothering with the condom since they'd had the I'm-clean-and-on-birth-control conversation. He squeezed his eyes shut as the sensations crashed over him. She was warm, tight, slick… it felt like coming home. He kept thrusting until he could tell she was almost ready to come. By now, he had her little tells memorized— the hitches in her breathing, the tightening of her fingers into his shoulders, the way she threw her head back. He slid out, and her eyes flashed open. Looking as though she was ready to scream anything but his name.

Before she had a chance to curse, he grabbed her hips and flipped her over, then pulled her ass up, palming the perfect, heart-shaped flesh. Entering her from behind, he continued to thrust with his body bent over her back. One hand tweaked her nipples, and the other hand fingered her clit. It didn't take long for her body to tighten. Just before she cried out his name, her inner muscles tightened on his eager cock. He followed her over the edge of the cliff, his roar now filling the small room as he continued to pump until every drop was emptied.

Her arms slid to the side as she flopped forward, and he crashed on top of her. Barely able to catch his breath, he managed to roll to the side so she could drag air into her lungs.

After a moment, she grunted, "Umph."

Chuckling, he rolled over and pushed her hair away from her face, loving her eyes open and staring at him. "I've gotten pretty used to everything about you, Abbie, but I have no idea what that grunt meant."

"It meant a lot of things because my brain was too tired to get them out at the moment."

"Going to have to break it down for me, babe."

She huffed. "That grunt meant thank you for a great orgasm. My body has never been so sated. I think your cum is dripping out of me, but then I don't care. And I'm pretty damn sure I could stay in this bed forever and not want to move."

"All that was in one grunt?"

"Uh-huh. Do you have a problem with how I speak in grunts after great sex?" she asked, quirking one side of her lips upward.

Laughing, he wrapped his arms around her and pulled her close. "You can speak to me any way you want to after great sex like that. Hell, I'd listen to you speak in grunts, squeaks, and squawks after great sex if you'd stay right where you are."

"Don't tempt me." She laughed.

"I'm not lying, Abbie girl. I'd be a happy man if we never

left his bed. Whatever we have going on, I wish things were different so it didn't have to end." The words had slipped out unbidden, but he had no desire to take them back because the sentiment was true. They hadn't defined what they were, but there was no doubt emotions were shared.

She lifted her hand and smoothed it over his face, and he leaned into her palm. His heart pounded as he stared at the beautiful gift lying in his bed. So caught up in the feelings that were swirling all around them, he almost missed her next words.

"I want to be honest with you, Rick, so I need to tell you something. The last time I was in town, Mace and I chatted about the possibility of LSI needing someone with my unique skill set. I still had so much time left on my CIA contract I didn't do more than just listen. But I went to talk to him yesterday evening and found out that he was interested in my skill set, and I want to take him up on his offer. I still have to return to Cairo to finish my contract, but then I'd like to become a Keeper."

His heart was already pounding but now erratically beat as he listened to what she was telling him. *I'm coming back. I'll be staying. I'll be working for Mace.*

She smiled as she continued, "I didn't want to keep this from you, and we certainly haven't defined that we're anything other than a really good time. But in case it's a problem, I want to be up front."

He knew beyond a shadow of a doubt that if she had come into his life two months earlier, he wouldn't have entertained the idea of moving to California and working for Carson. Maybe that didn't make any sense to others to change a career path based on a relationship he'd just started, but he was that sure of his feelings. But now? *Fuck!* There was no way he could go back on his word to Carson or deny how much he was looking forward to the move. Yet he would've given it all up just for Abbie. *Shit!*

He knew he should say something. Anything. Tell her what he was thinking. Tell her what was going on. Find out if they could see each other long distance. Or see if she might want to move. Or maybe…

"Abbie, I need to—"

The sound of tandem vibrating phones caused them to startle. She leaned over one side of the bed to grab hers while he reached over to the small table next to his side. They both spoke for just a moment, then disconnected and looked at each other.

"I assume that was Blake telling you there's a party getting ready to happen at the lighthouse," he said. Still trying to figure out the best way to tell her he was leaving, he hated that they'd been interrupted. She smiled, and his heartbeat stuttered in his chest.

"Yeah, it was." She inclined her head toward the phone still in his hand. "And I'm sure that was Rank."

"Well, we'd better go. Sylvie always puts on an amazing party along with Marge. If I had to guess, everybody will bring more food and beer than we can consume."

"Damn, I feel like I should bring something."

"Don't worry about it. You're still a guest."

She wiggled her eyebrows. "Maybe not for long." After a few seconds, a frown settled on her face, and she cocked her head to the side. "Rick, you didn't say anything when I told you I wanted to come back here to work. I thought that might be seen as a good thing, but if it's going to be a problem between us, I'll back away. I don't want anything—"

"No, no. It's just that I know we have things to talk about. Let's go and have a good time, and then we can come back here."

"Chances are I won't be able to do that since Blake will be at the party."

"Maybe I can take tomorrow off, and we can see each other then. That way, we'll have longer to talk about everything."

She smiled and nodded. "Okay. Let me get dressed, and I'll head over there first so we don't arrive at the same time." Leaning closer, she kissed him.

They dressed quickly, and he watched as she brushed her long hair before pulling it up into a ponytail. Everything about her called to him, and with each passing moment, his gut clenched more. *I'll tell her. I'll tell her tomorrow and get it out into the open. Then we can figure out where to go from here.*

With that decision made, he kissed her hard and fast, then watched as she jogged to her car in the parking lot. Giving her only a five-minute lead, he locked his apartment and followed.

6

The lighthouse made an impressive background for the picnic, and Abbie had to admit she couldn't wait to be back here. Unlike at the embassy, here she didn't have to hide who she was. There was a freedom amongst the other Keepers and their significant others. A camaraderie that she'd only found in the military, but even then, she'd often felt left out. Here, she felt equally at ease with the other Keepers and their spouses.

She was introduced to Carson, finding out he was a friend and now business partner of Mace's, who was starting his own Lighthouse Security Investigations business in California. This party appeared to be an impromptu goodbye since he was heading back to the West Coast the next day.

Her gaze had followed Rick, but she was careful not to make it obvious. She could tell he was doing the same, always aware when his eyes were on her like a secret caress. As they moved through the food line, their bodies gravitated together in a way that looked casual yet made it easy to stand next to each other. A strong breeze blew loose tendrils toward her food, and he reached out to tuck a strand of hair behind her ear. Smiling, she loved the simple touch, then realizing someone might have seen the gesture, she shot a quick look around the gathering. But there was no indication that anyone was staring.

She couldn't wait until she was a part of this team, sharing a relationship with Rick in the open. *If that's what he wants.* She'd considered that he might not want that relationship, but everything he'd said and done for the past couple of weeks indicated that he was all in.

She watched Mace and Sylvie, Drew and Babs, and Josh and Pippa, knowing that they worked together successfully as well as being in a relationship. Looking at the other couples, she could tell how they all fit together seamlessly.

While she and Rick had not talked of the future, he'd made it evident in every caress and longing look that he wanted more. In fact, she'd wondered how to tell him she was thinking of staying when he'd admitted he didn't want her to leave. She wished they'd had more time to talk earlier, but just like when she started working here, there would be times when they would have to wait until work was over.

To keep their relationship from being too obvious, she didn't sit next to him, but he'd snagged the seat across from her at the picnic table, sending a grin her way. Occasionally, he'd stretch out a long leg, his booted foot sliding along the inside of her calf. Tingles erupted every time. Hell, it had been like that for the past two weeks, and she wondered if it would always be that way.

If she had longer legs, she would have slid off her shoes and dragged her toes along his thighs toward his cock. Instead, she simply had to imagine it, but as her cheeks warmed, she glanced up to see his heated gaze on her and stifled a giggle at the realization he knew what she'd been thinking about doing. She'd gone into this relationship with the idea that it might be a one and done. Now, she hoped it would never be done.

By the time they finished eating, she relaxed with the laughter and conversation of the gathering. As people began to stand to dispose of their trash, Mace called out for their attention.

"I know everyone has places to be and things to do, so I'll make this quick. As always, I want to thank everyone for coming and for Sylvie and Marge gathering the forces to put this party together. Maybe I don't say it often enough, but I work in the best place with the best people and count myself a lucky man every day." He lifted his hand toward Carson, who was sitting across from him, and Carson rose to his feet.

Mace continued, "Carson will be traveling back to California tomorrow, but this won't be the last time you see him. With him as a partner in the new Lighthouse Security Investigations West Coast office soon to be opening, we'll be sharing information, sharing missions, sharing resources, and working together to make sure all LSI is successful. Who knows? There could be more LSIs on the horizon."

At those words, the gathering broke out into thunderous applause and cheers.

Lifting his hands to quiet everyone, Mace continued. "I've got a couple of personnel announcements to make, and then we'll call it a day. It's been great to have Blake's sister, Abbie, visiting us on her leave from Cairo. She and I have talked, and she's interested in joining the Keepers once her CIA contract ends."

More applause resounded all around, and congratulations were called out. She beamed, unable to keep from looking across the table at Rick, hoping to see him equally excited. Instead, the expression on his face appeared strained, and her stomach flip-flopped. Hoping she hadn't misinterpreted his desire for her, she only felt a modicum of relief when his lips curved an inch into a semi-smile that didn't reach his eyes. *I couldn't have misunderstood. He said he wanted me to stay. He said he didn't want me to leave this bed.*

Mace wasn't finished, and as the enthusiasm settled once again, he continued. "And, while Carson didn't come here to recruit anyone, I knew that it would benefit him if he could start his business with someone from here. I always hate to lose a member of my team, but then considering they're still going to be a Keeper, I'm not losing anyone."

Abbie looked around, wondering who'd decided to transfer to California.

"At this time, I'll announce that Rick has talked with both Carson and me, and he'll make the move to LSI-WC. Rank is upset that he'll lose his free babysitter, but I know Rick will bring his special qualities to the new partnership."

Thunderous applause broke out again, with Keepers coming over to slap Rick on the back, shake his hand, and offer their congratulations. From the looks all around, it appeared no one was surprised at the news. Except for Abbie.

Her breath halted in her lungs, and it wasn't until she was jostled from the side as someone moved from the table that she remembered to breathe. But the air was thick, her lungs barely able to fill. People's voices and sounds all around battered her ears, but the only thing she could hear was his voice from earlier saying, "I'd be a happy man if we never left this bed." *Oh, God, he just meant sex. He liked being with me, but it was always just going to be temporary. Christ, I'm an idiot!*

She heard someone call out his name, and her gaze jerked upward, finding him staring at her. She somehow managed to make the corners of her mouth turn upward but knew it was lopsided, much like his had been only a moment earlier. Giving herself a mental shake, she forced a wider smile. As a covert CIA employee, she knew how to play a convincing part. And right now, she was going to do just that.

"Hey, Blake! Bet you're glad your sister isn't heading to California, right?"

William came over, wrapped his arm around her shoulders, and squeezed. "I just wish I could convince her not to go back to Cairo and start now!" Turning toward Rick, he grinned. "And, Rick, you'll kick butt in California, breaking hearts there just like you did here."

Of course, her brother was just joking, having no idea her heart was broken. She smiled through her anguish as the others laughed, then glanced at Sara standing next to her brother. Sara's eyes were filled with pain, seeing straight through Abbie.

Rank clapped Rick on the back and laughed. "I guess he's gone through all the snow bunnies in Maine and now has to check out the beach bunnies on the other side of the country."

Pain scored through her, and her smile was so brittle she was afraid her face might crack. She hated hearing everyone joke in such a cavalier manner about his past. She knew none of these men would have wanted their past sexual escapades flaunted so publicly or embarrass their women, but since no one knew she and Rick had been together, he was ripe for the teasing.

"Oh, Rank, shut up," Helena whispered to her husband. Abbie looked over to see Sara's and Helena's concerned expressions as they stared back at her. She wondered how many of the other women could guess her feelings. One thing was for sure… she wasn't willing to stick around and find out.

Not willing to expose her heartbreak nor fake her way past it, she nodded and then tried to slip away. Her quick escape was denied. She'd almost made it to the other side of the building where the vehicles were parked when her name was called out. She recognized the voice. Hell, she'd memorized the voice as it had whispered sweet words into her ear as they climaxed together.

Turning, she glanced around to see if anyone else was present, glad it was just the two of them because she wasn't sure how long she could keep up the pretense regardless of her special ops training.

Rick hurried to stand just in front of her, anguish in his eyes as well as his furrowed brow and frown greeting her. "Abbie. Shit," he began. "I'm sorry. I'm so fuckin' sorry. That's not how I wanted you to find out. That's why I wanted to talk about—"

She waved her hand dismissively. "It's fine, it's fine. I would've preferred to have not had it so publicly announced and be surprised, but it's fine. We had fun, Rick. It's all good."

"No, Abbie," he pleaded, bending slightly to capture and hold her gaze. "We were a lot more than just fun. You know what we felt."

The world stopped spinning as they stared at each other.

Finally, swallowing deeply, she shook her head. "Were we? I thought we were. So much so that when I had dinner with Mace and Sylvie last night, I thought I was making a smart decision. One based on my heart as well as my head. But obviously, I was wrong."

"No," he urged, his hand lifting toward her. "You weren't wrong. I made this decision right before I met you. If I'd met you earlier, I would've never decided to go to California."

Her body jerked back as though hit in the stomach. "So you knew you were going to move to California before you ever stepped foot on the deck to talk to me a few weeks ago?" She could see Rick's eyes widen as the realization that he was stepping into a minefield and couldn't come out unscathed moved across his face.

Sighing heavily, he nodded. "Yes. But at first, I didn't know how serious we would become. Then I knew after that first day that you were special."

Crossing her arms over her aching chest, she arched her brow. "So after the first day we were together, you considered me special and what we had to be special? And so for two weeks, as we got closer and continued to be intimate, you knew that you were leaving."

His shoulders drooped. "Yes, I knew you were going back to Cairo and—"

"Oh no, don't turn this back on me. I was honest from the beginning. You knew I was going back to Cairo to finish my contract, then coming back to the States as soon as I could. So after I talked to Mace last night, I informed you today. On the other hand, you've kept me in the dark about your intentions ever since we've known each other."

He reached toward her, anguish still written on his face, but she stepped back.

"Abbie, please, babe. Let's go somewhere and talk."

"Talk about what, Rick? I agree with you that we started off as fun. What happened between us grew into a lot more for me, and from what you indicated, it had for you, too. But now, I think we should just part ways and not make this any more difficult on ourselves."

"Abbie, I don't want this to end! We're good together. We can figure this out—"

The sound of other voices coming toward the parking lot caused her to back away. She blinked furiously to keep the tears at bay, and her voice quivered as she said, "I think it already has ended, Rick."

RICK

He looked over his shoulder, then turned back quickly as the sound of approaching voices grew louder. "I'm coming over tomorrow. I don't care if Blake is there or not. I'm coming over, and we're going to talk."

She turned away just as others from the group came toward their vehicles. Climbing inside, she managed another smile and tossed her hand up toward anyone looking, trying to hide her pain. Pulling out of the parking lot, she chanced a glance into her rearview mirror and saw Rick standing there, hands on his hips, his eyes boring into hers.

She had a feeling that Sara would keep Blake away for a little while, which was exactly what she wanted. To be alone. Just like always, solitude was best when life was shit.

The following morning, Rick knocked on Blake and Sara's door, determined to talk to Abbie. He hadn't slept a wink that night, his chest hurting, his stomach in knots, and his head pounding. There was no way he was going to give up on them. He had a plan— to continue their relationship through communication as long as she was in Cairo, then date long distance when she came back to the States. Once the time was right, he could either move back to Maine or see if he could convince her to join him in California. But either way, he was not giving up on them and prayed she wasn't, either.

Knocking again, he was surprised when the door

swung open, and Sara stood before him. Glancing at his watch, he realized it was butt early. "I'm so sorry, Sara, but I really need to talk to Abbie."

"Oh, Rick, I'm sorry, but you're too late."

Shaking his head, he plunged forward, not caring if Blake was just inside and heard everything. "No, I'm not. I know she was upset with me yesterday, and I never meant for all that to come out the way it did. But I need to talk to her—"

She reached out and placed her hand on his arm, halting his words. "No, you don't understand, Rick. She's not here. She's already gone back."

His chin jerked backward. "Gone back where?"

"She left for Cairo in the middle of the night."

Now, his entire body jerked as though punched. "I don't understand."

"Come on in," she said gently. He followed her inside, trying to wrap his mind around the information she'd just shared. She moved into the kitchen and poured a cup of coffee. Looking over her shoulder, she asked, "How do you take it?"

"Splash of cream," he replied on automatic pilot. She doctored the cup, then handed it to him.

She sat down at the table and inclined her head toward one of the chairs, indicating he should do the same. He followed suit, but only because he felt like she needed to be comfortable before she gave him the information he was after.

"Let me begin by saying that I know something happened between the two of you. Abbie never told me anything, but I could see that she was very taken with whoever she was meeting up with. I happened to overhear her talking on the phone last week and heard your name, so I figured it was you. I didn't say anything to Blake because whatever was going on between the two of you wasn't my business. Before we had dinner with Mace the other evening and she mentioned that she'd like to come back and work here, I was so excited and had no doubt that you played a part in that decision. I also could tell that she was unprepared for the news that was shared at the picnic about you going to California."

He sighed heavily, the weight settling on his shoulders uncomfortably. "I was going to tell her, Sara. I just… I don't know. I just thought I had more time before I needed to do that. I know now that was a huge mistake." He leaned forward, his forearms resting on the table as he held her gaze. "But she was supposed to have more time here before she went back. I never wanted her to feel like she couldn't stay. Christ, I've not only fucked things up between her and me but I also messed up the time she had here with her family."

"Don't take that on, Rick. That's not your fault. She got a call in the middle of the night and packed her bags. She woke us up and said that her boss at the embassy needed her immediately. He'd already made arrangements for a private jet to get her to Paris, where she would catch another flight to Cairo."

Feeling as though pummeled after a fight, he leaned back in the chair, the air rushing from his lungs. "What the fuck? She had another week of leave. Hell, why did she need to rush back?"

"I'm afraid that information wasn't divulged to me. And I can tell you that Blake doesn't know, either. He drove her to the Portland airport and should be back soon." They were quiet for a moment, sipping their coffee before Sara tilted her head to the side and held his gaze with intensity. "I will tell you that I know she cares a great deal for you. Not that we spoke of it, but I could see it on her face when she came back from having been with you. And it was plain on her face yesterday that your omission cut her deeply."

"I never meant to betray her. I should've told her from the beginning, but I just wanted to stay in the little bubble we'd created." He shook his head in dejection. "I was fuckin' stupid."

"Then I guess the big question now is, what are you going to do?"

Hefting his shoulders, he said, "I don't guess there's much I can do. I leave for California in two weeks. But I don't plan on giving up completely. I care too much for her. If she needs space, I'll give her that. But I'm going to keep contacting her and hope that by the time she comes back to the States, she'll give us a chance."

"That's a perfect answer, Rick." A smile curved Sara's face, and he had no trouble at that moment knowing exactly why Blake fell for the beautiful, caring woman he'd rescued in French Guiana.

A few minutes later, he walked out, deciding not to wait on Blake. He wanted to be alone with his tumultuous thoughts.

7

CAIRO, EGYPT

When Tom called her after midnight, Abbie's first thought was to argue when he requested that she return to Cairo. As if her day could not get any shittier, she'd been furious that her leave would be cut short. While she hadn't looked forward to dealing with Rick the next day, she knew they needed to talk. If nothing more than to clear the air. She'd come home from the party angry and more than a little hurt, but by the time she'd lain in bed going over everything in her mind, she'd realized that as new as they were, he'd owed her nothing. *God, I told him I wouldn't become clingy... and then after two weeks, I started thinking about us being together. I do need to talk to him sometime.*

But all that fell to the wayside when Tom had said the words, "An employee is dead under suspicious circumstances, and we need you back." She'd immediately jumped up from bed and, while still holding the phone between her shoulder and ear, grabbed her suitcase and began tossing clothes inside. She'd only told

Blake that an emergency assignment had come up, and she was needed. He didn't ask her for the details, knowing the state of play with missions.

During the long flight across the ocean and then south to Cairo, her heart was sad at the thought of someone's death. He didn't divulge their identity, and she wondered if she knew them. And considering she was still gutted over the loss of Rick in her life, she wasn't sure things could get worse.

Tom sent a driver to pick her up at the airport and drop her off at the embassy, informing her that the luggage would be taken to her villa in Ma'adi and turned over to her housekeeper. She simply nodded, being too tired to think of an alternative plan. What she'd love more than anything would be a shower and a meal, but she knew she needed to talk to Tom. Grabbing the few things necessary from her luggage and shoving them into her travel bag, she tipped him before making her way inside. She'd managed to get to her office, where she was met by Sam.

His face held sympathy as he offered a one-shoulder hug, then led the way up the back stairs to Tom's office. Exhausted, she nonetheless walked in, determined to wrap her body in professionalism, hoping that would work to shut down her dark mood.

Michael was present as usual, but this time, Sam also stayed. Tom looked her over, then said, "I'm sorry to have had to cut your leave short."

She waved her hand dismissively. "It's fine. I enjoyed most of it, but it was time to come back. What have you got for me?"

If he was surprised at her curt acquiescence, he didn't show any emotion. "We have something that you need to analyze," he began, opening a file and pushing the papers toward her.

She glanced down, seeing hand-drawn maps, graphics, and what appeared to be a crudely drawn blueprint of a building's floor. Looking up, first at Tom and then Michael, she said, "It will take some time. These are going to be difficult to analyze. Can you give me more information?"

"They came from Anne Mills. She worked in food service requisition here at the embassy."

At that, she shook her head, indicating she had no idea who Anne was.

Michael continued the explanation. "She was on a Nile cruise organized by the employee recreation office and fell overboard. There had been a party the night before, and it was assumed by all that she was inebriated. It's not known the policy and procedures the embassy undertakes to understand why an employee might have died. A blood test revealed that she had barbiturates in her system even though there was no indication that she'd ever used drugs. Her apartment was searched, and the maps and drawings were discovered there, hidden under a desk drawer. It's vital for us to discover what she had, and then we can figure out why she had them. That's why you were called back. We need your skill set to try to ascertain what they were."

"Where did she live? I only ask in the event this helps to narrow my focus in case she had something local."

"She lived in a small apartment building in Ma'adi."

This information didn't surprise her, considering most embassy employees lived there. Ma'adi was large enough that you'd never know who all lived there unless you ran in the same circles. Her brow scrunched as she turned the information over in her mind. Unfortunately, it mingled with fatigue, hunger, and a headache threatening to bloom.

"I'll get started. I understand the importance of time constraints, but I'll let my programs start while I head home. I need food, headache meds, and sleep. Then I'll be ready to continue first thing tomorrow."

He nodded, and she walked out with Sam on her heels. Once in her office, she turned on her computers, then scanned the images into her geo-imagery comparison software.

As she waited to make sure the programs were running, she studied the papers in front of her. It would be a long process, and it normally helped if she had some idea of what she was looking at— a city or neighborhood, a geographic area, or even a specific type of building.

She enjoyed the challenge, not minding the work. From the drawing, it appeared she might be looking at tombs. Snorting, she rolled her eyes. This was Cairo, Egypt, where tombs had been built for five-thousand years, many still undiscovered.

Looking at the drawing of the building, she wondered if it had been built near the tombs. In certain areas in Cairo and along the Nile, buildings had been built a hundred years ago without full excavations underneath, providing areas where tombs could be hidden, so this supposition hardly narrowed down her focus.

Once sure that her computer would run all night, she locked up and headed back downstairs, where another driver was waiting for her. What she'd told Tom was right… shower, food, pain pills, and sleep. As far as her aching heart, she couldn't do anything about that.

Once in her villa, she climbed the stairs and pulled out her phone, glancing at the screen and seeing several missed calls and messages. She quickly replied to the ones from her brother and parents, assuring them that she was back in Cairo and safe. Then looking down, her finger hovered over the button, indicating the message from Rick. Finally clicking, she read it.

Rick: Hated that you left before we talked. So much to say between us. I don't want this to be over. But mostly, I wanted to say I'm sorry I wasn't up front with you from the beginning. Please let me know if you're okay. I miss you.

Plopping down on her bed, she reread his message several times. She wanted to be angry with him, wrapping her righteous indignation around her like a cloak to protect her heart. But in truth, she already missed him. Missed their easy conversation and fun banter. Missed their kisses and definitely missed the sex. But mostly, she just missed that she'd hoped to have him in her life, and now it was uncertain.

Typing out a response, she hesitated, then hit send.

Me: I'm fine. Work called, but by now, you know

that. I accept your apology. I guess the timing was just all wrong. Be safe moving to California.

Tossing her phone onto the nightstand, she lay down on top of her covers, not bothering to change out of her clothes.

Maine

A few weeks later, Rick walked into Rank and Helena's house, his heart heavier than when he usually visited. Saying goodbye was never easy.

He greeted them, then headed directly to his niece, Eleanor, sitting in her little bouncy seat. Picking her up carefully, he cooed, loving her wide gummy smile. Cuddling her close, he'd wondered not for the first time if he'd made the right decision to move to California. He sure as fuck had wondered after meeting Abbie. But now, he wondered again while holding his niece close to his chest. Closing his eyes for a few seconds with his back to Rank and Helena, he gave himself over to the sweet baby smell, knowing that his decision was going to keep him from being close while she grew up.

But he knew he'd made the right decision. In fact, as she got older and would turn to her Uncle Rick for advice, he'd give her the same. *Follow your heart. Be your own person. Forge your own destiny.*

"You're going to miss her."

RICK

He turned around and watched as Helena offered a sweet smile, her gaze moving back and forth between her beautiful daughter and Rick.

Without hesitation, he nodded. "I absolutely will miss her. And you. And even Rank."

Rank chuckled and shook his head. His brother didn't mention that he could change his mind and stay. As a former SEAL himself, Rank understood dedication and following your own path. Rick knew he was lucky. Many people didn't have the kind of relationship with their family that made it hard when they separated. So he figured the twinges on the left side of his chest were because he had that kind of family.

They soon sat down to the dinner Helena had prepared, easy conversation ensuing. No one mentioned Abbie, and he didn't either. For his part, he was glad to spend his last evening in Maine trying to focus on the future.

After dinner, he kissed Eleanor good night and offered Helena a heartfelt hug. She lifted on her toes and, with tears in her eyes, said, "We're going to miss you. You're always welcome, and I hope you'll take us up on that."

With his arms wrapped around her, he pulled her tight. "The same goes for you in California, sweetheart. I'm trusting you to take care of my brother and my niece."

She nodded, then lowered her heels back to the floor, wiping her eyes. She headed toward the nursery, leaving the two brothers alone.

Rank walked over to the liquor cabinet and poured

two fingers of whiskey into a couple of tumblers. Offering one to Rick, they walked outside and stood looking over the water before tapping their glasses together. "When I came here, I never expected you to join me," Rank began. "But I'm glad you did. You're the best brother anyone could hope for and a hell of a Keeper."

"Thanks to you, big brother, I always had an example to follow that was worth following. First in school, then as a SEAL, and then as a Keeper. You've had more influence over my life than anyone else besides our parents, and that's saying a lot because I've had some fuckin' good mentors."

"Then I'll give you one more piece of advice," Rank added.

Rick steeled himself, sure that he knew the subject of Rank's guidance. He wasn't wrong.

"We get used to relying on ourselves and relying on our team, whether SEALs or Keepers. But don't ever underestimate the power of relying on a partner. In my case, I found it in Helena. And when that partnership clicks, there's nothing in the world like it. Helena had filled me in that you were seeing Abbie when she was here. Don't worry, I haven't said anything to Blake. But whatever happened, you were really happy during those weeks. So if you can make that happen again, I hope you do."

Rick heaved a sigh and nodded. "I plan on it. I fucked up by not telling her ahead of time that I was leaving. Mace let the cat out of the bag before I took the opportunity, and she felt betrayed. In all honesty, she was right. That's not something I'm proud of."

"Men fuck up," Rank said, shrugging. "Believe it or not, women expect it at times even though that doesn't make it better. If we're lucky, we find the one who forgives us."

They tossed back the rest of their whiskey and set the tumblers on the railing. Facing each other, they hugged. It wasn't the backslapping, hoorah hug that men often give. This was just arms wrapped around each other, pulling in tight, familial emotions flowing between two brothers who were getting ready to separate. *Hell...* Rick had to battle back tears. Finally pulling apart, they shook hands, and Rank walked him to the door. "Don't be a stranger."

"Same to you." He walked halfway down to his car, then turned around and added, "I'll say it now because I might not say it again, but you're a helluva brother."

Now it was Rank's turn to grin and nod. "Same to you, bro. Same to you."

With that, he climbed into his SUV and drove back to his tiny-ass efficiency that was now much lonelier with Abbie gone. With her on his mind, he typed a text.

Me: Moving tomorrow but I'm only a call or text away. Hope you're okay and taking care of yourself. If you ever want to talk, I'm here. Miss you.

For each text he'd sent, she'd replied but gave him little to go on. *At least she hasn't cut me out completely.* Sighing heavily, he grabbed a beer and sat alone on his last night in Maine.

8

CALIFORNIA

Rick had made the move to California and settled into an apartment that was much larger than his efficiency in Maine. He'd now been at LSI-WC for several weeks, and the time had passed quickly with nonstop activity. He was excited to see Carson's setup was much like Mace's, although that shouldn't have surprised him. Carson had purchased a small, decommissioned lighthouse tucked into a hillside that overlooked the Pacific Ocean. The compound included seventy-five acres of undeveloped land, mostly part of national forests. As Carson explained, it afforded privacy, a place to train, and included a house. Then he'd had a compound built into the hillside near the lighthouse.

The other Keepers included Theodore Bearski, known as Teddy. The former sniper was in his sixties, never married, and was now LSI-WC's weapons and equipment manager as well as the caretaker of the property. Rachel Moore was another good find. She was a former Naval Intelligence officer, widowed, and didn't want to sit at home and wait for grandchildren during her retirement. She filled the same role that Sylvie did for Mace, which was administrative manager.

Lionel Parker, Leo, was a former Delta and had worked for Carson in a security capacity before becoming a Keeper. It was evident he was Carson's right-hand man and deserving of that honor. The other Keepers besides Rick who Carson had hired included Jeb Torres, a former SEAL, their communications expert and computer guru. Frank Hopkins, known as Hop, was their pilot. Adam Calvin was a former Ranger, as well as Terrence Bennett, a Ranger sniper. Frederick Poole was another former SEAL. Jonathan Dolby was Army Special Forces like Carson.

Carson was using the old house at the base of the lighthouse as his personal home. The compound building was built behind the lighthouse and into the hillside. It included their work areas, rooms for equipment, weight room, locker rooms, and anything else Carson thought of. The security was tight, but they were working on making it tighter after Carson had visited LSI in Maine and seen how secure Mace's compound was.

LSI-WC had already started taking basic security contracts, and Rick jumped in with the rest of the Keepers, staying busy every day. That was fine by him. Staying active helped keep the thoughts of Abbie from creeping in. But at night, nothing held the memories and regrets back.

After a few weeks of security system installs for a

few divas and entitled pricks, Rick was thrilled when Carson called the team together.

"We've got a contract that aligns with the kind of work I want us to be able to move into. The kind of work that Mace pulls in. We'll be partnering with the FBI and DEA. The assignment is to monitor two wineries owned by two brothers. One in California and one in Mexico."

"You mentioned DEA," Jeb commented. "Are we talking drugs?"

Carson dipped his chin. "They are suspected of transporting drugs over the border from Mexico. DEA and FBI can't get a lock on how they're doing it. But then they're hampered by regulations that we're not." A grin slid across his normally stoic face. "So let's get planning and get a team with eyes on these wineries."

Rick joined in the cheers, ready to prove that he could be just as valuable a Keeper to Carson as he was to Mace.

That night, he reread the last text he'd received from Abbie.

Abbie: Glad all is well in California and with your new job. They are lucky to have you. Things are the same here - nothing new. Take care.

It wasn't much more than she usually replied, but he took heart in the fact that she was still communicating, however brief. *At least she doesn't hate me.* And he planned on continuing the texts, eventually hoping she would let him back in and praying to have her in his life. *Whatever it takes, I'm all in.*

Cairo, Egypt

Abbie made the return trip up the back staircase to Tom's office after she'd completed her assessment. As usual, she once again saw Michael sitting with Tom. One thing she appreciated about the two men was that they hadn't continually bugged her every day for updates. They trusted her work. They trusted her process. And they had to have known she was handed an impossible assignment. Or rather, an *almost* impossible assignment.

Without wasting time or preamble, she sat at the table and opened the folder, as well as the laptop she'd brought with her. She skipped past the boring TMI of how she came to her conclusions. She knew they wouldn't give a fuck. They just wanted to know what they were looking at.

"Heliopolis."

With that one word, she had their attention. Heliopolis, like Ma'adi, was a suburb outside of Cairo, though it had now been merged as a district of the city. As one of the more affluent areas of Cairo, it held the Egyptian military and Egyptian Air Force headquarters, as well as the residences of Egyptian presidents and many other leaders. Newly developed metro stations linking it to the other areas of Cairo had been well documented for archaeological finds.

"While it's not drawn to scale, I eventually discerned that the rudimentary map is one of the main areas of Heliopolis. But while I'd like to tell you that I have identified the building in the same place, I haven't. The hand-drawn image could represent numerous buildings in Heliopolis as close matches. Probably at least nine buildings, and possibly a lot more, would easily fit the description, depending on the ability of the originator's skill in drawing."

"And the tombs?" Tom asked. "Are they underground in that area?"

She shrugged. "They don't appear to represent any known archaeological dig that I can find. But then, you have to admit that the drawing is also very rudimentary. Could it be something that's underneath one of those buildings? Certainly a possibility. Could it be somewhere else in the city? Also, a possibility. There's no way I can give you that information with any accuracy."

"If you went to Heliopolis and looked at various buildings that you identified, would that make a difference in discerning the street and building drawings? I realize that wouldn't help with the tombs, but it would with the others," Michael asked.

"Possibly. I didn't do that ahead of time because I didn't want anything to influence the imagery comparisons I was making with my analysis. If you'd like me to do a face-to-face visual, we can get more information."

"Yes," Tom said without hesitation.

"All right. I'll go tomorrow."

"On a Saturday?"

"It's probably better for me to go on a Saturday. That

way, I'm not missing time out of the office here, so no one questions where I am."

"Report back here on Monday as soon as you have more information," Tom concluded.

With that dismissal, she gathered her papers and laptop after leaving copies for them. Going back down the staircase, she rolled her mind to the change in her weekend plans.

Passing through Michael's office on her way to her own, Sam looked up and smiled. "I'll stop by your villa tomorrow on our way to Heliopolis. Just let me know what time you want me to be there."

She caught her halt in time so that she didn't stumble but turned and lifted a brow. "I see news travels fast."

He offered a grin that she felt sure had worked on many women before but did nothing for her. "Michael would prefer that you be accompanied."

"You know, as a former Army intelligence captain, I can handle myself."

"And *you* know what the deal is here."

The embassy encouraged its female employees to limit their unaccompanied touring and trips. Assaults were becoming more and more frequent, particularly to lone women. She sighed. Refusing would be pointless and a waste of time. "Be at my villa at oh seven hundred hours. Bring running clothes and a change."

She turned, but not before she saw his smile. In truth, the young lieutenant was cute. Tall, blond, blue-eyed. Lean muscles, a dimple in one cheek, and a killer, white-toothed smile that would be the envy of any dentist. But at five years younger than her, he was looking for fun, and she wasn't looking for anything. Been there. Done that. Bought the fuckin' T-shirt. Then burned it.

Once again, she secured her office, locked everything into the safe, and then began the commute back to Ma'adi and her peaceful villa.

She had to admit that Sam was prompt. When she walked out of her villa at seven the next morning, he was at her gate. He wore cargo shorts and a T-shirt with aviator sunglasses covering his eyes and a ball cap for shade. He also had a small sports bag slung over his shoulder. As soon as he spied her, he grinned.

"Good morning," she greeted.

"It is now that you're here," he quipped.

She rolled her eyes but couldn't help but grin in return. "We're going to the Ma'adi American School to run first." She also didn't ask him if that was all right. If he was going to invite himself along on her day's mission, he would have to follow her lead.

It wasn't a long walk down the streets to where the American school's campus was located in a park-like setting, surrounded by a tall wall bordered with lush trees. The private school housed kindergarten through twelfth grade and was where most of the American Embassy and expatriate children attended, along with a diverse student population from other countries. The campus included a large swimming pool and track that was available to the students and families, as well as a few select American Embassy employees.

Showing her ID, they were waved in by the smiling guard and walked past the playground equipment to the track. Reaching the small bench, she pulled off the flowing skirt she wore, revealing modest running shorts underneath. Dropping her bag and skirt onto the bench, she began stretching. Out of the corner of her eye, she noted Sam followed suit.

Soon they fell into a rhythm as they made their way around the track in the cool early morning. But Sam was a talker and kept up a continuous dialogue. Laughing aloud several times, she had to admit his company was less obnoxious than she thought it would be.

It didn't take long for the heat to rise, and by then, her muscles were loose, and she felt more relaxed. Running had always done that for her. Growing up in a family where her two older brothers were athletic, competitive, and adventurous, she'd often felt the same drive, but she leaned more toward solitary pursuits. She ran cross-country in high school and college, enjoying the team spirit while continuing to strive to beat her personal record. Now, usually running alone, she used the time to think, often analyzing work problems or getting lost in her own thoughts.

Slowing down, they stretched before heading into the locker rooms. It didn't take long for her to reemerge, her modest skirt flowing below her knees and a clean, loose T-shirt covering her arms to the elbows. A few female tourists would dress in short shorts, tank tops, and halters— styles that worked in other environments but could lead to unwanted attention in a conservative country. She was always careful to dress in a manner that was respectful of where she was stationed. She didn't waste time being concerned that she drew less attention to herself with a man at her side. Each culture had its own idiosyncrasies, and she was well-versed in getting the job done in the most covert manner possible.

They caught a taxi to Heliopolis, giving an address that was near the area of one of the buildings she wanted to look at. Over the course of the next few hours, they walked the sidewalks of the beautiful district, but she grew more frustrated. The architecture was picturesque. Some of the buildings were much more modern than in downtown Cairo. Yet while they were walking around the area indicated on one of the drawings, she couldn't find a building that matched the particular image she had on her phone.

"Let's stop and get a bite to eat," Sam said, halting her hurried pace with his hand on her arm.

She wanted to refuse but had to admit she was hungry. "Do you mind if we get something from one of the street vendors? I have dinner plans, and I'd rather not eat a large lunch."

They were close to a small restaurant serving takeout lamb shawarma. The scent of the grilled meat and spices had her mouth watering. With their pita wrapped in paper, they walked back down the street, coming to the last place she wanted to observe. Still not satisfied that she could positively identify the building she was looking for, she finished her meal, wiped her mouth and hands on her napkin, and tossed the refuse into a nearby trash can.

Sam hailed another taxi, and they made their way back to Ma'adi. He got out of the vehicle with her and walked her to the gate. "I'm sorry we didn't find what you were looking for."

Hefting her shoulders in a shrug, she said, "That's how research and analysis goes. Sometimes you get a hit, and other times you don't. But thank you for coming out with me. I know you gave up a Saturday morning."

"Well, I would ask you to dinner, but you said you already have plans." His words were casual, his smile quirking on one side.

Her plans were fictional, but she wasn't in the mood to have dinner with anyone, even a friend. He didn't seem to have trouble finding other women to occupy his time, so she knew he'd have company without her. With a casual wave, she said, "Have a good weekend, and I'll see you on Monday." She walked through the gate, turned to wave again, and then headed straight to her house.

That night, she looked at her phone and read back over the past texts between her and Rick. They were short, yet she looked forward to them. At first, she hadn't responded to each one, but now she made sure to reply, even if it was just to let him know she was well. Somehow, the simple line of communication had become important. Smiling at his last missive letting her know he was back from Mexico, she typed out a new one.

Me: Spent day visiting area of Cairo I hadn't been to before. It was good to see new things. Glad you're back from your trip. Can't wait to hear more about it.

She hesitated for a moment, debating whether to add more. Then making her decision, she typed, **Miss you, too,** at the end and hit send. Blowing out a long breath, a little smile slipped out.

9

CALIFORNIA

Rick followed the other Keepers into their local watering hole. It was Friday night, and the others were all ready to kick back, drink cold beer, eat mounds of nachos and wings, laugh, flirt, and maybe dance with a woman who was as funny as she was good-looking.

He grinned as Teddy held the door open for Rachel. She sailed right on by, but he wondered if she was as unaffected as she pretended to be. He never thought it was an odd thing for older people to have romance. His parents had been married for a long time, and they were just as much in love and just as frisky with each other. Although, that last thought made him shiver. Somehow it was easier to think of Teddy and Rachel being frisky than his own parents.

Stepping inside the bar, he looked over at the table, and another grin crossed his face. Carson was already claiming the spot next to Jeannie. The mission to Mexico and the winery in California had been successful in more ways than one. Not only did they catch the cartel's movement of drugs across the border but Carson had also met the beautiful Jeannie, a nurse trapped in the middle of their mission who had to be rescued. They were now married, and just like with Mace and Sylvie, Carson now seemed more at ease with life.

"Hell, Leo! Let's show them how it's done!"

Looking to his left, he chuckled at the newest Keeper. Natalie had been Leo's best friend for ten years since they'd served in the Army together. When she'd gotten out, she was doing basic security and ended up in Guatemala, where she witnessed a kidnapping and called on Leo and the Keepers to help. It was obvious that wild horses couldn't keep Leo from racing to her side. LSI-WC had been successful with that mission, also, and Leo had now followed in Carson's footsteps. He and Natalie were engaged, and she'd joined the Keepers. She was a petite, ballsy bundle of energy who could curse with the best of them, drink most of them under the table, and shoot pool like a shark.

The rest of the Keepers sitting at the table were still single. It made it easy for Rick to enjoy his night out with the other singles, glad that everyone wasn't trying to match them up with someone. The truth was, his heart was still with Abbie. Time and distance hadn't made a dent in how he felt about her. He hadn't mentioned it to any of his new coworkers, considering they often were talking to the original LSI Keepers. The last thing he wanted was for someone to mention it to Blake.

Abbie and he continued to text and now occasionally chatted on the phone. Between his missions and the time difference, it wasn't always easy, but he made sure she knew he was still there for her. She'd softened toward him but still hadn't indicated when her time in Cairo might be over. Even if she came home to Maine, across the country would be a hell of a lot closer than halfway around the world.

It didn't take long for some of the women in the bar to notice the table that was occupied with mostly big men who looked like they were out for an evening of fun. He leaned back in his seat, drank his beer, and enjoyed shooting the shit with the others. Jeb, Poole, and Bennett hit the dance floor with a trio of hotties who reminded him of the frog hogs who used to hang around the SEAL bars. He always had a good time whenever they went out, but in truth, he hadn't taken anyone home since he'd been in California. There was a time he would've thought celibacy would've been more difficult than it was. But when his heart was in Egypt, nothing in California tempted him.

"Care to show a lady a good time on the dance floor?"

He looked up to see a pretty woman standing nearby, her heavily made-up eyes on him. It was on the tip of his tongue to refuse, but at the encouragement of the others, he pushed back his chair and stood.

She laughed and looped her arm around his, leading him to the area behind the bar where a band was playing, and others were dancing. She immediately plastered her front against his, pulling in tighter than he was comfortable. He stepped back and took her hand, giving her a twirl so that her body was no longer quite so close. With one hand on her waist, and the other one clasping her hand between them, they were still dancing close without him feeling quite so violated.

She laughed and giggled, chattered and flirted, tossed her hair incessantly, winked, and made sure to wiggle so that he'd admire her body. He felt guilty because if she was with one of his friends, they would probably show her a good time and maybe even take her up on what she was offering. But all he could think about was a soft-spoken, dark-haired beauty with gray-green eyes who could handle herself in a bar fight as well as make him forget his name when she was in his arms.

If the woman he was with just wanted to dance, he would've been cool with that, but she was practically begging him to commit to taking her home. She tilted her head to the side and eyed him carefully. "Not to be conceited, but when I cast my line, I usually have no problem reeling in a man. So what's the story with you?"

He shook his head. "I've got to tell you, my heart is somewhere else. I can honestly say it's not you but me."

She softly smiled as she lifted up on her toes and kissed his cheek. "Well, thanks for the dance. And I hope the lady knows how lucky she is." She dropped his hand and moved through the crowd, already scanning to see who her next conquest might be.

As he made his way back to the table, he thought of her words. He wasn't concerned about Abbie thinking she was lucky. He was more focused on hoping that if

Abbie would ever give him a second chance, he knew he'd be the luckiest man alive. Once home, he typed another text.

Me: Had you on my mind tonight… what else is new? lol Let's talk this weekend. Stay safe. Miss you.

Cairo, Egypt

Pressing her lips together to keep them from quivering, Abbie held Tom's gaze. "What happened to Mary? How did she die?"

"She was on a tour arranged by the Embassy Employee Recreation office. She was crossing a road and was struck by a taxi."

As horrific as the accident sounded, a cold sliver of dread moved through her. Tom would never have called her back to the embassy in the pre-dawn hours of the morning based on just an accident. "You're going to tell me it was something else, aren't you?"

"The previous evening, Mary was at a party with some expatriates. A few teachers at the local university and American school. An engineer for an oil company. Several others."

Abbie didn't attend parties often, finding that she didn't seem to have much in common with most of the others. But she'd occasionally gone out with Mary and then hated the few parties that were overly crowded.

Tom lifted a brow and continued. "A blood test also revealed that Mary had barbiturates in her system. The same type as Anne Mills had."

Visibly jerking from the shock, she shook her head quickly. "Mary did not use drugs. In fact, I never even saw her inebriated from alcohol. Going to a party, dancing, enjoying herself, having a drink... yes, to all those things. We were rather close, but I confess that in the past couple of months, we hadn't spent as much time together." Her brow furrowed as she cast her mind back. *Not really since I got back from my leave.*

"Nonetheless, barbiturates were found in her system."

She jerked her attention back to Tom. "And you think this is tied to Anne's death?"

"By the time the embassy police made it to her apartment, it appeared that someone had already been searching, although the place was not trashed. We, of course, are trained to be able to discern that. We investigated but found nothing unusual."

Her mind raced, but no coherent thought came forward. Letting out a deep breath, she recentered her focus. Work the problem, narrow down the possibilities, and come to conclusions. Slowly steeling her spine, she nodded. "Okay. I'll begin work immediately. But I have to ask, other than the barbiturates, working in the embassy, and being out on a tour, was there another connection?"

"Did you know Mary was taking a class at the American University here?"

Nodding slowly, she replied, "Yes. I once asked her

about it, and she said she was trying to keep up a few classes so that she could apply for a better job with her next State Department assignment."

"Anne had been in the same class with her last semester before she was killed. We have checked their emails and determined that the women occasionally studied together."

The air rushed out of her lungs at that news, but she remained quiet, knowing Tom wouldn't believe in coincidences. She waited, wondering what was coming next. In typical fashion, he didn't make her wait long.

"Both women worked at low-level State Department jobs at the same embassy. Both women were in the same class at the university. Both women had attended parties with the same people. Both women were on tours arranged by the embassy staff recreational office. Both women are dead with the same barbiturates in their systems. The deaths occurred just three months apart. I want to know why. What were they doing? What were they involved in? And why did Anne have a map of a building in Heliopolis, a drawing of a tomb, and another map that you haven't been able to identify yet?"

Michael looked over at her. "Our fear is that someone is using these women for some unknown purpose."

She sucked in a quick breath. "And then killing them?"

Both men nodded, and Sam remained still.

"And you need me…?" She left her question open-ended, uncertain how her skill set was going to be used in determining the answer to all his questions.

"Your assignment will focus on this. We need to know the location indicated on the other map. But also see what you can find out from the staff from the embassy recreation office. Learn everything you can about the tours they were on. We need you to go back over all the information you can gather about those maps and drawings you analyzed a few months ago to see if we have any new information. I want to know what building in Heliopolis is involved. You will also attend a gathering of Mary's university friends meeting tomorrow for a wake. Go, observe, listen. You will be fitted with surveillance equipment. If anyone so much as blinks, I want to know about it. Those two women were involved in something that got them killed, and I want to know what. "

Sam finally spoke. "I've arranged to be at the wake also under the guise of being a work acquaintance of Mary's. You won't be there alone."

It was on the tip of her tongue to argue that she didn't need his company to do her job, but by now, her stomach was churning from the news of Mary's death. With the demands Tom was making, she could barely follow along. Knowing he expected cooperation, as well as honesty, she said, "Tom, I promise I'll do everything I can to find out what's going on."

He eyed her for a moment, then nodded. "Today, go home. Tomorrow, go to the wake with Sam. The following day, you'll report here in the morning to continue work on the maps. Then spend your lunchtime with those in the recreation office."

She stood, nodded toward the others, then headed to the door. Following Sam down the stairs, she moved to her office, wanting to check her equipment before leaving, aware he was on her heels.

"You okay?" he asked.

She cast her gaze around her office. She had no idea why that seemed important, but considering the amount of time she spent alone in the small room with just her computers and analysis equipment, it felt like checking on friends. And maybe, after learning that Mary had been murdered, she just needed to be grounded in something familiar.

She nodded absentmindedly but replied, "No. Overwhelmed with the idea of a friend being killed." Crossing her arms over her chest, she asked, "So what do I need to know about the wake tomorrow?"

"From early investigation, it appears that both women partied with a group of people from the university and others in the area. We'll go, mingle, see what's said, hear what people are surmising, and just check it out."

"Fuck…" she cursed under her breath. Finally, straightening her spine, she nodded. "Okay. I'll see you tomorrow."

"I'll pick you up at eleven hundred hours."

Nodding, she walked out and headed back to where a driver would take her home. *Home.* She loved her villa, but it felt increasingly more lonely. *My whole life seems more lonely.* Shoving down those thoughts, she climbed into the vehicle.

Arriving at her villa, she dismissed Sabah for the day and grabbed a bottle of wine, pouring a full glass. Finally, alone, she allowed a tear to fall as she drank a solitary toast to Mary. But while filled with sadness, she wondered what Mary had been involved in. *Did I really know her? Do I really know anyone?*

As frustrated with Rick as she had been and as much as she had doubted her short-lived affair with him, she couldn't stop from grabbing her phone, desperate to reach out to him.

Me: Had sad day - a friend died. Just feel down. Miss you.

Tossing her phone to the side, she drained her glass and leaned her head back, fatigue seeping into each muscle. A vibration caused her to look down at the return message. Instead of a message, her phone vibrated again, and she realized it was a call. Seeing the caller ID gave her heart a little start. Connecting, she whispered, "Hey, Rick. You didn't have to call—"

"I'm right here for you, Abbie. Whatever you need," he vowed.

She hesitated. "I think I just need to talk, but—"

"Then, babe, you just talk. Doesn't matter what about. It can be something or nothing. But I'm here for you."

She felt those words down to her very bones and closed her eyes as silent tears fell. And then she began to talk. And when she went to bed, nothing tangible had changed… Mary was still dead. Her job still had to be done. And her time in Cairo was still filled with investigating.

But something deep inside had changed. She could no longer deny what she felt for Rick, a man who cared enough to give of himself as he listened to her ramble. And when she fell asleep, her heart was a little lighter.

Abbie looked around the room of the large villa in Ma'adi, filled with people. She didn't recognize anyone and realized how much of Mary's life she wasn't part of.

"Think they're mostly from her college classes?" Sam whispered into her ear.

"I don't know. I don't recognize them."

"We can split up and mingle."

Barely nodding, she moved toward the food table, smiling slightly as she made eye contact with several others.

"Hello," greeted one of the women standing nearby. "Are you a student at the college also?"

"No, I knew Mary from work."

"Oh. Doesn't seem like there's a lot of people from her workplace here today."

"I think they were having a separate wake for her there," she murmured.

"Oh, that makes sense," the other young woman mumbled as she continued to munch on the food she'd put on her plate.

Plunging forward, Abbie asked, "So you knew her from the university?"

"Oh yeah, she was a lot of fun. She was the leader of our study group."

"I didn't realize how involved she was with her classes." It surprised her that Mary had never mentioned much about the college to her when they were together.

The young woman nodded with enthusiasm. "Professor Adamson always liked to get groups of students together. Sometimes we'd even meet at his house. He thought it helped us figure out who would like to be group and project leaders. Mary was definitely one of his favorites as a stand-out."

The name Adamson struck Abbie as being familiar, but before she could ask more, several other people came to the food line, interrupting their conversation. She moved to the side, then listened as a woman with a heavy German accent appeared to be in a deeply heated conversation with a man speaking with a British accent. "I don't even know why you're here, Giselle," he whispered loudly. The woman stalked away, her face red.

Abbie realized that with Mary taking classes at the university, her friend had rubbed shoulders with not only those working in the embassy with the State Department but also a large number of expatriates from many different countries. That realization opened up a host of complications in trying to ascertain who Mary might've been with and what she would have been doing when she was killed.

Glancing to the other side of the room, she watched as Sam maneuvered amongst some of the others at the gathering. Abbie preferred small groups or one-on-one conversations. Large crowds didn't frighten her, but she hated trying to think of small talk or witticisms. Tired of nibbling on a cracker, she moved to the drink table to snag a bottle of water.

"I don't believe I've met you," came a voice from just behind. Turning, she looked up at a man who appeared to be in his forties, wearing a button-down shirt and slacks. Tall but wiry, he had a runner's body. His brown hair was slightly long and looked messy as though he'd run his fingers through it a few times.

"I'm a friend of Mary's. We worked together at the embassy."

"Oh, I see. I'm Jason Adamson, her academic advisor and one of her professors. Such a tragedy," he said, shaking his head. "She was so close to having all the credits she needed to graduate."

"I'm afraid I didn't know her in a student capacity, other than to know she was looking forward to completing her classes."

"When she came to me last year, I evaluated the credit she had taken Stateside before coming here. She only needed three more classes to complete her degree. She was on the last one and said she hoped to be able to apply for better positions."

"I take it she was a good student?"

"Excellent," he enthused. "She led one of the study groups that I organized."

"I heard that she was on a tour. I wondered if any of her friends were with her when she was killed."

"No," he said, shaking his head. "It's my understanding that she was by herself."

She started to ask another question when an attractive woman from across the room waved, and Jason excused himself. It appeared the woman with a German accent was no longer arguing with the man, so Abbie sidled up next to her. "I couldn't help but notice you seemed to be upset earlier. Are you okay?"

The woman shrugged, her expression pinched. "I'm fine."

"Did you know Mary from classes?"

"Yes, but to be honest, I wasn't Mary's biggest fan. I detested the way she sucked up to Jason. Not that she wasn't smart, but it seemed she always wanted to be better than the rest of us. But her death was tragic, and that's why I'm here." Giselle inclined her head toward the man with a British accent, now standing with another group of people. "Paul was letting me know he thought I shouldn't be here just because Mary and I had had words the day before she died."

Before Abbie had a chance to speak again, Giselle moved away, leaving her staring in her wake. Sighing, she spent the next hour moving around the room, forcing small talk and discerning what she could from the group. Finally catching Sam's eyes, she jerked her head slightly toward the door, indicating she was leaving. After walking out, she made her way down the street to the place they agreed to rendezvous. It only took a few minutes for him to come jogging up to her side.

"You okay?" he asked.

"I will be." They walked down the street toward his vehicle. He drove them back to her villa in silence, and she was ready to go in and crash.

"You want to go over what we learned?"

"Tomorrow. Right now, I just want to go in, process everything, and make some notes. Tomorrow will be soon enough when I get into the embassy and see what my programs have come up with for the last map that I haven't been able to identify."

He nodded and then waved as she climbed from the vehicle. Walking into the cool interior of her house, she was still exhausted, and a nap was calling. Closing her eyes, she drifted to sleep only to have her dreams invaded by images of Mary dying on the street, the faceless Anne falling into the Nile, and a nightmare of being buried in the tomb.

10

Abbie sat at her desk, alternating between staring at the computer screens and the paper she'd scribbled on. The computer screen was not coming up with anything new other than what she'd discovered before— one hand-drawn map was from the Heliopolis area, but she had no idea what was the location of the second map. And the paper where she'd scribbled her impressions from the wake.

She'd listed names and then drawn connecting lines between the characters. Anne and Mary worked for the US Embassy. They also attended classes at the American University of Cairo. They knew some of the same people. Tapping her pen on the paper, she suddenly stood and walked to her door. "Hey, Sam?"

He looked up expectantly.

"Can we find out if there have been any other accidental deaths recently?"

He barked out a rude noise. "Seriously? This is

Cairo. There are probably five-thousand road deaths in Cairo each year."

Huffing, she shook her head. "Not just anyone, but other expatriates. Maybe those who had a connection with the university."

"Sorry," he mumbled. "I see where you're going with that. What could seem like independent deaths could be tied into our two."

"Exactly."

"I'll see what I can dig up. I'm sure Tom will get a few agents on it."

She nodded, then returned to her office. By lunchtime, she headed to the cafeteria, easily finding the staff members from the recreation office. Sitting with them, she pulled out the lunch Sabah had fixed for her. After a moment of small talk, one of them said, "I'm Betty. I just wanted to say how sorry I am about Mary. I know you used to have lunch with her. I didn't know her well, but what happened is horrible."

A flash of grief struck her, and she sucked in a deep breath, offering a nod. "Thank you. I was surprised because she didn't mention going on a tour. We usually went together on our outings."

"She didn't book it very far in advance, did she, Sue?" Betty commented, turning to the woman sitting next to her.

Sue shook her head. "No, actually, she was a late-comer. Cora likes to fill the tours and then close them out a couple of days ahead of time if possible. That way, she can make sure that there are plenty of amenities, water, snacks, and guides. But I think Cora added Mary's name the day before the tour."

"Cora?"

"She's the head of the Embassy Employee Recreation Office," Betty answered. "She's amazing. She's the most organized head we've had here, and I've been in this office for five years."

Abbie was surprised, considering foreign service assignments were usually shorter in duration. "That seems like a long tour."

"It is." Betty nodded. "My husband works for a civil engineering company that has a contract with the Egyptians for road building."

Abbie thought of Paul White, the man Giselle had been arguing with at Mary's wake. Even though she hadn't talked to him, Sam was able to have him identified based on the visual and audio intel they'd gathered. She chewed slowly, her mind connecting with more people who knew Mary. "Um, are the tours usually safe? I seem to remember hearing about someone who fell overboard on a Nile cruise."

Betty's brow furrowed, then shook her head as her lips pinched. "Oh, that's right. The woman was drunk. That was so stupid of her."

"Where was the destination of Mary's tour?" she asked, even though she'd read the report.

"The Citadel," Betty replied. "It was a full-day tour."

"Didn't they take a side trip to the City of the Dead?" Sue asked, looking at her coworker.

"Oh, that's right." Betty nodded as she stood to toss

her refuse into the trash can. "It wasn't on the original tour itinerary, but Cora added it at the last minute. I suppose the guide wanted to include it. The more he can show, the larger his baksheesh will be." She lifted her hand and rubbed her fingers together, indicating a tip.

The lunch had come to an end, and Abbie wasn't sure she'd learned anything worthy, but smiled her thanks and hurried back to her office. Sam looked up as she entered. "Any luck?"

Shrugging, she said, "Maybe. At this point, I'm just trying to get a feel for everything, and while there are connections, nothing makes sense."

"Tom wants us in his office in thirty minutes to review what we have."

She had just enough time to grab her notes and the latest information from her computer printouts. Glancing at them, she winced. *Not much to go on.*

Soon, she was ensconced in the room with Tom, Michael, and Sam. Not wasting time, she and Sam laid out their information from the wake, as well as her conversation from lunch. "I don't have any specifics on Anne, but I do find it odd that Mary was added late to the tour even though they said the head of the recreation office didn't usually do that. Was that just as a favor to her, or was she specifically put there for a reason? But if so, then why would the head of recreation want her on that tour?"

Tom's expression rarely gave anything away, but she could see the analytical wheels turning behind his eyes. He opened his laptop and, with a few clicks, lifted his brow. "Cora Adamson. Head of Embassy Employee Recreation Office."

Abbie and Sam looked at each other, both speaking at the same time. "Jason Adamson."

Abbie continued, "He's a professor at the university. Knew both Anne and Mary. He was at the wake."

With a few taps on his computer, Sam nodded. "Jason is Cora's husband."

Brow furrowed, she murmured, "It doesn't prove anything—"

"No, but it's a damn interesting coincidence," Michael added.

"What do you have on those drawings?" Tom asked.

Inwardly wincing, she shook her head. "Nothing so far, but I've concentrated my searches in Heliopolis—"

"Go wider," he curtly ordered.

Nodding, she stood and walked down the stairs to her office, Sam on her heels. "We need to lock this down, Abbie. You need to talk to those women again."

Frustrated, she turned and glared. "Look, I get it, Sam. You're anxious to get promoted and keeping Michael and Tom happy will go a long way to that. But I can't create intel where I don't have it. I do the behind-the-scenes imagery intel, not covert, in-the-field-operator investigations."

"He's not going to trust too many people on this right now, so we need to do what we can."

"Stop telling me what *I* need to do. I know *my* job." With that, she walked into her office and closed the door. Plopping down at her desk, she was reminded of a conversation she'd had with Mary before she went back to the States on leave where she'd wondered how long she wanted to stay in this job. She loved the mathematics of imagery analysis, yet the push to become an active CIA operative was not the direction she wanted to go.

An hour later, she reset the parameters of her computer program so that it would look for more information that was beyond Heliopolis. Needing a mental break, she moved to her laptop and sorted through emails, seeing one from Rick. Her lips curved upward as she clicked on it and grinned at the funny meme he'd sent, as well as a link to one of the houses he was looking at purchasing. He'd asked for her opinion, but she hesitated. It would be difficult to look through the photographs of the kitchen, living area, outdoor area and views, and especially the bedroom and not think about him being there, possibly sharing that space one day with another woman.

With her eyes tightly shut, she propped her elbows on her desk and rested her forehead in her hands. She had forgiven him for not speaking up sooner about taking the job with Carson in California. She'd also admitted that since they were so new, he'd been under no obligation to divulge his life plans to her.

Her chest squeezed just thinking of him. He'd found a place in her heart and had taken up permanent residency there. They'd corresponded, keeping things light, although he ended each email with how he looked forward to seeing her again. Her finger hovered over the house real estate link, then clicked off the email, not willing to go down that path at the moment.

Needing something to distract her, she clicked onto the embassy news, scanning the information to see if anything was pertinent. Her gaze couldn't help but snag on the tours offered by the recreation office. Trips to the pyramids and Sphinx. Trips to the Cairo Museum. Overnight trips to Luxor or Alexandria. Even cruises down the Nile.

Seeing those brought Mary to mind, making her sigh heavily at the loss of her friend. *I don't make friends easily, and the one good friend I had is gone.* As soon as that thought hit her, she winced, glad it had been private and not said aloud to anyone, considering it made her sound like a selfish bitch.

Tired of looking at the embassy news, she started to turn off her laptop when she decided to take a look at local news just to kill a few more minutes before she checked on her computer analysis programs.

Her gaze scanned the headlines. A Nile dam dispute. The unveiling of a massive sarcophagus find. An Egyptian recycling company was turning waste materials into plastic. Farmers are planting rice in Egypt's Nile Delta. Efforts to clear the Nile of houseboats. The threat of demolition looming over the City of the Dead. Egyptian Bank to offer—

She startled, jerking her finger back over the previous article about the City of the Dead. That's the tour Cora added on the trip Mary was on. Knowing that tidbit didn't have to be significant, she was suddenly set on finding out more about the area. She'd never toured there but was now fascinated to see why it was in recent news. Settling in, she began her research.

The southeast portion of present-day Cairo was an important ancient burial site from the seventh century. Prominent figures were buried there, new areas were added, and the monumental cemetery, known as the City of the Dead, now extended over two-thousand acres. While many tourists focused their interest on Giza and the other sites of ancient Egypt, the City of the Dead was often overlooked even though it is a medieval necropolis filled with historical and artistic value.

Of course, what the government would prefer not to mention was that over the years, the necropolis had developed from a solemn expanse into one of Cairo's largest, most run-down slums. Beds and ovens were pushed up against marble tombs going back into the catacombs and mausoleums. While no one had ascertained the exact population of those who live there, it was assumed that over one million individuals lived in the City of the Dead. Many displaced people had taken to squatting in the claustrophobic crypts as an escape from homelessness. The area wasn't authorized by the government for living quarters but was tolerated due to the housing crisis.

Abbie doubted if any of those sections were visited by the tour group. Now, reading the news article about the demolition, she leaned closer to her laptop, her gaze scanning over the words and images. The government was embarking on an ambitious road network project which would cross, encircle, and penetrate the City of the Dead cemeteries. The potential for hundreds of valuable treasures and Muslim architecture would be bulldozed in an effort to alter Cairo's urban landscape.

A civil engineering company based out of England was taking the lead, working in concert with the Egyptian government. The planning was already complete, and it was anticipated the demolition would begin within the next several months.

Civil engineering company. Paul White from the wake. He knew Mary. Could very well have known Anne.

Moving to her bank of computers, she changed the parameters of some of the images to include the City of the Dead. It wasn't too far from the Khan el-Khalili, the famous shopping area, the Citadel, or the Mosque of Mohammed Ali. While the one hand-drawn map had definitely been from Heliopolis, since she'd been unable to ascertain the other graphics, she had nothing to lose in following a new path. After all, Tom had instructed her to expand her search.

Three hours later, she raced out of her office and past Sam, calling out, "Follow me!" She took the stairs two at a time and burst through the doorway into Tom's office. "Tom. Michael. I've found something."

She had their undivided attention immediately. Sliding into one of the chairs, she pulled up her laptop and sent the images to a screen on Tom's wall. "We know the one map drawing is in Heliopolis even if we weren't able to discern the individual building. But the other one is somewhere off El-Soultan Ahmed… in the City of the Dead. The same place Mary was visiting when she was killed in the accident. The area that Cora Adamson added to the tour."

11

CALIFORNIA

Rick checked his email as soon as he'd plated his breakfast, sighing when he saw that Abbie had not replied to the last one he'd sent— the email where he included the real estate listing the house he was considering. "Fuck," he said aloud, plopping down on the stool at the counter in his apartment.

He'd filled his plate with eggs, bacon, and toast but was rapidly losing his appetite. He was already second-guessing sending the listing. He really wanted her opinion, hoping that when she left Egypt, she'd visit him in California. Of course, he wished for a lot more than a visit but was willing to take whatever he could get from her.

Maybe she didn't reply because she's halfway around the world, living in a third-world country, and didn't care about real estate in California. That thought made him wince, wondering if he'd been insensitive by sending it. Eating only half the food he'd made, he dumped the rest into the trash can and rinsed the dishes.

He debated sending another email, perhaps one just to see how she was doing. Their communication had gotten better over time. They talked about what was happening in their lives, enjoying their conversations as much as when they were together in Maine, but neither could discuss their job over the nonsecure lines. He felt that separation in closeness, wishing they weren't continents apart.

Deciding on a text instead, he thought carefully about what to say. **Miss you. Think of you all the time. I know you can take care of yourself but I worry. Hope to talk to you soon.**

Deciding he was satisfied with the text, he hit send. Pouring a travel cup of coffee, he headed out the door. His day was spent with another security walk-through, designing a state-of-the-art system for a newly elected state senator. It wasn't a difficult assignment, and he found the young man to be enthusiastic about his new job and interested in the system Rick was suggesting.

But by the afternoon, he was glad to head back to the LSI-WC compound. Just as he was climbing from his vehicle, his phone rang. Wishing it was Abbie, he saw it was Rank and hoped everything was all right. "Hey, bro. What's up? Is everything okay?"

"Yeah, we're all fine. Helena is great. Eleanor is precious. Everything's good. But I wanted to ask you about Abbie."

His feet stumbled to a halt, surprise hitting him like a punch to the gut. "Abbie? What's going on?"

"Blake just mentioned that he was worried. He said

his sister had told him that a friend of hers had been killed."

"Yeah, she mentioned it to me, too. She said the woman was killed in a pedestrian traffic accident."

"Well, Blake is concerned because the last thing he heard from her was that she's been pulled into the investigation because it turns out not to have been an accident."

Rick's veins filled with cold as the air rushed from his body. "What the fuck?" He couldn't believe Abbie hadn't given him that news.

"I knew that you and she had been talking, so I just thought I'd check to see if you had heard from her recently. And for full disclosure, bro, I haven't said anything to Blake about you and Abbie."

"I appreciate it. If anything needs to be said, it would be best to come from us. But right now, we're just friends, although I'd like it to be a helluva lot more. We email back and forth, call when we can, and text. She'd mentioned her friend, but we didn't go into a lot of detail. I'll see what I can find out."

"Sounds good. Take care of yourself, Rick."

"You, too. Kiss Helena and Eleanor for me."

Disconnecting, he walked into the compound, frustrated. *Hell, I've been worried that she didn't want to respond to my email about real estate, but she's been dealing with something much more serious.*

Tapping into his phone quickly, he fired off another text. **Heard through Rank that your brother is worried about you. That means I'm worried too. Let me hear from you soon.**

Walking inside, he made his way through the security system, past Rachel's office, and into the workroom. Plopping down into a chair close to Leo, he scrubbed his hand over his face.

His friend looked over, concern on his face. "What's up, man?"

"It's Abbie. Blake's sister." He knew that Leo had met Blake when he'd made a trip to Maine with Carson before Rick had signed on with LSI-WC. The others knew he was friends with her, but he'd never spoken to any of the Keepers about having had a relationship with her.

"What's going on?" Leo asked.

He looked around, seeing that he had the attention of several others. Sighing again, he said, "Don't know. She and I've talked since she's been back in Cairo, but I just got a call from my brother asking if I'd spoken to her recently. He knows that she and I are friends. Anyway, Blake's worried, and so am I. A good friend of hers died in an accident that they now know wasn't an accident. Her boss has her working on something, and I'm not crazy about her possibly being in danger. It's probably nothing, but I'd like for this assignment to be over for her. At least if she's in Maine working for Mace, I can be a lot closer if she needs me."

Carson spoke up, "If you're needed now, you only have to ask. She's one of us even if she's connected to the Maine LSI."

Seeing the nods from the others around and hearing Carson's vow, he says, "Thanks, boss. I appreciate it." He hoped she wouldn't need help simply because he didn't want her to be in danger. But knowing he could leave instantly to go to her side made him feel a helluva lot better.

Natalie walked over and shot him a smile. "Come on, big guy. Bennett and Hop are on their way home from their mission. The rest of us are finished unless Carson has something else on the books. It's time to hit the bar after work."

He had no desire to go but wasn't ready to go back to his apartment alone. Soon, sitting with the others at a table in the bar, he ignored the women who came around, preferring to nurse his beer in sullen silence. He was miserable and knew it showed to everyone. Finally, after letting Leo know he was leaving, he walked out.

As soon as he stepped into his apartment, he checked his email, his heart leaping when he saw he had one from her.

I'm fine. Just trying to do my job. Please don't worry. But know that I think of you often, too. I haven't had a chance to look at the real estate listing, but I promise to do so soon. It's exciting to think of you finding a place to call home. I'll be out of the office tomorrow, still working on the investigation. I hope we can tie things up soon so that I can think about what's next for me. Take care, and I miss you, too. Abbie

He reread her email several times, heaving a sigh of relief. Glad she wasn't upset with him, he was nonetheless frustrated. This wasn't the way he wanted their relationship to progress. Emails and texts. An occasional phone call. Separated by time zones, oceans, and continents. Yet for a man used to action, he had no idea how to fix things.

Cairo, Egypt

The next morning, Abbie looked over at Sam's eager face and sighed. She was torn between the natural elation that came from discovering a possible clue to Mary's death and the sadness that still pulled at her.

The embassy driver stopped just outside one of the gates at the City of the Dead and let them out. Dressed modestly with her head covered, she climbed from her side and slung her cross-body bag over her shoulder. Excitement scored through her. Even though she wasn't trained in boots-on-the-ground CIA operations and hated the small talk at Mary's wake, she was fascinated with the buildings in front of her. She had no idea if they'd be able to find the location of the drawing that Anne had hidden, but she was ready to see what they could find.

Met by an Egyptian guide with a wide smile on his face, he offered his welcome. "Ahlan wa sahlan! I am Achmed. Please to come with me. Follow. Follow."

They entered through one of the gates, walking along the concrete paths that led into the cemetery. In many ways, it looked like any other slum area of the city. Dirt, dust, and sand covered the walkways and buildings, giving everything a monochromatic beige appearance. Garbage and refuse were tossed to the sides of the mud and stone walls. Dogs slept in the shade of the buildings, lacking trees to give them any reprieve from the heat.

Children laughed and played, then looked at the strangers and scrambled away. A few adventurous ones would run over, their hands out for money or sweets. Achmed chased them away, shouting, "La! La!"

Abbie hated not to be able to offer something to them, but the embassy warned against giving to beggars, even children. It could encourage a swarm that could become dangerous.

Her head swung back and forth as they continued walking, taking in the area. Above ground crypts and mausoleums held the remains of the long dead. Amongst them hung laundry, firepits nestled in open spaces with pots of bubbling food hanging over them, and stone ovens baking bread.

"I will show you inside," Achmed said, waving to a nearby woman. They spoke in Arabic, and she nodded, standing to the side of an open doorway into one of the mausoleums.

Curious, Abbie followed the woman inside the crypt that had become her home. Crude beds were pushed against the corner, used as couches during the day and sleeping quarters at night. Bright, patterned cloth hung as room dividers. The stone crypt that held the remains of someone buried centuries before was used as a table for holding household items.

A small shelf with cooking utensils and several plates and cups sat against another wall. The woman turned and poured several small glass tumblers full of dark liquid. She handed the strong tea to them, a hopeful expression on her face.

Abbie thanked her in Arabic while taking a sip and nodding her appreciation. "Shukraan."

The woman's smile widened, her eyes bright as she nodded before taking the cups back.

Back out on the street, the trio continued, but with each step, Abbie began to lose hope that they would identify a specific building considering the labyrinth of the necropolis extended in all directions, everything looking much alike. After an hour of traipsing around the area, she was fascinated but no closer to determining why Mary would have been interested in the City of the Dead.

Sitting on a small bench, she drank thirstily from the water she'd brought as Sam and Achmed talked to a man standing to one side. Several minutes later, Sam walked back over with a smile on his face.

"He must've had good news," she said, curiosity filling her.

"The man we were talking to? He said he remembered seeing an American woman coming here with an Egyptian. He doesn't want to show me now where she'd gone, but I'm coming back later this evening."

Nodding, Abbie didn't voice the dreaded idea of a

return visit later in the day when it would be even hotter.

As though reading her mind, Sam added, "Please don't take offense, but he says he only wants me to come alone. I'm not sure he has much respect for women."

"Is that safe? To come alone?"

"I'll be fine." He laughed. "Anyway, you can see this is more of a housing area than it is a scary cemetery."

"Well, if I'm not coming, did he mention where you'd be going?" She knew Sam would be security conscious, but she wanted to have that information, nonetheless.

Lowering his voice, he glanced around. "I'm to meet him here, and he said it's just on the next street."

Unease slithered through her, but to offer more warning would be insulting. Nodding, she stood, and they walked back with Achmed to the gate where the embassy driver was waiting. Tipping their guide well, they waved goodbye and climbed inside the van.

Abbie jerked awake, sitting up in bed, shoving her long hair back from her face as she tried to discern the source of the loud banging noise. Untangling her legs from the covers, she ran to the top of the stairs, finally hearing someone knock with force on her front door. It was still dark outside, and she had no idea what time it was.

Hurrying down the stairs, she glanced at the clock

on the microwave in the kitchen to see it was two in the morning. Hesitating, she didn't want to throw open the door. "Who's there?" she called out.

"Sergeant Martinez and Sergeant Washington, ma'am. We've been sent by Mr. Olsen to escort you to the embassy."

Tom? Peeking through the security hole, she could see the man and woman in fatigues with military IDs held up in their hands. She unlocked the door and opened it, stepping back to allow them entrance.

The two hastened inside, the female sergeant standing with her as the male made a sweep through the downstairs. She looked at the name over the breast pocket. "Sergeant Washington? What's going on?"

"You'll need to get dressed, ma'am, and come with us. Mr. Olsen will give you the necessary information once you arrive at the embassy."

She pressed her lips together. She wanted to protest but knew they were following orders. Nodding, she jogged up the stairs, aware that Sergeant Washington was on her heels. Once in her bedroom, she grabbed her clothes and hurried into the bathroom, almost surprised when the sergeant didn't follow her in. Quickly using the facilities, she dressed and ran a brush through her hair, pulling it back into a ponytail.

Stepping back into the bedroom, she asked, "Do you know if I need to pack anything?"

"I'm sorry, ma'am, I don't. If there's anything you'll need, I'm sure Mr. Olsen will make arrangements."

Slipping on her shoes, she grabbed her phone and laptop, placing everything into her bag. Glancing around her room, she tried to still the pounding of her heart, unable to imagine what was happening but knowing no answers would come from the two who'd been sent to collect her.

She made sure to lock the door when they left, and on the street, she was placed into the back of a military SUV. The drive seemed to take forever, even with the ease of traffic in the middle of the night. She focused on breathing steadily, hoping to ease her racing heart. The vehicle drove to the back of the embassy, clearing the guard gate before moving onto the compound.

As soon as they alighted from the vehicle, the two sergeants escorted her inside, taking her directly up the elevator to the seventh floor. The Marine guards outside the elevator stepped to the side as soon as they walked out. Arriving at Tom's office, they knocked, opened the door, then stood on the outside as sentries as she stepped inside, seeing both Michael and Tom inside. The expressions on their faces caused her to stumble as she entered.

Unable to remain quiet, she blurted, "What? What's going on?"

"We needed you here for your own safety," Tom said, his jaw tight.

"I don't… but why…?"

"It's Sam," Michael said, swallowing deeply. "He's dead. He was killed tonight. His body was found near one of the crypts in the City of the Dead."

"Oh God!" she cried, her chest squeezing as her legs threatened to give out on her. "He went back to talk to someone. Was he robbed?"

"No… it wasn't random. He was stabbed. But there was no evidence of a fight. We had an initial test ordered. He had barbiturates in his system, which would have rendered him slow to fight back."

Grateful for the nearby chair, her ass hit the seat as her legs collapsed.

12

CAIRO, EGYPT

Rick slept little on the flight over the Atlantic but was grateful for the private jet provided by Carson and Mace. When he'd received the phone call yesterday from Abbie, he hadn't hesitated.

"Rick, something's happened!"

"What? What's going on?" *He was immediately on alert at hearing the strain in her voice.*

"The man I was working with on the investigation was killed tonight—"

"I'm coming." *The words bolted from his lips as he headed to his bedroom, grabbing his duffel bag from his closet.*

"I'm sorry," she said, and he immediately halted.

"Why?"

"I didn't mean for you to come. I just meant that I... I... shit, Rick, I don't know."

This didn't sound like the decisive Abbie that he knew. "Talk to me, babe." *He hadn't used that endearment since she'd left, but it fell easily from his lips. Not as a throwaway but because in his heart, she was dear to him.*

"I knew if I called my brother, he'd want to come, but with Sara pregnant, I don't want him to make the trip. Or he'd insist on one of Mace's Keepers, and I don't want that either. I was just calling to let you know, but I didn't mean for you to—"

"I'm coming, Abbie. Carson already said that you have LSI-WC at your disposal when I mentioned that things were rough. So right now, I'm packing. I'll text you my flight information."

"I don't need a rescue, Rick. I'm capable of handling things on my own. I just wanted to talk."

"Then we can talk in person when I get there. And just because you can handle yourself doesn't mean you always have to. Why do you think we Keepers are always there for each other?"

She had no response to that, so he kept pressing as he continued packing. "So I'll come. If you need an extra pair of hands, or just someone you can trust, or just nothing but a friend, then I'll be there."

At the hiss of a breath she released, his shoulders had slightly relaxed as he felt her capitulation.

He was going no matter what the obstacles, but Carson had talked to Abbie's boss. Now, he had official approval for LSI to assist. He'd taken a private plane to Maine, where a tight-lipped Blake listened as he explained how he and Abbie had become friends when she was visiting, and she didn't want her brother to come since his wife was expecting. He didn't go into details, and if Blake made an assumption about how close he and Abbie had actually become, Rick was glad he didn't call him out. Now, on another private plane nearing Cairo, he was glad the trip was taking much less time than flying commercial.

He looked out the window. It wasn't the first time he'd flown over Egypt, but he'd never spent time in Cairo. He observed as the green near the Mediterranean gave way to the endless drab beige of the vast desert. As the plane descended, he spied the pyramids at Giza, noting how the city limits crept closely on one side. Turning his attention from the window, he looked at his phone, re-reading the last email sent by Abbie detailing what she could about the investigation. His fingers curled into fists at the idea that she'd been put in danger. Forcing his body to ease, he knew he'd get answers from her superiors but also figured he wouldn't like what he'd hear.

Two hours later, he'd landed, made his way through customs, and now walked toward the doors leading to the outside.

"Mr. Rankin!"

He jerked at the sound of his name, seeing a casually dressed Egyptian man standing nearby holding a hand-written sign with his name on it.

The man grinned widely. "Mr. Rankin? Yes? Yes?"

He nodded and stepped forward. "Yes."

"I'm to drive you. I am Baniti. Come, come. Follow me."

They stepped through the sliding glass doors, and a blast of oven-like heat hit him from the unrelenting Egyptian sun. He slid on his sunglasses and continued to follow Baniti down the sidewalk teeming with people, at times having to use his bulk to maneuver through the masses. Finally coming to a beat-up taxi that had seen better days... maybe better decades, he stopped and pinned the man with a hard stare.

"Come, come," Baniti said. Just as Rick was going to demand some ID, Baniti stepped closer as he popped open the trunk and whispered, "Ms. Blake's office sent me. They thought it would draw less attention than an official embassy vehicle."

"Thank you," he said, hefting his bag into the back of the taxi. Sliding into the back seat, he watched out the window as Baniti darted in and out of traffic, using his horn as an extension of his driving skills. At one point, they bounced up on the median to get around a slow-moving donkey cart and then whipped back into traffic.

He'd been in a lot of crazy-ass vehicles all over the world on missions but was more than ready to get out of the taxi as soon as Baniti stopped outside the embassy. It was all he could do not to rush into the large, multistoried building, calling Abbie's name, regardless of where she might be. Hefting his duffel onto his shoulder, he followed Baniti to the security checkpoint. Showing his passport and ID to the Marine guards, he was quickly searched and then continued to the elevator. Stepping out on the seventh floor, he and his intrepid companion were met by more armed Marine guards who checked his passport against their list.

He understood the procedures, the need for protocol to be followed, and the need for security. But all he wanted was to get his eyes on Abbie and his arms around her.

Finally, ushered into a large office, he spied her sitting on a leather sofa. Face pale. Dark circles under her eyes. And holding her body stiffly as though she was trying to rein in emotions.

It had been over six months since he'd last seen her, and she'd never looked more beautiful. His heart threatened to pound out of his chest at the sight. He called out, emotions pouring into her name. "Abbie."

Her head jerked around, and as her gaze landed on him, her mouth opened for a second before she cried, "Rick!"

Faster than he thought anyone could move, she flew from the sofa, barely giving him time to drop his duffel and brace before she slammed into him. His arms wrapped around her and held her tight, pressing her safely against his chest. With her tucked against his heartbeat, he felt his world click into place.

Looking over her head, he spied a tall, middle-aged man in black slacks, a white shirt with the sleeves rolled up, and a tie loosened around his neck. His gut told him this was the embassy CIA chief of special operations. The man's sharp gaze raked over Rick with Abbie in his arms, and he knew he was being assessed as well as doing the assessing.

Abbie stepped back and drew in a breath before letting it out slowly. "Rick, I'd like you to meet my boss, Tom Olsen. Tom, this is Richard Rankin."

He stepped around Abbie and lifted his hand. Tom offered a firm shake, and Rick was glad to see the gesture was just as he hoped— neither limp nor too hard as though trying to assert whose dick was bigger.

"Richard Rankin," Tom said. "Former SEAL. Now employed with Lighthouse Security Investigations, first in Maine with Mace Hanover and now on the West Coast with Carson Dyer."

Rick didn't reply. There was no need to. This was a dance that they needed to go through where Tom proved that he understood who Rick was. Rick knew he'd been approved to come, or he wouldn't be standing in this office.

Tom continued, inclining his head toward Abbie. "She wants you here, so you're here. I'm sure you've got questions, and you'll need to be brought up to speed."

Deciding the best course of action was to gather all intel first so he knew what Abbie was dealing with, he simply nodded. Feeling the fatigue in Abbie's body, Rick nudged her toward the sofa, settling in next to her as Tom sat in one of the padded leather chairs nearby. Rick reached over and linked fingers with Abbie, not caring if it seemed unprofessional but willing to let go if she appeared upset. He hid his sigh of relief as her fingers curled around his. Still giving his attention to Tom, he waited to see what was coming next.

"I called Abbie back from her leave when we had the death of an embassy employee while on a Nile cruise. With first intel, it seemed as though Anne Mills had been drinking and fell overboard. But it wasn't difficult for our medical examiner to determine she had barbiturates in her system even though she'd never had a history of drug use. When the guard and embassy personnel went into her apartment, papers were also found in her possession. She worked in a nonsecure section, but there is always a danger of someone getting their hands on security documents. There were hand drawings of a map, crude blueprints, and a few other drawings, but not enough information to understand what we were looking at. The items were given to Ms. Blake for her analysis. We needed her skill set to ascertain what they were. She was eventually able to determine that the map was an area in Heliopolis, but there was no other discerning information to let us know any specifics or significance. Abbie and Lieutenant Sam Broadman went to Heliopolis to see if they could discover which building might be in question, but they were unable to determine the exact location."

Rick glanced down toward Abbie. "And your friend?"

She nodded. "Mary was next, several months later."

Tom continued, "Mary was another employee in a nonsecure section who was killed while on a tour. She also had been at a party the night before, and it was determined she had the same barbiturates in her system—"

Abbie shifted slightly to look at Rick. "Mary was not a drug user. Absolutely no way."

"Barbiturates would make it hard for someone to fight back," he surmised, gaining both Abbie's and Tom's agreement.

"This time, though, by the time the Marine and embassy personnel made it to her apartment, it appeared that someone had already been searching. She shared her apartment with two roommates, but one was on leave, and the other one was working an evening shift and wasn't home. We made the connection that both she and Anne were taking classes at the American University here."

Rick had been turning the information over in his mind, connecting the dots as he knew the intelligence chief in front of him had been doing for months. But not knowing all the players and understanding their significance, he still lacked the necessary information to fully grasp Abbie's involvement.

She looked over at him again. "Sam and I went to Mary's wake, meeting and mingling with some of her friends from the college. We were hoping to see if we could understand the connections better."

He held her gaze for a moment, then speared Tom with a pointed glare. "What I don't understand, Tom, is why you sent someone who, while more than capable, is trained in geospatial and photogrammetry and not CIA special operations? I have no doubt you have numerous operators at your disposal who could be sent out to search for the same information."

He watched as Tom stiffened ever so slightly and felt certain the CIA officer was rarely questioned or had his judgment doubted. But Rick didn't give a fuck. He wanted to know why Abbie had specifically been sent into the field and placed in danger.

Before Tom had a chance to reply, Abbie's brow furrowed. He was glad she didn't appear angry, just thoughtful.

"It was thought that if I could see the architecture and the actual buildings in Heliopolis, I might be able to make more of a connection with the images I had studied," she said. Shrugging, she added, "And because I was Mary's friend, it made sense for me to go to her wake."

"Understood," Rick said. "But I still think your boss put someone with a very special skill set into a dangerous situation."

A muscle ticked in Tom's jaw. "I understand why you'd have that opinion, considering your feelings for Abbie. Your relationship with Ms. Blake can work for you or against you."

If Tom thought Rick would shy away from admitting he had feelings or be embarrassed about them, he was wrong. Rick had no problem making a public stand. "You're right. I do. And I might be here to assist with whatever investigation you need and provide cover, but I'm here because of her. First and foremost, only because of her. So upfront, you know what my mission is."

Tom held his gaze for a long moment, but Rick remained unfazed. Finally, Tom nodded. "Understood." He shifted his gaze from Rick to Abbie, then back to Rick again. "I've never met Mace Hanover, but he's known to me. I talked to Carson Dyer, as well, and have no problem working with LSI. I want to be in the loop with everything LSI processes. I've let them know that."

Nodding, he swung his arm around Abbie's shoulders, pulling her close. "Then, Mr. Olsen, we understand each other."

13

Abbie sat in Tom's office, her mind swirling. When she'd looked up at the sound of Rick's voice, her heart leaped in her chest and her vision narrowed only to him. And when his arms closed around her, the disjointed pieces of her life clicked into place. *He's here, holding me... in Tom's office.* The surreal experience had her lift her gaze to his face to make sure it wasn't all her imagination.

Seeing him staring back down at her, she sucked in a deep breath, fighting to clear her mind. She was torn between relief that Rick had flown halfway across the world to be with her, grief over the death of Sam as well as Mary, and frustration that the men in the room seemed to be talking over and around her.

Finally, she released Rick's hand and shifted to one side, her gaze peering up at his face before swinging over to her boss. "Let's get one thing straight. I'm a part of this investigation because I want to be. Something is going on. These people were involved in something.

Sam and I obviously got too close to the truth, and he paid the ultimate price. But do not sit here and act as though I don't have a say in what's happening."

Looking back at Rick, she added, "I told Tom that I wanted you to come because I know that in this country, I'm going to get a lot further if I have a male at my side. And I need it to be somebody I can trust. Right now, I don't know any of the operators."

She swung her gaze back to Tom. "Now that I think about it, you agreed rather quickly to have Rick come, which tells me you weren't going to force one of your operators on me. So what's the deal? Uncertain of your own people?"

Again a muscle ticked in Tom's jaw. "Very few people knew of the trip you and Sam took yesterday. Right now, I'm trying to keep our cards close to our chest. And someone from the outside fits our needs. For all intents and purposes, your boyfriend has come to visit you. That's all."

"What trip was yesterday?" Rick asked.

Abbie sighed, both dreading to go into the story that she knew would undoubtedly piss Rick off, but more because it was painful thinking of Sam being alive only yesterday. Knowing she could go into more detail later, she brought him up to speed on discovering one of the maps was actually located in the City of Dead and how she and Sam went to see if they could make a closer identification of the specific location. "It's very difficult in this country for a woman to travel alone and certainly not be able to ask questions or get into certain places without a man with me. So Sam and I went

RICK

together with the guide. One of the men we met pulled Sam over to the side and said that if he'd come back later alone, he would show him the building where an American woman had gone."

Rick stood and held his hand toward her. Without hesitation, she placed her hand in his and allowed him to pull her to her feet. They locked gazes, and it was so easy for her to feel safe and comforted even though it had been months since they'd been together. Not willing to analyze why, she looked back toward Tom. "Right now, I want to go back to my villa. I'll get Rick settled in and continue to bring him up to speed on everything I've found. Perhaps a fresh pair of eyes might help us know what's going on in both Heliopolis, the City of the Dead, and even the coincidence of those at the university."

Tom stood as well and nodded his agreement. "I won't place a Marine guard outside your villa, but you'll be on their rotating patrol. LSI-WC has already assured me that I'll be in on all the secure communications." Looking up at Rick, he added, "It may not have seemed like it earlier, but I'm glad you're working with us."

Abbie led the way out of Tom's office and past the Marine guard at the elevator. Once they were given clearance, they entered the empty elevator and remained silent all the way down to the first floor. From there, they were ushered toward the back and out a different door where a taxi appeared to be waiting for them. A driver hurried over, and she hesitated.

Rick leaned down and said, "That's Baniti. He met me at the airport and was given specific instructions to be my driver. He's not your average Egyptian taxi driver but works for the embassy. More specifically, I think he works for Tom."

She nodded, thinking it was odd that her boss had not given her that information. Climbing into the back seat, she tried to tamp down her irritation, only succeeding when Rick looked over and said, "I don't think he was trying to leave you out. I'm not crazy about your boss, but I don't think this was personal."

She rolled her eyes and sighed. "I guess with everything else going on, it's pretty stupid to be irritated about something so minor, isn't it? But sometimes, I feel like I only have half the information I need."

Baniti climbed behind the wheel, and she and Rick remained silent during the drive to Ma'adi. The silence was easily filled by Baniti's constant commentary, pointing out things Rick might be interested in. By now, Abbie had been awake for almost thirty-six hours and had reached her limit of rational thought. She glanced to the side, wondering what Rick thought of Cairo, but found his gaze on her. Self-conscious, she tucked a strand of hair behind her ear, knowing she looked like shit but was too tired to care.

When they pulled to a stop outside her villa gate, Baniti jumped out and opened the trunk, allowing Rick to grab his duffel. Thanking their driver warmly, she led Rick through the iron gate and into her garden.

"Damn, this is beautiful," Rick said. "It's like each of the houses around here has their own little oasis."

She looked up and offered a little smile, realizing it was the first light emotion she'd felt since being given the stunning news of Sam's death. "It is lovely, isn't it? I like to sit out here in the evenings. Actually, Mary would come over, and we'd enjoy having a glass of wine out here."

He wrapped his arm around her shoulders. "Come on, babe. Let's get you inside."

She unlocked her door, feeling perfectly safe since she knew the embassy had Marine guards in her neighborhood now, keeping an eye on her villa. When she stepped inside, the scent of freshly baked bread and lentil soup sitting in a pot on the counter greeted them. "My housekeeper, Sabah, has been here. Are you hungry?"

"I think what's more important is when was the last time you ate?"

A rueful snort slipped out. "I munched on crackers and had some tea at the embassy. Before that, it was sometime yesterday. Or maybe the day before. Now, I can't even remember when I was hauled out of here."

Rick soon made himself at home and opened cabinets until he found two bowls. She stood and stared, once more hit with how surreal it was that he was here, in Cairo, in her villa. And seemingly so at ease.

He smiled over his shoulder toward her, then ladled warm soup into each one. Refusing to remain stuck in place in a stupor, she grabbed a couple of bottled waters from the refrigerator. They sat down at her small table, saying little as they both devoured the savory meal.

"Will Sabah be back tomorrow?" he asked.

"Yes, she should be. She usually comes in the morning and then leaves whenever she's finished. I have a feeling that she'll be surprised when she finds you here." Using her bread to sop up the rest of the soup from the bottom of her bowl, she explained, "When I first came here, I had no intentions of having a housekeeper or a gardener, both seeming rather pretentious. But I quickly learned that it was expected of those of us in the foreign community to help the Egyptian economy by hiring when we could. When I was assigned this villa, Sabah and Mustafa worked for the previous employees, so it was easy to keep them on. Now, I have to admit it would be hard not to have them. The garden is way more than I would be able to keep beautiful, and while I could cook my own food and clean my own house, she does a wonderful job, and I know it helps her family to have this employment."

He grinned as he sopped up the last of his soup. "If she cooks this good all the time, you'll hear no complaints from me."

She chuckled, then stood and took the bowls to rinse them out. Leaning her hip against the counter, she allowed her eyes to feast upon him. It had been months since they'd seen each other. Kissed. Made love. Laughed. Talked. She'd never thought to see him standing in her house in Cairo, yet here he was after only one phone call when she said she needed him.

He stepped closer, still giving her space. "What are you thinking?"

Her head leaned back as she stared into his eyes. "I was thinking how long it's been since we've seen each other. It seems like forever ago and just yesterday, all at the same time."

He didn't respond but slowly nodded as he closed the distance between them, wrapping his arms around her and tucking her head underneath his chin. They stayed pressed together for several long minutes, her cheek resting against his heartbeat, steady and sure.

Finally, he said, "You need to rest, Abbie. We'll take a look at things tomorrow. Start fresh. Bring LSI-WC up on what's happening and see where to go from there. But now, we both need sleep."

She nodded, knowing he was right and touched that he was so concerned, thinking of her needs. She walked toward the stairs, and he followed after grabbing his duffel bag. As she ascended the staircase, her heart pounded, uncertain how to handle the sleeping arrangements. She had one small guest room with a bed and dresser. There was only one bathroom upstairs, so they would have to share, but it was not knowing what he expected that caused nerves to flow through her.

Her feet stumbled at the top of the stairs, both from fatigue and uncertainty. "Um… there's only one bathroom," she said, lifting her hand to point toward the doorway at the back of the hall. "That room is the guest room." Clearing her throat, she chanced a glance up at his face. "The bed's not large, but if you want—"

"It's fine, Abbie."

"Oh, okay… yeah… sure. Well, I'll see you tomorrow," she stammered, strangely let down that he so easily agreed to use the guest room. She knew it was ridiculous to hope that he would still be interested in sleeping with her. She rubbed her forehead, exhaustion pulling at every fiber of her body.

"Why don't you use the bathroom first," he suggested. "I really want you to get some sleep." He stepped closer and traced his fingertips along her forehead and down to her chin.

The touch was warm, sending tingles throughout her, just like the very first time. Nodding, she hurried into the bathroom, took a quick shower, then stepped out, seeing that he'd already opened his duffel and was sitting on the edge of the guest room bed. He looked up and smiled.

She wanted to say so many things but only managed to whisper, "Good night, Rick."

"Good night, Abbie girl."

With that, she turned and hurried into her bedroom, climbing into bed and pulling the covers up to her chin. She wasn't sure if she'd be able to sleep with all the thoughts tumbling through her mind, especially with the gorgeous man who had haunted her dreams for months just across the hall. Yet the realization that he was so close wrapped her in a blanket of comfort, and she closed her eyes. Soon, sleep claimed her.

It had taken every ounce of Rick's self-control not to crawl in bed with her just to hold her tight as they slept during the night. But he knew it wasn't the time. The instant he'd seen her sitting in Tom's office, he could see shock, grief, and exhaustion plainly on her face. He wasn't lying when he said he wanted her to rest and that they could deal with everything the next day. What he didn't tell her was that he'd decided that also included their relationship.

He'd already planned on attempting to renew their connection when she returned to the United States, but fate stepped in and offered him an earlier chance. One that he wasn't about to squander. He'd keep her safe, and they'd figure out what the hell was going on, and he wanted to prove to her that he was not going to walk away again.

Taking a shower, he washed off the travel sweat and pulled on a pair of boxers, hoping the housekeeper wasn't going to barge in too early. Flipping off the light in the bathroom, he stopped outside her door, noting she hadn't closed it all the way. Wanting to assure himself that she was all right, he pushed the door open a few inches, seeing her asleep by the sliver of moonlight peeking through the window. Her long dark hair spread across the pillow, and her beautiful face was now at ease in slumber.

Tiptoeing in, he leaned down and gently kissed her forehead. Her soft skin felt cool under his lips, and he once again battled the desire to crawl into bed with her, curl his body around hers, and protect her during the night. Releasing a long breath, he slowly backed out of the room and moved across the hall. The bed in the guest room was small for a man of his size, but he hadn't lied when he said he'd slept on rocks and dirt before. And just like her, it didn't take long for sleep to come.

14

The following morning, Rick woke early, hearing the sound of someone in the kitchen below. He climbed from bed and tiptoed out into the hall, seeing that Abbie was still asleep in her room. Quickly using the bathroom, he dressed and went back into the guest room, securing his items inside his duffel. Another noise caught his attention from outside, and he stalked over to the window, looking down into the garden. A man in a long galabeya was trimming the hedges, and he assumed that must be Mustafa.

Not wanting to feel trapped upstairs yet not wanting to frighten Sabah, he made sure he clomped down the stairs so that she would know someone besides Abbie was in the house. Sure enough, in the kitchen was a petite Egyptian woman wearing a blouse and long skirt, her head wrapped in a habib. Lifting his hands, he smiled. "Ahlan wa sahlan. I'm Rick. Friend of Abbie's."

Sabah nodded but continued to stare suspiciously with narrowed eyes. The man from the garden looked through the kitchen window, then walked to the back door. He spoke to her in rapid Arabic, and she nodded, going back to fixing breakfast.

The man dipped his chin toward Rick. "I'm Mustafa. Gardner to Miss Blake. Baniti said that you would be here."

Glad for Baniti's foresight, he nodded. "Ahlan wa sahlan, Mustafa."

Mustafa turned and went back into the garden, and Rick decided he would go back upstairs, seeing that his presence seemed to disconcert Sabah. Just as he turned, he spied a sleepy Abbie walking into the room. A braid held her hair away from her face, and she was dressed in a flowing robe over her pajamas. She rubbed her eyes and yawned, padding barefoot into the room.

She looked at Sabah and smiled. "Salam alaykum, Sabah." Receiving a greeting and a warm smile from her housekeeper, she turned and walked over to Rick. Reaching out to place her hand on his arm, she held his gaze.

He felt the same jolt as always. Time had not diminished their connection, and he longed to pull her into his arms again.

Looking up, she asked, "Did you sleep well?"

"Yeah, babe. How about you?"

"I didn't think there was a chance in hell that I was going to be able to sleep, but I did."

"You were exhausted."

She nodded, agreeing. Turning, she accepted two glasses of orange juice from Sabah, and they moved to

RICK

the table. Soon, they had plates of boiled eggs, toast, fruit, and tahini.

They kept the conversation light, and he wondered how free they'd be able to talk with the housekeeper close by. Even if she knew very little English, he wasn't inclined to trust anyone who could overhear.

Suddenly, Sabah gathered her bag and announced, "I shop."

She turned and walked out, and Abbie laughed. "She usually does shop today, but I have a feeling she thought we would want to be alone." Suddenly blushing, she shook her head. "Of course, we do, but not for the reason I think Sabah was thinking." With that, she turned even brighter red, and Rick laughed.

He'd love to be alone with Abbie in just the way that Sabah assumed but knew that he would have to wait for the right time. He just hoped the right time would present itself soon.

They made their way into the small living room and sat on the sofa. Abbie carried a folder with her and began spreading papers out on the coffee table in front of them.

He glanced at the papers and said, "I know Tom went through everything last night, but I'll have you repeat a lot of it as we look at this. It'll make more sense coming from you since you're the one who's been analyzing the intel."

She nodded again, then sighed, blowing out a long breath. Pushing her braid over her shoulder, she held his gaze, her smile gone.

"So far, there have been two deaths of Americans

associated with the Adamsons at the university. When Anne Mills had her accident, which we don't believe was an accident, she was on a tour arranged by the recreation office. She worked in food requisition, and it was the first tour she'd taken while here. She also took a few classes at the American College. And you'll want to remember that tidbit for later. She was the first one where barbiturates were found in her system. Certainly, she could have been partying on the boat and had more than alcohol, but the drug would have rendered her less likely to fight back if someone pushed her overboard. Here are the papers that were found at her place. They are of a hand-drawn map that I discerned was from an area in Heliopolis."

"Okay," he drawled, his gaze scanning the new papers she laid out in front of him. "Got it. What's next?"

She hesitated, then spoke, her voice cracking. "Then comes Mary."

He winced. "Shit, babe. I'm sorry. I didn't mean to be insensitive." He reached over and wrapped his hand around the back of her head, and applied just a bit of pressure. She easily fell forward, her head landing on his chest. They stayed like that for a long moment, and he wanted to keep holding her to take away any of her pain. She sighed, then leaned back and looked into his eyes. He swore he could see his future in the gray-green depths. "Tell me about her."

She reached for one of the papers, but he stopped her hand. "No, Abbie. Not this. Tell me about your friend."

She pressed her lips together and held his gaze before he leaned back and pulled her with him. After a moment, she sucked in a breath and let it out slowly, nodding. "It's hard… first in the military and now. Hard to make friends when you spend a lot of your career in a closed space, staring at computer screens and maps, analyzing images and pictures. My work wasn't in the field. I wasn't part of a big mission team. Sure, there was team building in the Army, but for my daily work, I was in a room with others like me who preferred the solitary environment to get the job done. Even in Afghanistan, I wasn't in the field but in a windowless room poring over intel. Here… the same thing. So friends… girlfriends were few and far between."

She pressed against him closer, her body now curled into his. "She was pretty, happy, soft-spoken. She worked for the State Department as an IT specialist. It was just a way to travel, and she was taking classes at the university here to finish her degree and then could have moved into a better-paying job. We met shortly after I began here and started having lunch together. She dragged me out of my villa to go shopping at the Khan el-Kahili or go to a museum. Hell, she was the one who had me out on a camel near Giza." She shifted around to look at him, a slight grimace on her face. "I can't say that I knew everything about her because I've learned things since she died, but for a somewhat solitary person, she was the one I was closest to while here."

They sat quietly for a moment, then she looked back down at the papers and continued. "Mary was killed when hit by a vehicle. She was on a tour, a last-minute addition from the recreation office. She had barbiturates in her system, which would slow her reactions, making her an easier target for someone to hit. She also took classes at the American University and knew Anne. After she died, I went back to look at the map from Anne that I hadn't been able to identify."

"And these papers are of an area of the City of the Dead?"

"Yeah. It's a necropolis that's now used to house about a million poor Egyptians in slumlike conditions."

"Christ," he muttered, looking at a few pictures she'd taken on her phone. "And her connections to Anne would be dying by accident, a tour with the recreation office, barbiturates, and college classes. And a hand-drawn map from Anne that included the area where Mary was killed."

"Yes."

"And then Sam?" An unexpected bolt of jealousy shot through him and was difficult to tamp down. He had no right to feel jealous, but the thought that Sam might be more than a work partner… or just that the man had the opportunity to spend a lot of time with Abbie was enough to make Rick have to force back the irrational emotion.

"Yes, Sam. Lieutenant Sam Broadman. He was assigned to Michael and was one of the few to know of my cover as working for Michael as an assistant."

"Were you two friends?" He couldn't help but ask as he tried to keep the edge out of his voice.

"Not friends. More like just friendly. He'd asked me

out when he first got here, but he seemed younger than his age, and I feel older than mine. It had awkward written all over it. Plus, I wasn't interested. He was so eager to please. So eager to move up and get a promotion. I mean, I get it. I left the Army as a captain, and I sometimes think he felt in competition with me. But eventually, we settled into a decent working relationship."

"Why did Tom have you go out to the City of the Dead? That seems fucked to me."

"Tours actually go there, so it wasn't a big deal. I had the knowledge to visually scan the area, much like with Heliopolis, to see if I could discern a building that would indicate what was on the maps. Sam didn't have that skill set. But as a woman, a *foreign* woman in this country, I needed a man with me to get me into places and not be hassled. So we went together."

"And weren't successful?"

"No. God, it's worse than the pictures show. It's like, you know there's great history there, amazing crypts and mausoleums, yet it's still a place of horrific poverty where people are living their entire lives in the shadows of the tombs." She shivered slightly. "Anyway, it's such a maze where so many buildings look alike that we weren't able to find any exact location that might have been indicated on the maps."

"He went back again that night?"

She nodded, twisting on the sofa to face him. "One of the men in the area pulled him aside. When Sam came back to me, he said the man would show him where an English-speaking woman and Egyptian man had come. But he'd only show him if he'd come back alone."

Rick rubbed his chin, thoughts moving through his head. "And Sam didn't think that was odd? Or dangerous?"

Snorting, Abbie scrunched her nose. "Sam was excited to be the one to find something. I think he always chafed a little at the trust Tom and Michael put into me. So this was his opportunity to be the one who came up with the information."

"Fuckin' idiot," he mumbled. "Never go in without the proper intel and backup."

She remained quiet, neither defending nor cursing Sam, but then since she'd known him personally, he understood. It was hard to lose someone on your team. They sat in silence for several moments, gazes pinned on the multitude of papers laid out in a neat arrangement on the coffee table. Two similar hand-drawn maps of an area in Heliopolis, the City of the Dead, and a drawing of what appeared to be tombs, a list of dates and times.

"I'm going to make a secure call to LSI-WC," he finally announced. "I want their input." Feeling her slump with resignation, he hastened to add, "They'll be fresh eyes, but I trust your analysis on these. Mostly, I want them to get all they can on the players in this."

"Okay," she agreed, "But I haven't told you all of it."

Eyes wide, he shot his gaze from the papers on the table to her. "Yeah? Guess you'd better get it all out."

"Mary's wake."

"Damn, I forgot all about that."

RICK

"So Sam and I went. It was surmised that the two of us could mingle easier than just me. Not a bad idea since I hate mingling, and Sam knew how to work a room. But, anyway, it was interesting."

His attention was riveted on her because, for the moment, her grief was set aside as she related what she had discovered.

"Mary and Anne knew each other through classes. They were part of a study group that one of the professors created by hand-picking the students. And that professor was Jason Adamson. What's also interesting is that his wife is Cora Adamson, the head of the Embassy Employee Recreation office and was the one who added Mary at the last minute to a supposedly closed tour to the City of the Dead."

Jerking his chin back, he widened his eyes. "No shit!"

"Oh yeah. So the plot thickens," she quipped.

"Anything else before I make my call?"

Her brow furrowed. "Only that I witnessed a heated discussion between a woman with a German accent, Giselle, and a man with a British accent named Paul. I have no idea why it seemed significant, but it struck me as odd at the time."

"You have last names for them?"

"Giselle Schmidt and Paul White. I know he works for a civil engineering company here."

Leaning over, he kissed her forehead. "You did great, but then you don't need me to tell you that. I'm gonna make the call now. You can stay, and I'll put it on speaker. That way, if they need anything clarified, you can answer." He hesitated, seeing a flash of indecision move through her eyes before she nodded.

"That'd be good," she agreed.

He released a breath, realizing how much he wanted her to get to know his coworkers. *She knows the Keepers in Maine... but I want her to be comfortable with the ones I now work with on the West Coast.* He had no problem admitting the reason because it was staring him in the face with gray-green eyes. *Because when all this is over, I want her to come back with me.*

15

Abbie wondered if it would feel weird talking to the Keepers on the West Coast. While she didn't know her brother's coworkers very well, at least she'd met them and had heard him speak of them. She'd met Carson, but the others on the conference call now were strangers. *Yet isn't that always the way in the Army and CIA? Meet people, make new connections, work for a while, get transferred, or they get transferred.* So in truth, she had to admit that just because she'd initially been hurt when Rick had not confided his move to her early on in their relationship, she had no reason not to get to know or to trust Carson's Keepers.

Rick had called to set up a secure conference call on his computer. She couldn't see their faces but could hear voices identifying who was speaking. Her imagination ran rampant at the sound of the men gathered back in California. She could only imagine the man candy in one room if they were anything like the original Keepers. *Sexist but true.* Rolling her eyes, she was glad they couldn't see her face.

She took a back seat during the call, allowing Rick to first make sure that Tom was patched into the call. Once given the all clear, Rick gave a succinct explanation of everything she had reviewed with him. Hop, Dolby, Chris, and Leo seemed to ask the most questions, and she imagined the others tapping away on their computers as she gave answers.

"My first thought," Hop said, "is that I'd like to get closer for backup if needed."

Her brows lowered as she looked over at Rick, and he said, "Hop is our pilot. It would be nice to have him as backup and not all the way in California."

She nodded but couldn't imagine that after months of these events taking place, anything was going to be solved quickly, especially since Tom wanted answers and had the CIA at his disposal. But she kept that thought to herself since Tom didn't question the suggestion.

Leo spoke next. "Odds are that Anne and Mary came across information or were involved in something. Maybe they discovered something that they shouldn't have and had to be killed because of it, or they were doing something they shouldn't have and became a liability that needed to be eliminated."

"It's hard to imagine Mary that way," Abbie confessed. "But in truth, how well do any of us really know someone else? She certainly was involved in something that I didn't know about."

RICK

"Did she ever seem like she was hiding anything?" Chris asked.

Jerking slightly, she wanted to immediately deny that was a possibility but couldn't. "Not that I saw, but then I wasn't suspicious of her in any way. I suppose it would not be beyond the realm of possibility."

Rick reached over and wrapped his hand around hers, giving a gentle squeeze as though knowing that the idea that one of the few people she considered to be a friend might not have been as good a friend as she thought.

"Of all the coincidences you mentioned," Dolby said, "there is another one. All of these were women. You can't count Sam because he wasn't involved in whatever they were doing. He was killed because you two were getting too close to something."

At those words, Rick's hand spasmed, and she jumped. While not painful, his squeeze was a reminder that he was there because she could have been in danger at the necropolis. *Damn, even Tom understood the risk, and that was why he brought me into the embassy in the middle of the night. And that's why he's agreed to let LSI help.*

Bringing her focus back to the investigation, she said, "Of everything, what's most suspicious in recent times is that Cora Adamson added Mary to what was supposed to be an already full tour. That doesn't make sense. But then, her husband made a comment at the wake that he thought she was on a tour by herself. I'm embarrassed to say that at the time, I didn't even realize I was hearing information that didn't add up."

"Don't take that on, babe," Rick said, shaking his

head. "You're personally involved, and it's hard to be objective."

"That's just an excuse," she bit back, glaring. "I'm a trained professional. I was there to gather information and completely missed the contradiction."

"Abbie." Carson's voice cut through the call.

She jumped slightly, grimacing that she'd given in to the urge to argue with Rick in the middle of a meeting. *God, is this what it would have been like if we'd both been Keepers in Maine?* She glanced up to see Rick's intense stare pinned on her face, almost as though he knew what was going through her mind. Jerking her gaze back to the computer screen, she said, "Sorry. Yes?"

"I've been on a mission where someone I care about was involved. In fact, that person is now my wife. So have Leo and Chris. Hell, for that matter, so has your brother and most of the Keepers with Mace. What I'm getting at is every one of us will tell you to cut yourself some slack. We're professionals, but we're human. Our emotions can get in the way, but that doesn't make us less professional."

Clearing her throat, she replied, "Thank you. I just wish she could have come to me if she was involved in something."

Rick jumped in and said, "I want to look into Cora Adamson—"

"Tom, can you help us with this?" Carson asked.

Up until now, Tom had taken a back seat to the proceedings, which seemed odd to Abbie, considering he'd always appeared in control.

"I can look at the computer logs. Give me a minute,"

Tom replied. After a moment of silence, he came back on. "The system just has lists of who is on official tours, but not all the information needed. I can see that Mary's name is on the list for the tour but can't see any other information, such as who or when she was added."

She thought about the wake again, poring over every conversation. "What about Giselle?" she asked. "While we're looking into everyone else, how about I meet up with Giselle to see if there is anything I can discern from her?"

"Let us do some digging first and figure out what you might be dealing with," Carson suggested.

"And look into Cora's husband, Jason," Rick said. "He's another link we need to investigate."

"Got it," Carson said. "Tom? Anything else?"

"No, but I want follow-up on everything you come across."

"Absolutely," Carson agreed.

As Rick disconnected the call, she sat for a minute and stared at the now-blank computer screen, her mind sifting through the rapid-paced information that had been discussed.

"Are you okay, babe?" Rick asked, drawing her attention back to him.

She nodded slowly, then finally let out a long breath. "It feels…" she began, searching for the right words.

She appreciated that he didn't try to throw descriptors at her, guessing what she was thinking. Instead, he gave her the time to sift through her thoughts. "It's not overwhelming because I've been on the front end of missions. But usually, my value added was in the imagery analysis that was then given to those who would actively investigate or plan missions. But this time, it feels relevant to be active in the investigation."

"You're good at this."

Her gaze jumped to his. "You think so?"

"I know so. I know you've always been a behind-the-scenes person, but I think that serves you well. You observe. You observe people and places carefully, logging the information in your mind. I think that's what we're going to need for this."

Glancing back at the computer, she asked, "So what now?"

"Why don't you show me part of Cairo? Tomorrow, we're going to get real busy, and time for ourselves will be minimal. But now, if anybody's watching you, they'll just see you showing your boyfriend the sights."

"I suppose it would be cheesy to take you to Giza to see the pyramids, wouldn't it?"

"Can I get on a camel?"

Her lips curved upward as she tried to stifle the smile but then burst out in laughter. "It'll be overpriced and smelly, but yes. You can get on a camel."

He stood and reached back, and she placed her hand in his. They walked up the stairs, disappearing into their separate bedrooms to change. Pulling out her messy braid, she brushed her long hair and braided it once again. She glanced at her bed, remembering their moments together in Maine when they'd spent as much time naked between the sheets as they could. Her body flushed, and she couldn't deny that she still wanted him.

"You ready?" he called from the hall.

With a last glance down at the bed, she shouted in return, "Oh, yeah. I'm ready."

Two hours later, tickets in hand for not only getting into the Giza Esplanade but also for entering one of the pyramids, they walked toward the one that allowed visitors inside. She waved her hand as several guides rushed up and called out, "La, la." Turning to Rick, she said, "You have to watch out for the scams. It's even worse outside the Esplanade. Almost anyone can tell you they're a tour guide and charge for their services. Most of the time, what they say isn't even factual. The information they give is what they've heard others say, but you learn nothing from them." Inclining her head toward the nearest pyramid, she said, "Let's go in first. Then we can take our time and walk around a bit more leisurely."

The line was not overly long, and soon they were entering. She was able to walk without ducking but looked over her shoulder and grinned as Rick had to stoop to keep from bumping his head. It was well lit, but the narrow passageway cutting through the massive stones gave evidence of the undertaking the ancient Egyptians went through to create such a world monument. They came to a ramp with wood slats that allowed their feet to keep from slipping on the steep incline of stone. Holding the metal rail on the side, she now had to bend over just to make it up the smaller passageway. The farther they ascended, the hotter it became.

Finally, they made it to a large room of smooth-cut stone walls, floors, and ceilings deep in the heart of the pyramid. The only light came from the wire of light bulbs attached to the walls. They could stand up straight, and she welcomed the feel of Rick's fingers lacing through hers. Spending several minutes looking around, imagining how far back in history they'd come from just their walk, they made it down the other side, mimicking the hunched position and careful placing of their feet to keep from sliding down the sharp inclines. "It's harder going down," she murmured, glad for his presence as her feet slipped several times. "At least the air gets cooler as we descend."

Once out, she breathed deeply, but the sun's heat bore down on them, giving no relief. She lifted her hand and pointed to one of the other pyramids in the distance. "We'll head there next."

"Pictures make you think this is so much closer than it is," Rick said, looking from the base of the pyramid to the others on the Giza Plateau.

"That's why a lot of people take carts to get from one to the other," she said, dipping her head toward one of the horse carts nearby. "Are you game?"

With a wide grin on his handsome face, he nodded, and her heart clenched. After paying the driver, Rick placed his hands on her waist and easily lifted her into the cart. They came to the area where men in galabeyas stood near their camels, offering the chance for visitors to get on a camel for photo opportunities. After he climbed onto the sitting camel, she cackled aloud at the sight of the large man almost falling off the front as the camel came to a stand by rocking forward first and then backward. Snapping pictures, she then accepted the assistance of another man as she climbed onto her camel and held on as he rose.

Looking over at Rick, she couldn't miss the way he was staring at her, his eyes twinkling and his smile infectious. Biting her lip, she refused to think of how wonderful it was to have him there with her and how lonely it would be when he'd left and returned to his life in California.

Back on the ground, they took numerous pictures, including selfies with the great monuments in the background. After another horse cart ride, they made it to the Sphinx. More pictures were taken, most with his arm around her or standing behind her with his arms encircling her. A vacationing family asked if Abbie would take photographs of them, and she quickly acquiesced. To reciprocate, the wife snapped several of her and Rick also. He cracked a joke, and she twisted her head to look up at him, grinning widely.

After leaving the esplanade, they caught a taxi, and she grinned. "I've got another surprise for you."

It wasn't far, even with traffic, and they arrived at the Mena House resort, the luxury hotel that overlooked the pyramids and sported green grass, tall palms, and beautiful restaurants. "I thought we could eat here," she said.

"Damn, Abbie girl. This is fuckin' amazing!" He

grabbed her and gave her a twirl, setting her feet down on the lush grass.

As they sat down in the cool shade with the spectacular view out the window and the delicious food served, she said, "I've only been here once before."

"The location is perfect," he said.

"It was originally a house that was enlarged over the years, and the new owners turned it into a hotel. Of course, it's on a slightly different level now, but it's still the best hotel in Cairo."

They finished their meal and strolled amongst the gardens with the sun setting behind the pyramids. She was still exhausted and knew they had a lot to do and plan for their investigation, but for now, it was nice to just pretend that they were a couple enjoying a day out. She closed her eyes, giving over to the feel of a light breeze against her skin, the touch of his hand wrapped around hers, and his shoulder pressing into hers. And wished it didn't have to end.

"Why California?" The words slipped out before she could hold them back.

16

Rick stood in the lush, grassy courtyard with palm trees swaying in the evening breeze. The setting sun sent brilliant yellows and oranges across the sky, and in the distance sat the pyramids as they had for thousands of years. His fingers were laced with Abbie's, and her side was pressed against his. The gentle breeze picked up the loose tendrils of her hair, and he tucked them behind her ear. Her green tunic blouse fluttered around her hips, and he longed to peek behind her sunglasses to see if the color reflected in her eyes. Her cheeks were kissed by the sun, a few freckles dotting her nose. He closed his eyes, wanting to hold on to the memory of this day and this moment.

"Why California?"

At those barely whispered words from her, his eyes shot open, and his stomach tightened. He knew they needed to have a conversation but didn't want to have it there. Looking down into her eyes, he said, "I'll tell you everything, Abbie. But can we go back to your place first?"

She held his gaze, seeming to study him before nodding her agreement. He had no idea what she was thinking, though. With their hands still linked, they walked back to the front of the resort and hailed a taxi to Ma'adi. The ride was made in silence, yet it didn't appear to be uncomfortable, which he hoped was a good sign. Once they arrived at her villa, he paid and tipped the driver while she walked through the gate into her garden.

He followed, and she looked over her shoulder. "How about some wine? We can sit out here if you'd like."

"Sounds good."

After a minute, she returned, and they sat next to each other on a wicker settee near a hedge of fragrant flowers. Linking fingers with her again, he began. "I didn't want to put you off, but we'd had such a good time at Giza. I guess I just wanted to preserve the good memories."

"And you're afraid that what you're going to tell me will ruin everything?"

"I hope not. I don't think so, but I just preferred being able to sit very close to you as I tried to explain." She nodded and leaned her shoulder against him, and the tightness in his chest eased. "You've met Rank. I love my brother, and he made it easy for me to appreciate him. He was never a jerk, which I know some older brothers can be. And I would never say that he didn't have to work hard for everything he obtained, but sometimes it seemed like everything he wanted just came to him. In high school, he played every sport and excelled. I only played football but knew what it was like to be compared to my older brother by the coaches."

"You felt lacking?" she asked softly.

"Do you remember what you said about your two older brothers?"

She grinned and nodded.

"So yeah, the same kind of thing. Neither he nor our parents ever made me feel less. In fact, to be honest, no one ever did. But it always seemed like I had to work harder to get some of the same things that came naturally to him. He was accepted into BUD/S on his first try. Me? I was turned down twice before finally being admitted on the third try. He was able to get on the ground level with Mace in the building of LSI. The first time I came out and he showed me around, I was stunned. I had a strange sensation of being both thrilled and uncertain when asked if I'd like to work there also."

She nodded, and he felt her cheek rub against his shoulder as they pressed closely together. "I understand completely," she said. "There's a desire to follow in your older siblings' footsteps, yet a desire to forge your own path."

"Absolutely. LSI was such a unique opportunity that I would've been a fool to turn it down. And there were a lot of good advantages to it. I love my brother, so I got to see him and work with him. Helena is a beautiful and smart woman, and I couldn't ask for a nicer sister-in-law. And hell, just being around Eleanor was wonderful.

When our parents came from North Carolina, they could see everybody. And working for Mace and the other Keepers was a great career. Yet..."

"You wanted something for you."

He nodded, encouraged that she appeared to understand. "When you're blessed, it's hard for others to see that you might want more. Not more money or more glory. But more can just mean the chance to be your own person instead of an extension of a sibling."

She held his gaze and offered a little smile.

Emboldened, he continued. "When Mace started talking about taking on a partner and creating a West Coast LSI, I was intrigued. To start on the ground level and help someone build it was exactly what Rank had done with Mace. But I didn't figure I had a chance. Until Carson came out, and I talked with him and Mace, and I also talked with Rank. The only doubts I had about making the move was just missing out on family time. But everything else about it made me want to leap at the opportunity."

Abbie shifted slightly and held his gaze, reaching up to caress his jaw with her fingers. He leaned into the warmth of her touch.

"Abbie, I never planned on you. I never planned on meeting someone who made me want to be with them more than anything else. And yes, I knew you were special right away, but I told myself it was temporary. You were going back to Cairo, and we were having fun. It was a helluva lot more than a one-night stand, but..." He sighed, shaking his head slowly. "By the time I realized my heart belonged to you, and that I needed to talk to you about what was happening with my career move, the cat was let out of the bag, and everything fell apart. Maybe if you'd been able to have that last week in Maine, we could have talked more, cleared the air, and discussed how to move forward. But I fucked up, then you got the call to come back."

"It's not your fault, Rick. I acted like it was because I was hurt and disappointed. But you're right, we started out as fun, and then friends, and then we figured out it was more than that. The timing sucked, but you did nothing wrong."

He searched her face, her words giving him hope. "Abbie, this doesn't have to be the end. There's no reason we can't work to move forward once we get past all the shit swirling around right now."

She nodded slowly, her gaze boring intently into his, a puff of breath leaving her lips. "I have no idea when that will be or how that will happen, but I'd like to move forward with you. Because I'm no longer willing to not have you in my life."

"Thank fuck," he groaned, pulling her close and covering her mouth with his own.

He lifted her easily with one hand under her ass and the other banded around her back as he stood. She didn't hesitate to wrap her legs around his waist, and her hands clutched his jaw. As soon as he made it through her door, he kicked it shut with his boot and then carried her up the stairs, their lips never separating. Not hesitating, he walked into her bedroom and then pulled back slightly. Her eyes were hooded, her lips plump and wet. She tried to pull him back to her, but he resisted, hating every second the kiss wasn't continuing. But he had to get the words out… she had to know.

"Abbie, I need to tell you, and I need you to really take this in."

Her breathing slowed as she pressed her lips together, a crease marring her forehead. Her eyes looked deeply into his, and he knew he was drowning but didn't care if he never came up for air as long as she was in his arms. Swallowing deeply, he said, "You are no fuck. This isn't just for fun. This is as real as it gets. I've been miserable without you and have plotted and planned for when I could see you again. I didn't want it to be because something happened, but I'll take any excuse for being with you now. But, babe, you have to understand that I want you in my life. And when we make love, I'm making a commitment. However we have to work that out, we will."

"Wow…" she breathed, eyes now wide. "When you have something to say, you really get it all out, don't you?"

"I'm not making the same mistake again. I'm all in, and I need to know how you feel about that."

A slow smile curved her lips as she wrapped her arms around his neck and pressed tightly to his chest, her core nestled against his cock. "I'm all in, too, Rick."

"You and me, babe?"

A soft bark of laughter left her lips. "Yes… you and me."

"Thank God," he groaned, then angled his head and slammed his lips over hers again. She squirmed against his body as teeth clicked, noses bumped, and hair was pulled. Just when he thought his dick would explode or have a permanent zipper imprint, he turned and sat on the side of the bed with her still in his arms. Falling back onto the covers, he pulled her along with him so she was now spread on top of his body.

Just when he was sure the kiss had taken on a life force of its own, she lifted, and he felt the loss immediately. Grinning, she straddled his hips, ground down on his erection, and unbuttoned her blouse, allowing the green material to slide off her arms and float down to the floor. He'd been right earlier... the green did bring out the color in her gray-green eyes.

His gaze dropped to her breasts, and he lifted his hands to trail his fingertips over the delicate flesh as she unfastened her bra and allowed it to follow her blouse. Now, he lifted her breasts in his palms, feeling their weight and circling her nipples. She threw her head back, and his gaze dragged from the pale column of her neck down to her breast. She had another smattering of freckles that danced across her shoulders, and he vowed to taste and memorize each one.

She dropped her chin and slid her hands underneath his shirt, her palms smoothing over his abs. "I want you," she whispered.

"Then that's what you get, babe." He grabbed her waist and lifted her upward, shifting so that she fell onto her back, and he bolted from the bed. Toeing off his boots, he stripped faster than ever and soon leaned over to pull her pants down her legs. With her clad in only her panties, he nuzzled between her thighs, inhaling the scent of her arousal. His cock ached, but he wanted to take his time and savor every moment.

Hooking his fingers into the top of her panties, he dragged them down her legs, his gaze feasting on her body and continuing to memorize each curve.

She spread for him, and he crawled over her, his hand cupping her mound, inserting a finger into her channel, finding her wet and ready. Biting her bottom lip, she half closed her eyes, and a moan escaped. He bent forward, capturing her mouth and swallowing the next moan she emitted. Working her sex with his finger, finding the spot that caused her to arch her back, he sucked a nipple deeply just as she cried out her release. Slowly, her body eased, and a lazy smile aimed at him made him smile as well.

"Please…"

"Always," he vowed, then hesitated. "Um… I've got a condom, but there's been no one since you."

"Not for me either," she whispered.

"So…"

"Yeah." She grinned, pulling him tighter.

He eased his cock into her sex, slowly moving until he was fully seated. "Christ, you're tight. So fuckin' tight." He thrust gently, allowing her body to acclimate, then grip him as he pistoned faster.

The feel of her was every bit as amazing as he remembered. The dance of the ages continued as her legs lifted, her heels urging him on, and he was only too happy to acquiesce. The pressure built, and he knew he wouldn't last long… not with this woman who had come to mean the world to him. It wasn't sex… it was a commitment. He communicated with his body what she meant to him and prayed she understood.

She grasped his shoulder, crying out her orgasm as her inner walls gripped him even tighter. He tightened his jaw as his entire body tensed, his release hitting him right after hers, and they flung themselves over the precipice together.

Rolling to the side as his cock slowly slid from her body, he gathered her in his arms. Holding her close, he fought to catch his breath. When he could finally speak, he mumbled, "I thought I might have died, but then if I did, I can't think of a better way to go."

She giggled, wiping the sweat from his brow. "La petite mort."

"Hell, forget little death. That was a big fuckin' fireworks explosion."

Her laughter rang out, and he swept her hair back from her face, thinking he'd never heard or seen anything more beautiful in his life. "I love you, Abbie."

She blinked, her obvious surprise written across her face, and for a second, he wondered if he should have remained silent on his feelings. *Too much, too soon?* But just as quickly, he dismissed those thoughts. He repeated, "I know what I feel. I love you."

Time stood still as he stared into the depths of her eyes. Then the air flowed into his lungs again as she smiled.

"I love you, too," she whispered as her fingertips lightly traveled over his face.

He kissed her just as the last syllable left her lips. Pressed together from lips to hips, he pulled her tight to his body. Their hearts beat in synchronization, pounding out a rhythm as old as time but new to him. Rolling over so that he was once again on top, his cock was ready to go just as his phone vibrated. He wanted to ignore the sound, cast out everything but the feel of her body nestled into his, but he couldn't. With a groan, he shifted to the side and reached over to grab it from the nightstand. "Yeah?"

"Meeting in five. We'll go over what we've got."

Disconnecting, he looked down at her eyes which had been filled with lust and now were filled with questions. Kissing her lightly, he willed his cock to behave. "Five minutes. Carson's got some intel."

With a quick nod, she said, "Got it. Just let me hit the bathroom first."

He rolled off her and stood by the side of the bed, reaching his hand down to her. She placed her hand in his, and he gently pulled her up. She hurried into the bathroom. The toilet flushed, and she came out naked. "Ugh, I wish I could shower first, but duty calls."

As his gaze raked over her, he considered calling Carson back to tell him that they needed more time… to make love again, shower, eat, and only then would they be ready to jump back into work.

As though reading his mind, she grinned and waggled her finger toward him as she dressed quickly. He did the same but vowed to get back to what they were doing as soon as possible.

17

Abbie sat once again in front of the computer that Rick had set up on her kitchen table. And while the faces of the Keepers were not on the screen, she listened with rapt attention to what they had to say, now starting to recognize their voices.

"I want you to know that Hop and Dolby are on their way to you. They left this morning," Carson began. "Tom, thank you for agreeing to my proposal."

"Good to work with LSI," Tom said.

She blinked in surprise. *Tom must really need assistance... I wonder why?* She had little time to process that information when Carson continued.

"We've taken a look at Anne and Mary to see what we could find that might give us direction. You were right with your connections... female, in their late twenties, single, in Cairo for about two years, taking classes at the American College, and in jobs at the embassy that, while giving them the opportunity to live and work in a foreign country, weren't overly ambitious, leaving little room for professional advancement. And of course, they participated in Jason Adamson's study group, seemingly hand-picked by him."

She pressed her lips together to keep from asking questions, wanting to know what new information the Keepers had discovered, considering they had just repeated what she knew.

"This is Jeb. Plus, both women had significant deposits from a Cairo International Bank account go into their bank accounts. Anne's parents were surprised to discover their daughter had such *savings* when she died. Mary had only a brother as a relation, and he had been equally pleased to be the beneficiary of his sister's money. Neither had any idea what their relations were doing other than working at the embassy."

"Oh God," Abbie moaned at the thought of what Mary had done to receive that money.

"Because of each woman's connection to Jason and Cora, we've focused on three things. Obtaining background on the Adamsons, looking into anyone who isn't part of the embassy community but fits into the pattern with the Adamsons, and checking on the French woman, Collette."

"There wasn't anyone else from the embassy who died, was there, Tom?" she blurted.

There were a few seconds of hesitation. "No other personnel have died in the past year," Tom said.

Her brow furrowed at Tom's reticence. The idea that her boss might be sitting on knowledge or had ignored information was more than she wanted to deal with at the moment. Looking over, she caught Rick's stare and shook her head.

"Go ahead, boss," Rick said.

"Bennett here. I've looked at the info on other women. Of course, in a city like Cairo, missing women and discovered bodies are commonplace, which, not to be insensitive, is unfortunate when trying to do any research or analysis. Almost twelve months ago, there was a French student who was studying at the university. Collette Chastain. She had nothing to do with the American Embassy, but she fit the profile, and the reason I picked up on it was that she was reported as missing by the French Embassy and then found by the Egyptian police outside her apartment building. She had been in a class with Jason Adamson. I can run through more programs to see if anything else pops up, but I think we've got enough to see the Adamsons are fuckin' suspicious."

"I asked Sam to do the same thing," she huffed, looking at Rick. "I had wondered if there was someone else who fit the profile. He said he'd talk to Tom to see if some agents could look into it."

Again, the video conference was silent for a few seconds.

"I never got a request from Sam," Tom replied curtly.

She managed to hide her frustration but held Rick's gaze before listening to the continuing report.

"Now for the information on the Adamsons," Jeb continued. "Jason Adamson. Forty-one years old. British passport. Professor of Ancient Middle Eastern History. He has been with the American College in

Cairo for eight years. Before that, he was at a British college in Alexandria. He was born and raised in Cairo by his parents. Father was with a British company, and mother was a socialite. He met Cora when he was traveling and lecturing in Boston. They married two years later. She is American and found work in the American Embassy as a contractor in minor offices. She has never been in an office with secure knowledge."

Abbie was used to taking time to sift through the information given to her to analyze, using her computer programs for accuracy, but now, she was struggling to make sense of everything being laid out for them. So far, though, there was no information that she thought was suspect until his next words.

"And the Adamsons have an apartment in Heliopolis."

"Heliopolis! I can't imagine that!" she blurted. "That's where some of Egypt's elite live, so I can't imagine the cost of real estate there. Even if someone is renting a small apartment, I don't know anyone who can afford to live in Heliopolis. Cora can't be making much money at her job, but maybe Egyptian college professors make more than I think." Even as the words slipped from her mouth, she knew they sounded ridiculous. There was no way Egyptian college professors made more money than their American counterparts, which she knew wasn't a lot.

Bennett confirmed what he said, "I've already looked at their salary since it's easy to find. They have money in the bank, but it doesn't come from their salaries."

"Can you see where the money comes from?" Rick asked.

"Cash deposits into their Egyptian bank account."

She snorted and shook her head. "Well, that's suspicious as fuck!"

She heard laughter on the other end and winced at her unprofessional comment. "I couldn't have said it better myself." Chris laughed.

She was already starting to pair their voices with names even though she couldn't see their faces. It was interesting how with just a couple of conference calls, she was already getting used to the different Keepers in California. Looking over at Rick, she asked, "So what now?"

Jeb added, "I was able to tap into her online calendar. At ten o'clock this morning, she's got listed, Giselle, Heliopolis Kaffee. You and Rick might want to decide you need coffee in Heliopolis this morning."

She looked over as Rick grinned but still needed to pass it through her boss. "Tom, is that okay?"

"Yes, but let me know once you've made contact."

"Okay," Carson said, "Abbie, Rick… try to make contact with Giselle and Cora this morning. See what you can find out. We're still looking for a way to get into the Adamsons' apartment."

Ending the call, she glanced at her watch. "Of course, it's the middle of the night for us, so we can get some sleep before we try to make an impromptu contact with Giselle and Cora."

"Is sleep the only thing on your mind, darling?"

Grinning, she shook her head. "Not at all!" She

leaped from her chair and ran a few steps toward the stairs, only making it halfway before Rick's hands wrapped around her waist and swung her up. She squealed and laughed as he carried her the rest of the way to her bedroom.

Tomorrow was going to be busy and undoubtedly stressful. But for now, the world fell away, leaving only the two of them in their own world.

The taxi dropped them off near the coffee house in Heliopolis. The area was teeming with pedestrians, many in modern clothing and women with no head coverings. The streets were cleaner than in downtown Cairo, and Abbie breathed in deeply before letting it out slowly. Closing her eyes for only a few seconds, she soon felt Rick's fingers wrapped around hers.

"I know this is hard on you," he said. "The last time you were here was with Sam."

It warmed her heart that Rick remembered, understood, and acknowledged. Giving his fingers a squeeze, she nodded. "Okay, off with the sadness. Now, let's go see if we can make contact." By the time they got to the coffee shop, it was a few minutes before ten, and she hoped that Jeb's information was correct and also that Cora was prompt.

Sitting at a small table where they could see and be seen, they ordered coffee and pastries, then sat close with their heads together, chatting. She couldn't help but smile. The cover was no longer just a cover. As though thinking the same thing, he touched his forehead to hers.

She glanced up to see Cora walking through the door. Jerking her eyes to the side, she indicated to Rick that she had entered. A few minutes later, Giselle walked in. After both women ordered at the counter and sat at a nearby table, Abbie waited until getting the sign from Rick that the time was right.

She looked over, catching Giselle's eyes, and then widened her own. "Hello!" Turning to Rick, she said, "I'll be right back, sweetie." Standing, she walked over to the other table, her smile still in place. "I'm not sure if you remember me, but we met—"

"I do remember you," Giselle interrupted with a smile. "You were at Mary's wake."

"That's right. I'm Abbie."

"You were very kind to listen to me rant on a difficult day."

Waving her hand dismissively, Abbie said, "It's fine. No worries." Turning her head toward Cora, she furrowed her brow. "You look very familiar. Do you work at the American Embassy? The recreation office, right? I work at the embassy, too."

Cora's face settled into a curious smile, but her eyes were sharp. "Yes, I do." Cora's gaze moved from Abbie and shifted over to the table she'd left, looking at Rick.

"I've been meaning to come in to see you. My boyfriend came over from the States for a visit, and we were hoping to take a tour while he was here. Plus"—she laughed and rolled her eyes—"I work in a stodgy office with stodgy people and was hoping to find something fun going on for us to do."

"You should come to hang with me sometime," Giselle offered. "I'm usually with people from the university."

"Oh, that sounds nice. Is there anything going on this weekend?"

Before Giselle could answer, Cora said, "My husband is a professor at the college here. We've invited some students over this evening. Our apartment gives us access to the rooftop of our building. It makes for a beautiful view of Heliopolis. You should come."

"Oh, that sounds wonderful. Are you sure you don't mind?"

Now it was Cora's turn to wave her hand dismissively. "The more, the merrier." She inclined her head toward Rick. "How long is your boyfriend going to be visiting?"

"His plans are a little fluid, but he'll have to be back at his job soon."

"Well, if you come tonight, you'll meet new friends," Cora said.

"I feel like I'm crashing a party, but it really does sound fun."

"Oh, don't worry. It's very casual and open-ended. Actually, the invitation was extended to most of my husband's students. You might find it a little boring because he'll slip in part of a lecture sometime during the evening."

Laughing, Abbie said, "I'm always open to learning new things."

Getting the address from Cora, she waved at the two before walking back over to Rick. "Are you ready to go, sweetie?"

He stood and smiled down at her. Taking her hand, he led her out of the coffee shop, and they walked down the street with their hands linked. Several blocks away, they caught a taxi back to her villa.

"Carson is never going to believe how easy that was for you to finagle an invitation." Rick laughed.

"I couldn't believe how easy it all came to me, either," she said. "Of course, the party is going to be on the rooftop and not actually in their apartment."

"No worries, babe. I'll be able to figure out what's going on while you circulate at the party."

Once they were back at her villa, Rick made contact with Carson and found out the ETA of Hop and Dolby while she made a call to Tom. Gaining his praise and promising not to speak to anyone other than him, she agreed.

Yawning, she accepted Rick's outstretched hand and allowed him to lead her upstairs. They took a nap in the cool afternoon, both tired from their lovemaking the night before and knowing they'd be up late while at the party. She woke an hour later, once again wrapped in Rick's arms, and closed her eyes tightly, breathing him in. The practical side of her worried that things were moving so fast, too soon. Yet she couldn't deny what she'd felt from the moment she'd seen him step onto her brother's deck.

Her heart had been given to him, and she didn't want it back. Because she knew beyond a shadow of a doubt that he'd guard it with his life. But storm clouds were churning all around them, and she prayed they'd stay safe.

Now, if we can just see this mission to the end and figure out how to make us work in a normal world. Snuggling closer, she smiled. *Because I can't deny I want things to work out with this man.*

18

Rick could not have asked Abbie to play her part any better. He knew she was nervous and out of her element, but the moment they stepped off the elevator and onto the rooftop of the beautiful building in Heliopolis, she'd smiled, made small talk, showed interest in Jason's comments about the history of the area, and seemed to be in her element. Without using too much PDA, she'd managed to stay close to Rick with little touches, occasionally looping her arm through his and sometimes leaning gently into his side. He wasn't even sure she was aware of those claiming gestures, but he wasn't about to complain.

As the two of them made their way back over to the food table, she kept a smile on her face, belying the seriousness of her tone. "I don't know that we're finding out anything, Rick," she whispered.

"You don't always get intel immediately, babe," he reassured.

"How are we going to be able to get a look into their apartment?"

"I've seen a couple of girls walk out together and come back a few minutes later. My guess is they're probably going to the Adamsons' place to use the bathroom."

Her eyes widened. "Of course! I didn't even think about that. I can do that—"

"I don't want you out of my sight, Abbie."

"I understand, but I don't know how else to do it. Most girls don't ask their boyfriends to go to the bathroom with them. If we leave together, it might look suspicious."

He started to argue, but she placed her hand on his chest in what would look to all as a loving gesture, and continued, "I'll ask Giselle to go with me. As you've already said, women often go to the bathroom together, and there's safety in numbers. No one will think anything about me going downstairs if you're still up here mingling."

He had to admit her plan was less suspicious but nonetheless hated to have her out of his sight. His finger traced along the chain around her neck, tapping the lighthouse. He'd given it to her before the party, explaining that there was a miniature camera as well as a tracer embedded in the lighthouse charm. "Okay, I don't think I have much choice. Remember, as you walk around, try to move in different directions so the camera in your necklace can gather as much detail as possible."

She nodded before they casually walked over to

RICK

where Giselle was standing near the table with drinks. Rolling her eyes in exaggeration, she said, "Giselle, I was going to ask Cora, but I hate to bother her. Do you know where the ladies' room is?"

Giselle smiled. "They're letting the students use the bathroom in their apartment. I've been there before and can show you." She glanced up at Rick and winked. "I'll bring your girlfriend right back to you."

He laughed and offered a one-armed hug to Abbie. "You'd better. I'd hate to have to search for you since I don't know this place at all."

"Oh, it's just down two floors. They probably have a person hired to guard the door to make sure no one walks off with anything since they have the door unlocked."

He watched as Giselle and Abbie walked to the elevator, and then he grabbed a water bottle and drank deeply. He headed over to where Jason was standing in the corner with several students. The professor was pontificating about how the modernization of Cairo was partly to blame for the dearth and ruin of some of the antiquities. Rick listened, giving the impression that he was fascinated with the topic while allowing the camera he wore to pan slowly around the gathering, sending the information back to LSI-WC.

He felt antsy, unlike any other mission he'd been on before, where calm confidence in the knowledge that his team was ready was the name of the game. Now, with Abbie no longer in his sight, he glanced at his watch, determined to only give her ten minutes before he went looking for her.

As Jason finished and several students began asking him questions, a man turned around and looked up at Rick. "I haven't seen you around before," he said with a British accent. "Are you new to the university?"

"No, I'm here with my girlfriend. I'm just visiting," Rick replied. Sticking his hand out, he smiled. "I'm Rick."

The man shook his hand firmly. "Paul. Paul Smith." He inclined his head toward Jason and said, "I'm not from the university, either, but I met Jason as a neighbor in the building."

"Have you been here long?" Rick asked.

"Almost three years. Jason and Cora lived in another building and moved here after me." His voice held a lofty air as though thinking he had a superior standing due to being in this particular building longer. Continuing, Paul smirked, then added, "I'm an engineer with a civil engineering firm. Egypt is always looking for road builders. Professor? Not so much."

Rick managed to make sure that the camera in the button of his shirt was pointed directly at Paul's face. The hairs on the back of Rick's neck stood up, and his distrust of the young man grew.

"I saw the girl you're with. I met her at a wake for a mutual friend who was killed in an accident. Saw her with Giselle earlier, too."

"Yeah," he acknowledged, not giving anything away.

"Giselle," Paul snorted, rolling his eyes. "Are they friends?"

"Just acquaintances, I think."

Paul nodded, downing the amber liquid in his tumbler. "Smart. Giselle is an opportunist."

"Well, I don't know anything about her. But my girlfriend doesn't have anything to do with the university, so I doubt their paths will cross often."

"Just watch her. Warn your girlfriend to watch herself—"

"Paul, would you like to have some water or maybe something to eat?"

Rick had clocked Cora walking over to them, but she had Paul in her narrow-eyed glare. He shifted his stance to make sure both were in his camera view. After Paul's warning, he wanted to find Abbie but needed to move carefully so as not to arouse suspicion.

"I'm doing just fine, thank you," Paul said, his words slurring slightly.

"Nonetheless, we want to make sure that all our guests have a good time and that no one makes poor choices that could have ramifications down the road." She looped her arm through Paul's and started to lead him away. Looking over her shoulder at Rick, she smiled, but it didn't reach her eyes. "You'll have to forgive him. He does tend to imbibe just a bit too much."

"No worries, Ms. Adamson. I just appreciate you inviting us to your get-together. I enjoyed listening to your husband's talk."

At that, her brittle smile seemed to ease a bit, and she dipped her chin before leading Paul over to the small group still standing with Jason. Glancing at his watch, Rick decided he wasn't going to wait anymore.

Tossing his empty water bottle into one of the receptacles, he had just made it to the door when Giselle and Abbie reappeared.

She smiled up at him, her countenance carefree, yet something was playing behind her eyes. Giselle giggled, then headed toward another group of women standing by the outer wall taking selfies. Leaning in, Rick whispered, "Do you want to leave?"

"Yes, but not so soon after coming back up. Let's mingle just a little bit more, and then we'll slip out."

As much as he wanted to get her away from the party, he admired her insight. They spent another twenty minutes nibbling on food, sipping drinks, making small talk, and then made their way to say goodbye to Cora and Jason. After thanking them for the invitation, they took the elevator back down to the first floor. Stepping out, they walked toward the exit, but suddenly Abbie grabbed his arm and pulled him back. Jerking his head around, he followed her line of vision and spied Giselle and Paul standing to the side of the apartment building's lobby behind a large potted palm tree.

Ducking to the corner where they could hear but not be seen, he pulled Abbie closer.

"They'd better watch themselves," Giselle said, poking Paul in the chest with a forefinger. "I know where things are buried." Then as though she'd made a joke, she snorted and giggled.

"Christ, you drank too much," Paul said, his voice haughty.

"Look who's talking," Giselle bit back.

"If you know what's good for you, you'll keep quiet."

"Just remember," she said, "I know what they have and where they keep it. And I expect to be paid for my part, just like everyone else."

"Oh, I have no doubt they'll take care of you," Paul said, still weaving slightly.

"Good, because like I said... I know what's under here and where you take it. And I know how they get rid of it. How they get rid of *everything*."

Rick grabbed Abbie's attention when he nudged her and stepped silently to the side, pulling her with him. They made it around the corner of the lobby and out a side door before hustling down the sidewalk. Hailing a taxi, they once again remained peacefully quiet until they arrived at her villa.

As soon as they made it inside, she whirled around, letting out a huge breath. Eyes wide, she said, "Good God, that was crazy!"

"We've got a lot to break down. But first, you seemed excited when you and Giselle came back upstairs."

She nodded quickly. "I think I may have found something."

He couldn't help but grin at the tenor of excitement that tinged her voice. He led her to the sofa and pulled her down with him. "Lay it on me, babe."

"I know you'll be able to see it from the necklace video, but standing outside their door was a man who greeted us warmly and said we were to use the guest bathroom toward the right. So when we entered their apartment, we were in a wide entryway. A long kitchen is on the left, with a pass-through to the dining room.

The living room is directly in front and connected to the dining room. A long hall to the right had two guest bedrooms, a bathroom across the hall, and at the end was the main bedroom and bathroom. We were instructed to use the hall bathroom, but Giselle didn't go that way. After wandering with me in tow as she talked about the expensive furniture and artwork the Adamsons had, she headed through the dining room on the left and went into another room. While Giselle was in the bathroom, I realized the room could have been another bedroom but was used as an office. I had no doubt we shouldn't have been in there."

"Do you think anyone saw you?"

She shook her head. "No one else came in. I didn't take the time to look around, but I made sure to walk to get everything on my camera. When Giselle came out, I went in but left the door open the tiniest crack so I could peek through. She immediately went over to the desk and started searching. Then she opened a planner on the desk and snapped a picture. I turned on the water so it sounded like I was washing my hands and made a lot of noise as I came out. By that time, she was standing at the doorway, looking innocent."

"Fuckin' amazing, babe. Let me put in a call to LSI-WC to make sure they got our video. They can run visual imagery through to see if anybody of interest was at the party and will get more information on Giselle."

"What do you think it means?"

"I don't know, but while you were gone, I had an interesting conversation with Paul." He relayed the comments Paul made about Giselle.

Abbie gasped. "That's who Giselle had words with at Mary's wake. They didn't seem to like each other at all."

"That kind of emotion usually comes from anger, love, or betrayal." Shrugging, he said, "I don't know. Maybe they just rub each other the wrong way." After a moment, he added, "I'll be curious to see what LSI-WC turns up on Giselle."

She placed her hand on his arm. "Did anything else happen while I was gone?"

"Just the way Paul was taken away from me by Cora."

Leaning forward, she asked, "What happened?"

He then related how Cora pulled Paul away and led him to Jason.

Abbie flopped back onto the sofa cushions and groaned. "This is ridiculous, Rick. Give me maps. Give me images. Give me architecture, buildings, and mathematical equations. And give me the computer programs to analyze that information. But trying to figure out who might have slept with someone… who was competitive with someone… who liked, or loved, or hated someone… I don't know how to do this! And for all we know, we could be looking in the completely wrong direction."

"I've got a feeling about Cora and Jason. Whatever is going on, I think they're at the center of it."

She pinched her lips together. "I'm gonna go in and talk to Tom tomorrow."

Rick raised his brows. "I'll go with you."

He thought she would protest, but she just pressed her lips together. Rubbing his chin, he pinned her with a hard stare.

She heaved a sigh and nodded. "You don't like him very much, do you?"

"I don't have to like someone to report to them. But right now, I put my trust in you, me, and LSI-WC."

"Ugh, I'm so tired of feeling like I'm running in circles." She covered her face with her hands, shaking her head slightly before looking back up at him. "Okay, what's next?"

"Let's get the call with the Keepers over with."

It didn't take long to set up the secure conference call. The Keepers had watched the video Rick and Abbie provided from the party.

"Giselle Schmidt," Jeb began. "German student studying at the Egyptian American University in Cairo. She's twenty-five years old. Has been in Cairo for over a year. She's studied in Germany, France, and now Egypt. A bit of a nomad, traveling from place to place. Nothing suspicious about her family or her background. Bank account shows some money from her family and from the few jobs she's had along the way. Worked for Jason Adamson as a teaching assistant last semester. Then two weeks ago, she had a cash deposit equivalent to about five-thousand dollars."

Eyes wide, Abbie said, "She didn't get that from being his assistant. What about Paul Smith?"

"Paul Smith. Thirty-six years old. Single. British passport. He's been in Cairo for thirty-four months. Lives in Heliopolis… the same building the Adamsons live in. Civil engineer hired by MacCauley Engineering Company, which currently has a contract with the Egyptian government for work on their major highway exchange extending lanes over and through the City of the Dead."

"I knew it!" Abbie said. "Something is going on with Paul, Giselle, and the Adamsons. But how do we prove it?"

Jeb continued, "We got the visual you provided and are looking at the Adamsons' apartment."

"I want to get in," Rick said.

"Hop and Dolby will be there in a few hours," Carson interjected. "I want you to wait until you have backup. No unnecessary risks. Too many bodies are piling up at this point."

Rick nodded, knowing his boss was right. "Are they coming here?"

"Yes. They've got Abbie's info, and Tom Olsen will have someone meet them at the airport and get them to you. They'll have the requested equipment."

At those words, he shot a glance toward Abbie, but her attention was elsewhere. "Roger that," he replied, glad his fellow Keepers were on their way.

19

Abbie wasn't sure what she expected, but the two men who arrived at her villa and were exuberantly greeted by Rick were so like the Keepers from Maine that she wondered if Mace and Carson had a tall-muscular-gorgeous clause in their contract for employment.

Blinking out of her exhausted brain stupor, she stepped forward to be introduced to Hop and Dolby. "Thank you for coming—"

Hop waved her thanks away, his boyish smile wide. "Darlin', don't thank us. Hell, I've been itching to get boots on the ground here."

His Southern drawl made her grin, and she had no doubt he hid a sharp mind behind his aw-shucks persona. Chuckling, she said, "You've got to be hungry and tired. I've got food ready." Waving them toward the table, she filled platters with some of the food that Sabah had left. The scent of the warm spices that coated the meat on skewers, rice, and steamed vegetables had the men quickly sit down, digging in with obvious pleasure.

As the four of them ate, they discussed the latest findings. "So we're going in? Into their apartment?" she asked, leaning back in her chair. It didn't escape her notice the three men at the table shared glances before turning their gazes back to her. She narrowed her eyes, and her words were sharp. "Is there a problem?"

Rick rubbed his chin and sighed. "Look, Abbie. Don't take this the wrong way, but you really need to stay back and let us go in."

She lifted her brows. "And why is that?"

"By your own admission, you aren't trained for active missions."

"Yes, but what do you call what I've been doing lately?" she argued.

"Only because your boss put you up to it first and then because of my cover as your boyfriend."

"And I can't offer any value added to this endeavor?"

"Babe—"

"Oh, hell no, Rick. There's a time and place for *babe*, but this isn't it!"

"Shit, Abbie. I'm sorry." He shot a glance over to the other two Keepers.

Blowing out a long, slow breath, she grimaced. "Hop. Dolby. I'm sorry, too. You shouldn't have to witness our argument."

Hop grinned while Dolby pressed his lips together in an expression of overt sympathy. "Don't mind us." Hop laughed.

Dolby glared at Hop before turning back to her.

"Abbie, in this case, I have to agree with Rick. We can get in and get out with the expertise and experience needed."

She battled the desire to keep arguing but knew he was right. Looking over at Rick, she nodded. "Okay. I'm sorry. I'll stay back."

"Actually, I thought that I'd like to have you close. Just not inside," he said.

She carefully watched him, but his words didn't sound placating, and his demeanor was as trusting as ever. And, in truth, she believed him when he said he'd like her close. "Okay. So what are you looking for?"

"We get in and get eyes and ears on their place."

Pressing her lips together, she nodded. "Will you be looking for anything special?"

"Rigging their place will be the quickest way to find out what they've got going on."

She nodded slowly, then asked, "What about their computers?"

He grinned. "We'll take care of that, too."

"Okay."

Brows lifting, he asked, "Okay?"

She snorted and glanced at the amused faces of Hop and Dolby before turning her gaze back to Rick. "Yeah, okay."

"Damn, bro," Hop said, still grinning. "I need to find someone like Abbie. Smart. Pretty. And knows when to give in."

Giving him the evil eye, she warned, "Just don't get on my bad side." Standing, she added, "And don't assume I'm giving in."

Rick belted out laughter as Hop shook his head.

"No wonder you can't keep a woman," Dolby said to Hop. "You can't figure out how to keep them from getting pissed at you!"

"I keep 'em plenty happy," Hop protested, a twinkle in his eye.

"Okay, boys," she said, turning and leaning her hip against the counter. "What's the plan?"

"Tom is offering access to a panel van that we can fit with some of the equipment," Rick said.

Eyes wide, she cocked her head to the side and battled to keep the glare from her expression. "And just when did *my* boss start coordinating with LSI-WC and not me?"

A muscle ticked in Rick's jaw. "I'm not keeping anything from you, Abbie. But Tom has accepted a contract with LSI-WC."

She didn't like Tom keeping her out of the loop directly but was determined to put her personal feelings aside and simply nodded.

"Dolby and I will go in, and Hop and you will stay in the van. We'll be able to slip in, set up surveillance they can't detect, and get back out. That gives us a chance to get eyes and ears on their place."

Trying to keep the bite out of her voice, she asked, "So it doesn't really seem like I'm needed."

"Once again, I want to take a look into the office and at their computer. If they have information there that perhaps only you can identify, that would be good to have your input immediately."

She couldn't argue with that, so another nod was her only reply.

Rick looked over at Dolby and asked, "You got anything for me?"

She didn't know what he was talking about, but it was obvious Dolby did when he reached into a bag at his feet and pulled out a small black kit and handed it to Rick.

Before she could ask what was going on, Hop and Dolby headed upstairs to change clothes while Rick walked over toward her. She glanced down at the small case in his hand. "What's that?"

He moved directly into her space, his chin dipping to hold her gaze. "Do you trust me?"

She didn't answer immediately, pondering the question and examining the possible reasons he was asking. Then, deciding it didn't matter, she nodded again. "Yes, I do." And at that moment, she realized how true her answer was.

He opened the case, and she spied a small syringe. Now, with wide eyes, she waited to see what he would do.

"I know there's a tracer in your lighthouse necklace," he began. "But every Keeper has a small tracer embedded underneath their skin. With your permission, I'd like to do that now for you."

Her breath grew shallow as the ramifications of what he was saying raced through her mind. *Is he acknowledging that I'll work for Mace when I leave Cairo? Do I still want to consider that as a possibility when all this is over? Is this an acknowledgment that he sees me as a Keeper?* Her gaze moved back to his, and she could see him patiently waiting as was his way when she was making a decision. She loved that about him. He didn't rush her. He didn't try to talk over her. He didn't try to force his opinion upon her.

Then she opened her mouth and gave the only answer she could. "Yes."

He appeared relieved, and no other explanation was needed from either of them. He wanted her safe. He wanted to make sure he could find her if needed. And she'd be a fool to refuse such an offer.

"I'll embed it into your shoulder. You can just drop your blouse off your shoulder enough to give me a little room."

With Hop and Dolby out of the room, she unbuttoned her blouse and slid the material off one shoulder to her elbow. Turning sideways, she presented Rick with the optimum position to make his task easier.

"You'll feel a prick, and I know it might be sore for a couple of days."

She said nothing, focusing on breathing easily as he inserted the needle just under her skin. Wincing at the small, sharp pain, it was over before she could take another breath. Glancing down, she spied the small red bump on her shoulder. Shifting her gaze back to his face, she recognized relief in his expression.

He dealt with the needle and then replaced the kit back into the bag and turned toward her, gently lifting her blouse over her shoulder and fastening up the buttons. Keeping his hands away from the injection site, he pulled her close and kissed her forehead. Hop and

Dolby came down the stairs a moment later dressed in black cargo pants, tight black long-sleeve T-shirts, and boots.

"The van is outside," Hop said. Glancing over at Abbie, he sheepishly shrugged, adding, "Not trying to bypass you."

She waved her hand, knowing that Tom would use her for what she'd been hired for, intel analysis, and let LSI-WC handle the logistics.

"We'll get changed now," Rick said.

She led the way upstairs and into her bedroom, deciding to dress in a similar fashion while keeping with the dictates she knew would be placed on her. She chose black leggings and a black blouse and paired it with a long black skirt. Choosing a black scarf, she quickly covered her head. Turning, she spied Rick as he pulled a black T-shirt over his chest and abs and, as always, appreciated the view. "This is surreal," she admitted, gaining his attention. "You, here in Cairo, like this. Some of Carson's Keepers are here as well. Doing the things that I know Tom directs others to do, but I've always been blissfully ignorant of, staying in my little office and handling my little corner of a mission."

"Are you okay?" he asked, tucking his T-shirt in before stepping closely again. He lifted his hand and then let his fingertips caress her cheek. "All I want is for you to be safe, Abbie."

"I won't be the one sneaking into a building," she reminded him.

Chuckling, he shook his head. "We've already checked, and I can tell you the security on that building is shit. Anyone could probably walk in, so it's hardly a high risk."

"Good. So how about we get this show on the road? The sooner we go, the sooner we can come back." She started to turn, then halted and looked over her shoulder, her brow furrowed. "By the way, where are those two going to sleep?"

"I figure one will get the guest bed, and the other one will get the floor," he said with a grin.

Her own chuckle slipped out, and she shook her head. "You don't seem too upset about one of your friends having to sleep on the floor."

Now his chuckle turned into a full-blown laugh. "I get to sleep in a bed with the beautiful woman I've fallen in love with. Being upset about one of them sleeping on the floor doesn't bother me at all."

Grinning as he grabbed her hand, she followed him down the stairs and out to the white panel van that was sitting just outside her villa. She climbed into the back, surprised only for a moment when she glanced at the driver and recognized Baniti. Looking around at what looked like a large, black suitcase, she found a place to sit as Rick and Dolby came in behind her. Hop climbed into the passenger seat, and they'd barely closed the doors before Baniti jerked onto the road and drove in typical Egyptian bat-out-of-hell fashion.

She looked over at Rick, immediately noting his attention was on her. "How are you going to get into their apartment without them knowing? "

"They're not home right now."

Not understanding how he would know that her

attention was diverted when Baniti chuckled from the front seat.

"I made sure," he said. "My brother-in-law has been outside their apartment for most of the day."

"How did you manage that?" she asked, unable to keep the incredulity from her voice.

"He pretended to work for a paint company. You know what it's like here. Men run around in uniforms, and no one asks what they're doing. Most of the time, they don't know what they're doing."

Her eyes widened, and she shook her head as she caught Baniti's gaze looking back at her through the rearview mirror.

Baniti grinned. "Am I wrong?"

The truth was, he was right. It was commonplace to see Egyptian men in work uniforms or galabeyas moving in and out of buildings, in and out of traffic, congregating or rushing somewhere, or just sitting and having their tea. It would be almost impossible to tell if someone was out of place.

"My brother-in-law will stay to make sure, but there will be no problems."

Glancing over Rick, she lifted her brow. "Somehow, I imagined LSI-WC would have a much more sophisticated way of seeing if anyone was in the apartment than just a random Egyptian man lingering outside the Adamsons' door with a paint can."

Laughing, Rick shoulder bumped her. "Never underestimate using anything at your disposal when on an active mission."

"Clearly, I hadn't considered everything." Against

her cautious nature, she found the circumstance ridiculous and somewhat comical, even though Rick was about to go into a situation that could turn ugly. But perhaps, levity was the best way to ease the tension she felt. Once they parked in Heliopolis, she barely glanced up before Rick leaned over and grabbed the back of her head and held her steady as he kissed her hard and fast.

"Stay here with Hop. As soon as I get visual, I'll let you start looking at things," he whispered against her lips.

Now, sitting in the back of the van while Baniti stayed behind the wheel, Hop began turning on some of the computer equipment that he had stored in the large case. Glancing toward her, he winked. "Don't worry about them. They'll be fine. And my guess is that it won't take long for us to begin figuring out what the Adamsons are up to."

She watched with fascination as the video camera on Rick's shirt soon started sending images that popped up on the screen in front of Hop. She leaned in close, anxious to keep up with what he was seeing.

"Walk me through this," Hop said.

She appreciated his acknowledging that she'd been inside before. "The building has a security person at the front desk, but when I was here before, it felt very lax. Sometimes I think there is the pretense of security just so a building can charge more rent when, in reality, as Rick said, it's easy to get into."

"Yep, that's pretty typical of a lot of places," Hop agreed. "That tells me that no high-ranking officials or politicians live in this building. As you say, it's expensive, and I don't see how a basic State Department employee and university professor can afford it if they weren't doing something on the side to bring in money. So the building offers a lot of nice amenities but no real security."

Keeping her eyes on the screen, she said, "They live on the fifth floor. There's one floor above them, and then there is the rooftop terrace."

"Okay, looks like our boys are getting off the elevator on the fifth floor."

A man in a paint-splotched uniform was in the hall, looking as though he'd probably painted the same area over and over. "That must be Baniti's brother-in-law."

She watched as Rick slipped inside the apartment with little effort at the door. Slowly nodding as he made his way through the apartment, she was startled when she heard his voice. "Abbie? Do things look the same or different to you?"

"You can speak in here, and he can hear you," Hop explained, holding a small microphone.

Nodding her thanks, she replied, "I was only in there one time, but the rooms look the same. Walk through the kitchen, and you'll come to the office."

The screen split as Dolby went in one direction, attaching an audio and visual recording device near the entrance to show who would come in and out of the apartment.

The other side of the screen showed Rick as he walked into the office. He quickly attached a similar device in that room as well. With gloves on, he moved to the computer on the desk. Inserting a special drive, he waited for a moment, then said, "Hop? You got this?"

"Give me a minute."

"What are you doing?" she whispered, then scrunched her nose, knowing she didn't have to lower her voice.

"With this, Jeb back home can get access to the history on this computer, plus be able to see what comes up at any time."

"You're kidding?"

"We've got the best toys, darlin'," Hop quipped, winking.

She knew the CIA could get their hands on just about anything, but considering that wasn't part of her job, she gave it little thought. She had been given images and maps to analyze, and that was what she focused on. But seeing what was happening on the screen, she realized there was a lot the Keepers did that she'd never considered. An excitement speared through her as she thought about what LSI could offer. *But LSI or LSI-WC?*

When that thought hit her, she jolted and then covered quickly before Hop could ask what she was thinking. She and Rick were in love, but what about after this case? It was too much to think about now. Glad that Hop was focused on the screen, she forced her mind to do the same.

20

When Rick climbed back into the van, his gaze immediately sought Abbie's face. She was as beautiful as ever, but the light in her eyes and the excitement she exhibited made her smile even more brilliant.

She waited until he and Dolby were safely inside and the door shut, and Baniti jerked out into traffic again before rushing, "Hop and Jeb are already working on the information from the computer, and I saw a few things of interest already!"

"I can't wait to hear about it, babe." He wrapped his arm around her, glad when she leaned her head against his shoulder. He knew she was tired and was looking forward to them getting home and being able to sleep. With Baniti at the wheel, it didn't take long to maneuver through the traffic and arrive outside her villa. Dolby and Hop closed up the equipment and carried it inside her house as she and Rick waved goodbye to their intrepid driver.

Once inside, Abbie pulled food from the refrigerator

and reheated it while Hop connected to LSI-WC on a secure line and sent information from the computer. By the time they'd eaten, Jeb had reported, "We can see where the money had gone into the Adamsons' account, and then from their account into one that doesn't have their name on it. Then that account fed into the bank accounts of Mary, Anne, and a few other current ones. And just so you know, Giselle does also."

Rick looked to the side, but instead of the excitement he expected to see on Abbie's face, she appeared pensive, with a touch of sadness in her eyes. She looked up, and hearing his unspoken question, said, "So that means Mary was doing something she shouldn't have. And then was killed for it."

"Come here, babe," he said, pulling her to her feet and encircling her with his arms. Looking over her head, he added, "Been a long day."

Dolby nodded, then stood and stretched. "If no one has an objection, I'm gonna go take a shower and hit the bed. We'll have a lot to look at tomorrow."

Rick grinned as he looked down at Hop. "Looks like you lost the bet."

"Yeah, I get the floor."

Abbie twisted around and looked at the others. "There are lots of blankets in the hall closet. Take as many as you want. You can make a pretty decent bed that way."

"Thanks, darlin'," Hop said. "I'll be fine. Blankets on the floor make a much better bed than some places I've slept!"

After checking the security of her villa, Rick linked

their fingers and led her upstairs. They chatted in her room until the bathroom was free, and she took a shower while Rick waited in the bedroom. What he really wanted was to take one with her, but he knew that time would come when the mission was over, and they were alone once again. Glad she wasn't embarrassed about their relationship, he soon crawled into bed with her, wrapping his body around her.

"How long do you think it'll be before we find out anything?" she asked.

"Honestly? In a case like this, it could be any time, but I've got a feeling that we're gonna learn some things pretty damn quick. Whatever Jason and Cora are doing, it's active and ongoing. My guess is that they talk freely in their apartment, and we'll find out something soon."

It didn't seem to take Abbie long to go to sleep, but it was elusive for Rick. Casting his mind back over the Adamsons' apartment, he'd noted the elegant but not over-the-top furniture. The artwork on display was upscale but not extravagant. It was as though every piece had been chosen to portray a successful couple while not being so excessive as to make others wonder where their money might come from. Certainly, their apartment rent must be expensive, but it wouldn't be too difficult to explain that they preferred to live in Heliopolis rather than somewhere else in Cairo.

He knew the Keepers were looking into their bank accounts, but he felt sure they'd only find cash deposits for the money they received from whatever scheme they were running. *Drugs? Human trafficking? Black market? Terrorism? Smuggling?* He shifted slightly, pulling Abbie in closer.

Whatever it was, her friend had been involved, and he knew that made it more difficult for her to process. And Sam had been killed for getting too close to the situation. *Does Abbie have a target on her back?* Just the thought of that made him sick, and he inwardly vowed to keep her safe.

For two days, nothing. They watched as Cora and Jason got ready for work, their conversations exactly what would be expected by any married couple planning their day. An Egyptian maid came while they had breakfast and stayed until the middle of the afternoon, cleaning the non-dirty house. Jason got home first on both days, and Cora followed not long after. Dinner was what the maid had left for them, and then nothing but boring conversation, reading, or watching TV.

On the evening of the second day, Abbie looked toward Rick and shook her head. He grinned, knowing what was coming.

"I thought something would happen by now," she said.

"Think about how long it takes you to decipher maps or images," he reminded her.

"Yes, but those are inert things. Not changing. These are two people who should be talking, planning, raiding, pillaging, or whatever the hell they're involved in. It's Saturday morning. Why aren't they doing something besides just drinking their coffee?"

Dolby chuckled, and Rick glanced over toward his coworkers.

"What?" Dolby asked, still grinning. "She's said the same thing we're all thinking. We'd like it to be faster, but right now, the Adamsons are the most boring as hell people to watch."

"Well," Abbie interjected with a shrug. "I have been looking at some of the images that have come from their computer. He has photographs of tombs. I can't identify them with my software, don't know where they're located, but they were scanned into Jason's computer. Of course, with his background in archaeological digs, they could be anything from anywhere."

Hop, who was monitoring the computers, called out, "We might have a hit!"

The others gathered around and watched as Paul White walked into the Adamsons' apartment carrying a small piece of luggage. He was greeted by Cora, who then called out to Jason. "Paul's here!"

Jason walked from the study and glanced down toward the luggage now sitting on the floor. "Are you ready?"

"Yes. The buyer has the money, and Giselle said she made contact."

Even from the angle of their camera, the Keepers could see Cora's narrow-eyed glare. "Good."

"This buyer is twitchy, but Giselle knows what she's doing."

"Yes, she knows what she's doing," Cora agreed. "We'll reward her with the cruise that we're taking."

Jason put his hand on Cora's arm and patted. "Oh, that would be nice for her."

"I'm sure," Cora said, but Abbie could have sworn she heard a hard edge to Cora's voice.

Paul nodded. "Are you ready for the cruise? It's important that you keep him happy."

"Oh, I have no doubt that he'll be happy with what we have for him."

Jason looked at his watch. "I've got a meeting on campus with one of the professors in my department. It should only last an hour or two, and then I'll be back." He kissed Cora and nodded toward Paul before heading out the door.

Cora stood for a few minutes, her manicured hands on her hips. Glancing at the case on the floor, she asked, "Is it all there?"

"Don't you trust me?"

"Oh, I trust you," Cora said, leaning in and sliding her tongue along Paul's lips. "I trust you to take care of me."

"My pleasure," Paul growled.

They fell into a clench, barely making it down the hall toward one of the bedrooms as her clothes began to disappear.

"Oh…" Abbie said, averting her eyes from the screen. "That was unexpected."

Rick looked toward a wide-eyed Abbie, who blinked several times as she peered up at him.

"O…kay," Hop drawled. "So not everything is peachy keen in paradise between Cora and Jason. Not if she's getting a little somethin'-somethin' on the side from Paul."

Abbie turned toward her door at the sound of a knock, and Rick's hand shot out to rest on her arm. "Let me," he said. Checking through the small door window, he said, "Baniti," before opening the door.

"I have news," the smiling Egyptian said.

Ushering Baniti inside, Rick moved back to Abbie's side, then wrapped his arm around her shoulders. "What do you have for us?"

"My brother-in-law went back down to the basement under the guise of washing out his paintbrushes. Besides the typical storage rooms, there is a door with a man sitting guard outside of it. When Ashraf began chatting to the guard, he was able to get him to talk some, but mostly the man just said that he was paid well to make sure only the tenant who owned the storage unit was allowed inside. So Ashraf had to leave once his brushes were clean. This is interesting, is it not?"

The others chuckled and nodded at Baniti's excitement. Rick escorted him back outside, then turned to see Abbie's brow furrowed as she chewed on her bottom lip. Suddenly she whirled around and moved to her laptop. He remained quiet, watching while shooting a glance toward Hop and Dolby. She settled in and appeared to be concentrating deeply. He moved over to the table where Hop was monitoring his screen. "We need to get eyes on the basement."

"Yeah, I was just thinking of that."

Abbie shook her head. "I want to get down into the basement. Can you get me in there?"

He looked over to see her gaze now intently staring at him. "You got something?"

Nodding, she said, "I think so. Take a look." She

turned her laptop around as he and the others gathered near.

Rick stared at the program she had displayed and shook his head. "Babe, you're going to have to break this down for me."

"For us, too," Dolby said, his brows lifted.

"Sorry," she mumbled. "Okay, so one of the graphics was of a square grid that appeared to be dug into the dirt. I had no reference to where it might be, so it was relegated to the back of my work while I identified the street views of Heliopolis and the City of the Dead. But I remembered that there are areas of more modern Cairo, such as buildings in Ma'adi and Heliopolis, that were built on top of un-excavated sites that probably held antiquities."

"You think that's what they might have?"

Hefting her shoulders, she replied, "I don't know. But I want to get in and look."

Rubbing his chin, Rick said, "Dolby and I can go in—"

"Rick, we don't have a lot of time. They're already threatening Giselle, and they obviously have something. Something down there worth guarding. And I've got a better chance of recognizing what is possibly under that building. Maybe that's what's happening there, or maybe it's just a storage place for whatever they're involved in."

"If she goes with you," Hop said, "we can have you on constant surveillance like before. Dolby and I'll be right there."

Rick hated the idea of Abbie going in but knew she'd

have a better understanding of the excavation map if that was what it was. Offering Hop and Dolby a hard stare, they held his eyes, and he could see they took her safety as seriously as he did. Turning toward her, he said, "Okay, but we go in and go in fast. We get whatever intel we can find, and then we get out of there."

"You know I have to tell Tom, right?"

"I'll tell him," Rick said. Looking toward the others, he said, "Let's get ready."

21

Abbie followed Rick through the back door of the Heliopolis apartment building. The building indicated on the maps, she now felt sure, was the one the Adamsons and Paul White lived in. A building that held something worth killing for. Dressed in a similar manner to the other night, she wore a calf-length skirt over leggings, flat shoes, a blouse, and a headscarf. She'd heard Rick on the phone to Tom, giving him their findings so far and plan. She trusted him but, like Rick, didn't understand why Tom was reluctant to send in operatives and rely on the outside Keepers instead.

Sucking in a deep breath, she let it out slowly as she focused her attention on Rick and where they were going. He held up a hand, and she halted as they peeked around the corner. The word guard was a relative term... the man was dressed casually in khaki pants and a shirt, sitting in a chair with his head leaned back and his mouth opened, emitting loud snores.

She placed her hand on Rick's arm and nodded. He'd

hated this part of their plan, but she knew it would work. The guard would be unarmed and would easily assume she was not a threat. Walking around the corner, she lifted her hands as the guard startled awake. When he jumped to his feet, she approached. "Elevator? Where is the elevator?"

As she continued to babble, the Egyptian guard didn't stand a chance as he waved his hands and tried to converse with her. She managed to move toward the door next to his chair, and he began shouting, "La, la." But with his back to the hall, Rick stealthily slipped behind him and took him out with a carotid hold. Binding and gagging him, he dragged the man into the closet that Baniti's brother-in-law had used earlier in the day.

The door was locked, but Rick was easily able to pick the lock, and they slipped inside. Staying behind him, she looked around at the inside of the room, unable to hide her surprise. "This is it?" The small room appeared to be nothing more than a storage area with concrete walls. Cardboard boxes lined two walls, and a couple of bicycles were propped against one another. "There doesn't look like anything is here that needs to be guarded."

"Nope, and that tells me there's something hidden. If there are tombs under this building, there must be an entrance." He began to shift the boxes away from the walls.

She had no idea what they were looking for. Nothing in the images she'd studied gave any indication as to what was in the buildings. "This is like looking for a needle in a haystack, and we don't actually know what the needle is... or where the haystack is either, for that matter—"

"I found something."

At his pronouncement, she startled and rushed over.

Hop radioed, "What have you got?"

"There's a door in the corner of the floor." Lifting the hatch, he leaned over, and she tried to peer over his shoulder, but all she could see was a black hole.

"What is it?" she asked, her hands resting on his shoulders as he crouched down.

"There's a ladder."

The idea of going down a ladder into a dark pit filled her with unease. Hoping he had another plan, he looked over his shoulder, and she held her breath.

"I've got a snake camera that will go down about ten feet."

As her breath rushed out in relief, Hop radioed, "Ready."

Rick uncurled the coil with a small light and camera on the end and lowered it into the hole, extending it the full length and turning it slowly. A small screen held in his other hand showed the image that was also being sent to Hop, Dolby, and she felt sure LSI-WC. Still balancing with her hands on his shoulders, she leaned closer to peer at the faintly illuminated image as well.

"There's a small light switch just inside," Rick announced. He shifted lower and leaned down into the hole, feeling around. Then suddenly, the space was lit with faint illumination.

Dirt walls greeted her view of the crawl space, and

she blew out another breath. "Whatever is there, it's not a lot of space to move around."

"I'm going down," Rick said, looking over his shoulder toward Abbie.

"Shit," she muttered.

"Stay here—"

"Nope. Not happening, no matter how creepy this looks."

She held his gaze, not backing down.

"Okay, stay close." Gaining her agreement, he climbed down the short ladder.

As he looked up, she climbed down after him, hating to be engulfed in the dim area. The space was illuminated by a few light bulbs strung along electrical wires, reminding her of the pyramid they'd been in a few days prior. Only this time, instead of smooth stone walls, it was a cave with dirt walls.

"This make any sense to you?" Rick asked, looking over his shoulder.

Her gaze scanned the area but saw nothing to indicate what they were experiencing. "I… no… no, not really."

They kept walking forward for about ten yards when his hand shot back toward her. "Watch your step."

She had noticed the walls were cut away in the direction they were moving but could now see that the floor had been dug out in long rectangles. *Shit, they look like graves.* They followed the only path available. But soon, they found more ladders that went deeper, with wooden poles holding up the dirt walls.

"These are empty," she said. "Whatever was in them for... God, probably centuries, have now been dug up."

"So do you think this is it? Do you think the Adamsons are dealing in antiquities?"

She chewed on her bottom lip before searching his gaze. She'd never suffered claustrophobia before, but then crawl spaces were not something she'd wandered in. Glancing up, she murmured, "It's really hit me that we're underneath a tall, concrete building in Cairo that was never built to a code up to American standards. Hell, maybe not even to Egyptian standards. Christ, Rick. We need to make this fast."

"Agreed," he said, his voice as sharp as his gaze on her face. "Whatever they've looked for, there's nothing left here."

"Wait!" She pointed downward into the shadows toward the right. As he aimed the light in that direction, they could see the glint of gold. They discovered the area looked like it was currently being excavated. In the dirt were pieces of pottery and jewelry, some still being cleaned and some still half buried. Moving closer, she said, "They did find something. Somehow they discovered tombs under this building, and they've been excavating, taking them away, and probably selling them to the highest bidder."

She began snapping pictures as Rick knelt to hold the light at the best angle. She couldn't imagine how the Adamsons had discovered the tombs, but as she focused her attention on the artifacts still half buried, she hurried to finish taking pictures of the evidence.

"Are you doing okay?" he asked, standing so close,

his breath whispered against her neck, sending comfort through her.

"I'll be a helluva lot better once we get out of here."

They finished with their photographs and sent everything to LSI, then retraced their steps and climbed back up the ladder.

"Coming out," Rick radioed.

Dolby replied, "Come to the back. Abbie's boss is here."

She looked up at Rick but shrugged, having no idea why Tom had left the embassy to meet them. He reached down and linked fingers with her as they walked up to the first floor, then out into the alley behind the building.

A large black van was parked behind them, the windows tinted, and two Egyptian men wearing suits standing guard. Baniti nodded toward the dark van and said, "I will follow, but you go there."

Hesitating for a second, she was propelled forward as Dolby opened the door, and she spied Tom and another man inside. Dolby climbed in first, then Rick assisted her up, staying right on her heels, while Hop brought up the rear. One of the men with a weapon climbed in next to the driver, and the other slid in behind Hop, closing the door. The driver took off, making his way through traffic, and she hoped Baniti could keep up.

"Tom, what's going on?" she asked, cutting to the chase as curiosity hit her and fatigue pulled at her.

His jaw was tight as his gaze moved over the group. "After Sam's death, my office may have been compromised. That was why I was eager to bring the Keepers on board and keep my operatives out of it. If I do have someone passing on information, I will find out who."

The suited Egyptian man sitting beside Tom nodded toward him, and Tom said, "This is Shakir Nassim. He is the head of the Egyptian secret police and is over the department of antiquities. His office has been following the trail that led him to Cora and Jason Adamson. I was only recently informed of his department's search into the two Americans."

Her gaze moved over to the handsome man who appeared younger than his silver-shot black hair indicated. His dark-eyed gaze was sharp but not unkind.

Shakir said, "We suspected Jason and Cora Adamson had been running an antiquities theft gang, but we didn't know where they were getting their items or how they were transporting them."

"And you do know where they're getting the items now, thanks to us," she stated, her gaze not wavering.

"Yes, that's true. When I contacted Tom yesterday, he informed me that a private investigation firm was working with you. We were willing to see what information you could discern." Shakir lifted his hand slightly, palms up in a sign of resignation. "Our government deals harshly with thefts of antiquities. Not knowing the Egyptian money backer behind the Adamsons' endeavors meant I had to tread carefully. I had a suspicion, and that's why I talked to Tom yesterday. I need help with this investigation, keeping the Egyptian secret police out of it except for those I trust explicitly."

"So what's going on?" Rick asked. "You didn't bring us here just to chat and share information. You want something, and I wanna know what it is."

Shakir and Tom shared a look before Shakir continued. "A small group of my men, who I trust, are ready to raid the Adamsons' building as soon as I give them the signal. But I do not want to tip them off too soon. Thanks to you, we know that Cora, Jason, and Giselle Schmidt are taking a boat tour down the Nile toward Luxor tomorrow to talk to their money person and to try to sell the largest sarcophagus. We need eyes on them, but I can't assign this to my people."

"Why do I get the feeling you want me on that boat?" she asked. As soon as the question left her mouth, she felt the air crackle around her as Rick nearly snapped.

"Fucking hell, no!" he bit out.

Shakir cut in. "You wouldn't be alone. My trusted men will be there but hidden. All of you will be on that boat as tourists. A disguise for you, Ms. Blake. Cora and Paul haven't met the other two men." He inclined his head toward Hop and Dolby.

"We work for our boss," Rick interjected, "not the Egyptian secret police or the CIA."

"Then I suggest we talk to him," Tom countered, "because we need you on that boat tomorrow."

22

Rick leaned over the rails, pissed as hell but unable to do anything about his mood. As the boat glided down the Nile, he stared into the distance, seeing the lush green vegetation and trees along the edge, farmers in their fields, and children playing at the river's edge. As he lifted his gaze to the horizon, the green morphed into nothing but the beige color of sand and dust for as far as his eye could see.

He was on one of the lower decks, staying out of sight since the group they were after had all met him in Cairo.

He hated hiding away but knew it was the only thing he could do. Carson had assured him that the Keepers were under no obligation to assist with the mission, but Carson and Mace had given LSI's full support wanting to keep Abbie safe. Blake was on pins and needles in Maine, gaining Rick's assurance he'd make sure her brother was in the loop with what they were doing.

Scrubbing his hand over his face, he thought of the

intense conversation he'd had with Blake, who now knew that he and Abbie were involved. He could tell Blake wasn't happy, but thank fuck it wasn't because of who Abbie was with, just that they'd kept it a secret.

Sighing, he pushed off the rail and walked back into his room. Even on the lower deck, the accommodations were decent, although the two double beds were small for him and Dolby. It killed him that Hop had been the one who'd spent the night in Abbie's room last night for her protection. He hated not being the one to make sure she was safe.

Dolby looked up from the computer screen. "How are you doing?"

"There's no reason to ask me that," he groused. "I'm stuck down here having to listen instead of being up there with Abbie, but I understand the mission."

"With her disguise, I don't think they'll recognize her."

It was surprising how quickly Abbie pulled together a blond wig, glasses, and dowdy clothes that would keep her in the background, not noticed by others. But with her body cameras, she could capture the conversations and had already discerned the man they thought was the moneybags behind the Adamsons' illegal endeavors.

Hop was on the upper decks, staying close to the action while keeping an eye on Abbie.

"I think the deal is going to happen tonight, considering Tom discovered Cora's tickets for transportation at the stop tomorrow," Rick surmised, praying his intuition was right so Abbie would no longer be away from his immediate protection.

"Why do you think they're conducting business on a boat?"

"I think it's to keep prying eyes off them. Everyone else here is on vacation. Tourists aren't looking at the other passengers. They're looking toward the banks of the Nile or waiting for the next stop. I think it makes it easier for the Adamsons to take care of business."

"And if they do plan on getting rid of Giselle, they can do it here just like they did Anne," Dolby added.

Rick growled, "I just can't stand the idea of Abbie around any of them. If they discover who she is, then I'm not wasting one second. I'm out of here and up there and don't give a fuck about Tom and Shakir's investigation."

"You got that right, man," Dolby agreed.

Frustrated but knowing there was little he could do at the moment, he sat down at the small table and stared at the computer screen while Dolby slipped out once they'd received notice from Hop that all the players were at lunch. He knew Hop would have Abbie in his sights, so he concentrated on the security that Dolby was placing inside the three cabins—Giselle's, Cora and Jason's, and the man identified as the money backer. *Dolby's job would go much faster if I could help*. But it was too risky for anyone to recognize him.

Keeping an eye on Abbie through the camera Hop was wearing, he spied her in her disguise sitting near the wall of the dining room, surrounded by several others traveling alone. She was perfect in the role. Even through the disguise, he could see her beauty but could easily understand how others would simply look over her. She wore the blond wig in a style that discreetly hid her face with hair hanging down the sides. The thick lens of her glasses gave her eyes an owlish appearance. And the dark-gray sweater and slacks didn't seem to catch anyone's eyes but his.

He watched as Cora and Jason left their table and sent a message to Dolby. "Adamsons leaving dining room."

"No worries, I'm finished. Heading back."

Abbie scooted her chair backward and walked out, appearing to wander along the rail and look out onto the setting sun over the water. Hop walked by and stopped near where she was standing. Knowing she was protected, Rick flipped his attention to the monitor that showed the inside of the three cabins. Giselle entered hers and walked into her bathroom before coming back into the main cabin just in time to throw open her door and greet Jason with a kiss.

As Dolby walked back into the room, Rick looked over and shook his head. "Looks like Jason is courting disaster with his side piece under his wife's nose."

Just then, they watched as Cora entered her and Jason's room, her head jerking around before she stomped to the bathroom.

"Fuck, she's got to know what he's up to," Dolby said, his brows lifted.

Rick flipped off the sound in Giselle's cabin and aimed the cameras to the side of the room, refusing to be a voyeur but also refusing to trust her or Jason.

Hop radioed, "We're staying up here on deck. I overheard Jason tell Khalil Hussein they'd meet in his cabin at nine o'clock."

"Got it," Rick replied. "Just so you know, Cora's pissed because Jason has disappeared, and he's gone to Giselle's room."

Hop choked out a laugh, and Abbie could hear as well. She shook her head as a small chuckle slipped out, and the sweet sound sliced through him. Unable to help himself, he asked Hop, "How is she doing?"

"She's a pro," Hop replied, answering for her.

"I know that," he huffed. "What I want to know is…" He faltered, not knowing how to put his worry into words.

"I'll be glad when this is over," she replied.

Hop jumped in again. "If I had to guess, it's mostly because she just wants to be with you."

He shook his head and chuckled as Hop's words hit him in the chest. He knew she was professional and could handle herself, but… *Damn, I'll be glad when tonight is over with.* Turning back to the cameras on Khalil's opulent stateroom, he counted down the time until they had the proof they needed.

Abbie thought about Cora finding out that Jason was banging Giselle and thought about Paul having been with Cora. *It could get interesting!* Rolling her eyes, she shook her head. "Don't care," she muttered to herself. *We get the intel we need for Tom and Shakir, then we're out of here!*

She walked along the deck unnoticed while in plain sight as Cora made her way to Khalil's room. She waited outside for a moment until Jason joined them. She turned to her husband and lifted a brow. "I was surprised you weren't in the room."

"I was headed that way when I decided to check out the beautiful view from the back of the boat. I'm afraid I got lost in thought as I stared out over the vista."

"It must've been quite impressive to hold your attention for almost an hour," Cora said, her narrow-eyed stare on her husband.

Continuing to lean against the rail, Abbie kept her gaze out over the water but was able to pick up their conversation. Not wanting to appear conspicuous, she walked farther and had just passed them when the sound of a door opened, and the others were invited inside. "You may come in. Mr. Hussein will see you now."

Knowing that Dolby would have the stateroom bugged, she started down the stairs when she spied Giselle standing near the railing on the deck just below, chatting with Hop. Or rather laughing and flirting. *Hmm... she just got finished with Jason and is ready to move on.*

Deciding to keep walking around the boat and take in the sights, she found it hard to concentrate. Thoughts of Anne, Mary, and Sam caused her body to tense. Closing her eyes, she breathed deeply and lifted her chin, letting the heat of the Egyptian sun cast its glow over her body. With a cleansing breath heaved from her lungs, she opened her eyes and started walking again.

"Babe? You okay?"

Rick's voice in her radio earpiece caused her to smile. "Yeah," she whispered. "Or I will be when I can hold you again."

"This is fuckin' killing me," he admitted.

"We're close, and then we're done." She was relieved when after half an hour, Hop walked by, no longer encumbered by Giselle, and stopped at the railing next to her again.

"We've got what we need," he said. "Rick just told me that Jason and Cora nailed down a deal with Khalil. Price, artifacts, everything. Cora just walked out, saying she'd leave the details to the men."

The initial glee they felt knowing they'd managed to get the information Tom and Shakir needed and had it recorded was tempered with the idea that Cora would leave something up to the men. "Didn't that strike you as odd? She doesn't seem like a woman who will walk out and let the men hammer out the details."

"Abbie, I've got no fucking clue why some women do what they do." Hop grinned and added, "Probably why I'm still single. But then, you're not like most women, and my buddy Rick seriously lucked out with you."

She laughed and shook her head. "Since you're still wired, you know he can hear you, right?"

"Sure. I figure that'll keep him straight. If he ever fucks up, then you know I'm right here waiting in the wings!"

Patting his arm, she smiled, enjoying the levity. "I'm

gonna head back to my room," she said. "Are you catching up with Rick and Dolby?"

"Yeah, I'm gonna be with them while they send everything to LSI, Tom, and Shakir. Once we have that, Shakir can move in on his arrests, and I figure you and the rest of us will be ready to wrap things up."

"Hell yeah." She tossed a little wave as she moved down the steps to the next deck. Passing the lounge where food and drink were offered all day, she decided to stop in for a bite to eat. "Guys," she whispered, "I'm going to get a snack in the lounge."

Only a few people were around at this time of day, but her gaze immediately fell upon Giselle at the bar. Turning so she could face her, she knew the Keepers could see what she was viewing.

"I'll send Hop back up," Rick radioed.

"No, don't," she whispered. "She was talking to him earlier, and I want to see Giselle when the others come back in without anyone around."

She didn't have to wait long as Cora walked in, spied Giselle, and made her way over to the bar. The two women greeted each other in a way that, while Abbie couldn't say they looked like best friends, there was no obvious animosity. *I guess Cora doesn't know about Giselle and Jason.*

Almost as if on cue, Jason entered the salon, walking toward the bar as well. Abbie made sure to keep the gathering in her hidden camera's sight. She steadied her breathing, forcing her body to stay in place.

"We're coming up," Rick radioed. "I don't want you there by yourself."

Jason greeted the women, then headed to the table containing the buffet.

As Giselle's gaze stayed on Jason's back, a sleight of hand behind her caught Abbie's attention as she spied Cora pouring liquid into Giselle's drink. Still smiling, Cora pocketed the vial before she walked over to the buffet table as well.

"Shit, I've got to go in," Abbie whispered into her radio, hoping the others were on their way.

Just as Giselle lifted her drink to her lips, Abbie stepped forward and placed her hand over the top of the glass. "I don't think you want to drink that."

"What?" Giselle startled, swinging her head around.

"If you want to stay alive, keep quiet, and don't drink that."

Giselle's gaze shot to Abbie, confusion marring her expression.

"Have we met?"

"I witnessed someone put something in your drink just now."

Since the only person who had been next to her drink was Cora, it didn't take Giselle but a few seconds to jerk, her eyes wide as they shot to the other side of the room where Cora held Jason's arm. Faster than Abbie thought possible, Giselle shot off the barstool.

"You bitch! What did you put in my drink?" she shouted, drawing the attention of others in the salon.

Abbie stepped back, willing to see how the scenario played out.

Giselle held up her drink, stomping toward Cora, a snarl on her face. "You put something in my drink!

What the fuck? Are you going to kill me like you killed the others?"

Cora's eyes narrowed. "Stop being ridiculous! You don't know what you're talking about! You're drunk!"

"No, I'm not, but you'd like that, wouldn't you? That would make things easier."

Jason's jaw dropped as he turned toward his wife. "You drugged her drink? What the hell did you do that for? We're so close, and you want to pull this?"

Cora glanced around. "Shut up! We've got too much riding on this."

"Then why the hell did you go rogue? Why her?" Jason bit out.

"Oh, I see you're more concerned about your fuck than you are your wife," Cora said in a whispered growl.

"You're one to talk! You think I don't know about you and Paul?" Jason bit back.

The news appeared to stun Giselle as she gasped, her wide eyes moving back and forth between Jason and Cora.

The doors opened behind them, and Khalil stepped through, his brow lowered and his expression thunderous. "What's going on? My manservant heard the loud voices. Is this how you do business?"

Abbie watched the train-wreck situation developing in front of her, and it was all she could do to keep up with the accusations flying. After all the years the Adamsons had worked on their perfect crime, it was all falling apart because of who was sleeping with who.

Jason turned to assure Khalil that business was fine and that it was just a slight misunderstanding. The doors swung open again, and a multitude of Egyptian police, some in suits and others in uniforms, swarmed in with their weapons drawn.

Abbie didn't have to turn around to know that Rick was right behind her. She felt his warm presence and let out a breath that was shakier than she would have liked it to have been.

"You okay, babe?" he asked softly, his breath against her cheek as he leaned forward.

Taking her eyes off the arrests and protestations going on in front of her, she peered up into his eyes and nodded. "I am now." Hop and Dolby stepped forward, flanking her and Rick on each side.

Giselle suddenly looked over at Abbie and gasped. "I knew you were familiar!"

Her declaration brought Cora's and Jason's gazes swinging her way, confusion knitting their brows. Jason shook his head, not recognizing her, and Cora was already being handcuffed, pulling her attention to her own predicament. Khalil was protesting loudly, his security guards standing nearby, their expressions slack as though not having a clue what they should do.

Rick pulled Abbie back gently and leaned down to whisper, "We need to get out of here, babe."

She nodded her agreement, glad to escape the lounge. Once back in her room with the others, she jerked off her wig and glasses, tossing them to the dresser. Taking the pins from her tight bun, she ran her fingers through her hair and groaned.

"How do you like field work?" Hop asked, his eyes twinkling.

"Oh God. That was crazy. Absolutely, fucking crazy. Give me my tiny-ass office, my images, and my computer programs any day!"

Rick moved behind her and began to massage her neck and shoulders. She groaned again, loving the feel and wanting his hands on more than just her neck.

Dolby looked at his watch. "We dock in about two hours. By then, they can unload the prisoners, and I'll see what transportation Tom can arrange to get us back to Cairo." With a wave, he and Hop headed back to the other room, leaving Abbie and Rick alone.

He wrapped his arms around her, and she relished the security she felt pulled back against his chest. "It's over. It's really over," she breathed.

"I fucking hated knowing you were walking around the boat and not being with you," he admitted.

She turned in his arms and peered up at him. "Well, we're together now, and this is the only place I want to be."

"Thank God, babe, 'cause I feel the same."

Grinning, she winked. "Gee, sailor. What should we do for a couple of hours?"

Bending, he lowered his face to a whisper's breath from hers and said, "Let's see if we can find something to occupy our time." Then he erased the space between them and kissed her.

23

Baniti had dropped them off and waved goodbye. "I will see you when I come to take you to the airport tomorrow."

Rick carried Abbie's bag into her villa as she walked in front of him, glad to be off the cruise boat and have the case wrapped up but wishing Baniti's words had been for all of them and not just the Keepers.

Abbie sighed. "God, it feels so good to have this case done with. I am so ready to finish my time here in Cairo."

Rick encircled her with his arms, pulling her back to his front. It was on the tip of his tongue to ask, 'Then what?' but he hesitated. It wasn't a conversation he wanted to have with others around. And, in truth, he was afraid of the answer. Kissing the top of her head, he simply held her close.

Dolby and Hop followed them into the villa, dropping their bags near the door before they headed to the kitchen, their noses leading them to whatever Sabah had left for them on the counter.

"You guys ever think about anything other than your next meal?" he asked, grinning.

Hop lifted his gaze and waggled his eyebrows. "Yes, but it's not polite to talk about it with ladies present."

Her phone vibrated, and she looked down at the text. "Hmm, it's from Michael. He said he's sending a driver here to give me something so I don't have to come into the office tomorrow. "

"What would he be sending?" Rick asked as she twisted her neck to look up at him.

"I don't know," she admitted. "I can't imagine, but I guess I'll see."

She pulled away from his embrace and started for the door. "I'm coming, too," he said.

"I'm just going to the garden gate—"

"Doesn't matter."

Laughing, she slipped her hand in his, and they walked through the garden to the black iron gate, stepping onto the sidewalk. A white panel van was parked just outside, and she started forward.

A sharp pain hit Rick in the neck, surprising him. "Umph… sh…" He reached out and grabbed at her, wanting to pull her back to his side.

"What—" she began as she turned.

He felt his weight already dragging her down but couldn't seem to let go. She twisted and grabbed him as he slumped forward, but they landed on their knees on the sidewalk. As though someone had the daylight on a dimmer switch, the illumination slowly disappeared, but her stunned expression was the last thing he saw before he faded into total black.

"Rick! Rick!"

He battled to open his eyes, hearing Dolby's voice close by. "Wha... the fu..?" he muttered, his words slurring.

Sitting up, he reached behind him and rubbed the sore area at his neck, feeling a stinging pain. He was in the garden, Dolby kneeling in front of him.

"Shit, somebody must have hit me with a tranquilizer." Suddenly as more clarity penetrated his brain fog, he jerked his head around, battling the dizziness. "Abbie? Where the hell is Abbie?"

"Fuck, we just got down here." Twisting around, Dolby called to Hop, "Rick's been hit by a tranquilizer. Probably a dart gun. Abbie is gone."

"She got a message from Michael. Michael Hawn."

"On it!" Hop called out.

"Come on, let's get out of here." Dolby hefted his shoulder underneath Rick's armpit and assisted him to his feet.

Taking deep breaths, he focused on standing and getting to Abbie. "Shit, how long was I out?"

"Couldn't have been more than five minutes," Dolby said. "You were gone, and I came out to see where you two were. I didn't see anyone."

"White panel van. Michael's message was that someone was coming here because he needed to get something to her." He squinted, willing the nausea to go away. "Christ, I didn't see anybody! We've got no fucking idea who's got her! Dammit, she could be anywhere!"

Hop interrupted. "Jeb just called. He's got her tracer and is sending me the info. I called Baniti. He's coming back. He was only a few minutes away. Let's go!"

Dolby grabbed his shoulders and shook him. "Come on. You're still not thinking clearly. With the tracer, we can find her location."

He looked up as the squeal of tires met their ears. Baniti was driving the van, jerking it to a stop next to them. The side panel door opened, and Dolby shoved Rick inside. He stumbled but managed to haul himself into a seat. "What the fuck happened? What did we miss?"

Hop was in the back, his gaze on the computer screen, but as he glanced up toward Rick, his tight jaw gave evidence that he was furious. "Fuck, I'm sorry, bro. For them to have a tranquilizer gun ready, they were ready for her."

Rick was sick, but not from the tranquilizer. Agony ripped through him that Abbie had been abducted right from his side. "Jesus, I fucked up. I fucked up—"

"Get that out of your mind," Dolby ordered. "She's on the move, and we can get to her."

He was barely aware of Hop giving Baniti directions, staring at the horrific traffic. As though reading his mind, Hop said, "They're in the same traffic. They can't get far."

"They didn't count on you being so large," Dolby

surmised, drawing Rick's attention. "That's why whatever they gave you wore off quickly."

"Shit, but did they do the same to her? The same amount would knock her out longer." Looking out the window, he growled, "Where? Where does it look like they're heading?"

After only a few seconds of hesitation, Hop replied, "The City of the Dead."

24

Abbie slowly lifted her hand to her forehead, not remembering the last time she had a hangover this bad. Dry, cottonmouth. A tongue that felt swollen. Stabbing pain in her head when she blinked open her eyes to the dim light. Battling nausea that made her want to roll over and heave. The dry and hot air made it difficult to breathe.

Memories floated through her mind, the pieces not coming together in a well-formed pattern. Memories of her and college friends as they stumbled back to the dorm, giggling as they held each other up. They were too drunk to be any good to each other, but they'd somehow convinced themselves they'd be safe if they stuck together. Next, memories of her Army teammates going out to a bar to celebrate their promotion when they made it through OCS.

No... I'm not drunk.

More memories pushed their way into her consciousness. Waking to Rick's face in his apartment with the sun already shining through the blinds, casting a glow over his beautiful torso exposed when the sheet had drifted to his waist.

Rick... Rick...

A movement out of the corner of her eye caused her to force her eyelids to stay open despite the pain. It was dark, but a small ray of light came from the distance.

As her memory sharpened, she recognized she wasn't in Maine. Taking a deep breath, the scent of spices mixed with perspiration and the decay of garbage gave her a clue about her whereabouts. *This is not Cairo*.

Her memory focused, and the sight of Rick slumping forward slammed into her. She tried to lift her hand to her upper chest, where a tingling pain lingered, but discovered her wrists were taped together. Fear jolted through her body at the realization that her ankles were also bound. Terrified, she squirmed.

"Nothing is broken, I assure you. Just a tranquilizer drug."

She tried to sit up, but nausea nearly forced her back down. Sucking in a deep breath through her nose, the scent of spoiled garbage sent a retching reflex through her. Determined to get oxygen into her lungs, she breathed deeply through her mouth. Looking toward the voice coming from the corner, she wasn't surprised when the man stepped out of the shadows. Paul White.

"What... what..." She tried to talk, but her mouth was two steps behind her brain.

"I knew there was a problem when I got notified of what happened on the cruise." He shook his head. "All that work. All that planning." Then a slow smile crossed his face. "But, lucky for me, I know where things are stored, so more money for me."

"You..." She cleared her throat. "What did you do to Rick?"

"Your boyfriend?" Paul snorted. "He'll be out for a while. And when he comes to, you'll be long gone in a place where he'll never find you."

"Why not just arrange another accident?" she asked, her mind clearing. She wanted to keep him talking, praying that Hop and Dolby would get to Rick and then to her. "After all, it worked for Anne and Mary."

He threw his head back and laughed, giving her a chance to glance quickly around to see that they were in a dark room with no windows, and... *fucking hell*—a mausoleum was just behind him. *Are we... could we be... oh, God... how will Rick find me here?*

Paul returned his attention to her, shaking his head. "You really are smart. But then that's why you can understand that while two accidents worked before, another accident of someone from the embassy would be too coincidental. No, much better for your disappearance to be blamed on someone who was close to you, such as your boyfriend."

"All this... for a few antiquities?"

His smile dropped, and he stepped closer. "A few antiquities? Oh no. The items Jason discovered buried under his building in unrecorded tombs contained jewelry, gold, treasure, and a sarcophagus, with the promise of more as we continue to dig."

"But how did you find out about those tombs underneath the apartment building?"

He grinned, and she could tell he was gearing up to impress her. "That was all Jason's doing. He and Cora lived in a shitty apartment in Ma'adi, but through his research, he determined that some of the buildings in Heliopolis were built over tombs. He'd spent years researching using texts and maps and discovered what he felt sure was the location of the one he thought would bring the most money with the least amount of work." Paul shrugged. "So he and Cora, with the backing of Khalil Hassein, who had deep pockets and few scruples, moved into that building, making sure to take over a large storage unit in the basement. Strangely enough, that was the difficult part. As you can imagine, the easy part was paying Egyptians to dig."

"How did they know that the whole thing wasn't going to fall on top of their heads?" she asked, thinking about how the workers could become buried in a tomb if the dirt walls or ceiling fell on them.

"Inshallah. The Egyptian workers didn't care. If Allah wills that it is their time to die, then they die. But that is where I came in," he gloated.

More understanding moved through her ever-clearing mind. "A civil engineer. Of course, you're a civil engineer."

He nodded, his smile calculating. "Ah, yes. You're making the connections now."

"And you were here, in the City of the Dead, where some of the mausoleums are being demolished for the new roads."

"What better place to hide something until we could

find a buyer than an area that I knew was not going to be demolished."

"But Anne? Mary? What do they have to do with all this?"

"Initially, they were couriers. But, eventually, they became expendable." He chuckled, seemingly proud of his wit.

"Couriers?" she prodded, wanting to keep him talking.

"They took photographs of the artifacts and met with potential buyers. They had no idea the worth of what they were showing. They simply thought their beloved professor was doing research, and they were getting paid to assist. So they would take the images to potential buyers and receive closed bids, and that was the extent of their involvement. And for that, they were paid handsomely. The first girl we used, a French student, became suspicious. She wanted out, so we arranged for her to get out. Permanently." Shaking his head, he sighed. "Such a waste. She was beautiful and so satisfying."

Abbie's skin crawled at the thought of Paul being intimate with anyone.

"Anne was next. She would've done anything for Jason, much to Cora's displeasure. Poor Anne was perfectly happy with the arrangement. She thought she was special to Jason. Of course, sleeping with her was a huge mistake. He greatly underestimated his wife's suspicions or what lengths she would go to."

"So Anne was killed because she was Jason's mistress?"

Paul roared with laughter again. "Mistress? What century are you in? She was nothing more than his occasional fuck. Cora put up with it just long enough to create the most elaborate accident. It was easy enough to get someone to put sleeping pills in the bottled water and pour drinks in her one night on the boat." His hands lifted, palms out as he demonstrated. "And then a little push over the side. That's one thing about living and working in a third-world country. Money can buy you anything."

"That's despicable."

"That's business, Ms. Blake."

"And Mary? The same thing with her?"

He snorted with derision. "Mary was desperately looking for a bit of adventure. Jason had his eye on her, but after what happened to Anne, Cora had him by the balls. But me? I was her secret lover. The one she was sure she might spend her life with."

"You? You were the one she was involved with?"

"Easy enough to arrange a meeting at one of Cora and Jason's parties. Easy to get her working for us. But it took a little longer than it had with the other two. She was cautious. I told Jason not to push it, but she became suspicious when Jason dumped more money into her account than he should have. You see, he's brilliant when it comes to ancient Egyptian artifacts but not so smart when it comes to people. So Cora and I had a chat, and we made another accident happen."

"It seems like a lot of work for what cannot possibly be much money." Shaking her head, she stared, still unable to grasp the time and energy spent on the illegal and risky endeavor.

"That's the thing about collectors who buy antiquities that are... shall we say, not on the legitimate market. They will pay much more than what someone would get otherwise. So this has been very lucrative for all of us."

"And Giselle. Cora tried to kill her on the cruise."

His chin lifted slightly. "Cora... brains, beauty, and smart. But she can't stand anyone getting to Jason. Well, as you witnessed, it was her downfall."

"But to kill so willingly—"

"This is Cairo. Shit happens. People go back to their homeland, and no one checks. Accidents are commonplace."

God, please let Rick be okay and let someone realize I'm missing! Keeping her voice steady, she continued, "Then why Sam?"

"I should hand it to him. Until he and you arrived here, I had no idea you were investigating. But he was too much of a fool. Easily led by dreams of solving a big case. I was sure I could frighten you, but he needed to be dealt with."

Another thought hit her, and she gasped, stunned that it had taken her so long to put the pieces together. "Michael. Michael Hawn. He's the one who sent me outside my villa." She blinked, her chest depressing as the air rushed out. "Oh God... he's the one who told you about Sam and me coming here. And... he's the one who told you what happened on the cruise!"

He stepped closer, his gaze moving about the shadowed room until falling on her again. "It's interesting to see the light dawn in your pretty head now that the fog of the tranquilizer is wearing off. You'll disappear, and I'll still be a very rich man with what we were able to accomplish before I leave this country tomorrow."

Hating the way her heart palpitated as he neared, she asked the questions burning inside. "Why did you bring me here? To the City of the Dead?"

"I should've known you'd recognize where you were. This has become a brilliant place to hide some of the artifacts and soon, your body as well."

"When I'm found, they'll know that it was you. They're already on to you."

"My dear, you're not going to be found, and I'll be long gone. We are in one of the sections that will not be destroyed for the highway. You will be entombed just like another ancient body." Pulling out a gun from a holster underneath his jacket, he lifted his brows. "I assure you, this is no tranquilizer gun."

From behind her, a man appeared and grabbed her, forcing her back into the stone crypt she was perched on. Screaming, she recognized him as the man who'd met with Sam. She battled, but with her wrists bound together as well as her ankles, she flailed before falling backward, unable to right herself. With another scream on her lips, a heavy slab was slid into place on top, plunging her into a dark tomb.

Her chest quivered as her nightmare came to life. *Buried alive!* Jerking her bound hands to her mouth, she covered her face, fighting the rising panic threatening to overtake all thoughts. Squeezing her eyes tightly shut, she finally let out a breath.

Think... think. Slow down and think.

When she'd become aware of her surroundings while talking to Paul, she'd barely been able to focus on anything due to the dim light in the room. She had been perched on a slab of stone, not realizing the crypt was directly behind her. She hadn't noticed anything specific about what she'd sat on, certainly not its thickness or size. *Wait! The man who pushed me back into the crypt moved the slab by himself! It must be heavy, but it can't be impossible to shift!*

Unable to see anything, she lifted her hands slowly until her fingertips touched the stone slab. She was never going to be able to press her palms flat against the slab with her wrists taped together. Gnawing on the tape with her teeth, she eventually managed to loosen it slightly, giving her a chance to move her hands around. Pressing upward, the slab didn't budge. She cursed her lack of upper body strength, remembering it was the hardest thing she'd had to overcome to make it through OCS. But as a runner, she had strong leg muscles.

Lying partially on her side, she worked at the tape on her ankles, managing to rip enough to get her ankle bindings a little looser as well. Now on her back again, she was thankful for her slender stature because she could cock her knees and get her feet on the slab above her. With the combined effort of her arms and legs, she pushed. But it barely moved.

"Again... do it again... don't stop... don't fucking stop," she chanted softly, giving a heave upward again, this time with more force. The slab shifted ever so slightly. Not having any idea which way would be the best for it to move, she concentrated. *Away from my head. He probably just covered the top with the slab, so it has less far to go nearest my head.* Slowly counting to three, she pushed upward with every ounce of strength and felt the slab move another inch. Taking a deep breath before letting it out slowly, she repeated the action one more time, her body straining with the effort, a grunt forced from her lips.

Still unable to see anything, a sliver of dark gray appeared near her head where before had only been solid black. Stretching out slowly to ease the muscles in her legs, she caught a whiff of a scent. Almost afraid to hope, she sniffed deeply. The familiar scent of garbage mixed with a wood-burning stove with meat cooking met her nostrils. Her breath caught in her lungs at the realization she had moved the slab enough to allow air to come into the crypt. And if air could get in, her voice could get out.

Abbie rose up as far as possible and listened, hoping to hear the sound of other human voices. At first, she heard nothing but her own raspy breathing. Then it dawned on her that nothing indicated that Paul was no longer nearby. *Or maybe he is, but he's just not speaking.* Uncertainty filled her for a moment, and then she decided to gather her strength and try to move the slab a little bit farther.

Lifting her legs again and with her feet pressed upward next to her hands, she strained her muscles and moved the stone another inch. Now, she was able to stick her fingers out of the small space and could tell that the slab overhead was only about an inch thick.

Of course, an inch of stone or concrete was still heavy, but at least she'd moved it a bit. Breathing easier now that air was able to get in, she spoke softly. "Hello? Hello? Can anyone hear me?"

Waiting in fear as her heart pounded, terrified that Paul or his accomplice would be close by and discover that she had moved the top of the crypt and decide to replace it with something heavier, she barely breathed, and she waited and listened.

When no response came, she took that as a good sign. Right now, no one being around was better than having him near. Taking a chance, she called out a little louder this time. "Hello? Hello?" She thought she heard more rustling but couldn't be sure. Hesitating for another few seconds, she tried again. "Hello? Help me... saeadani."

She tried to push upward again but felt a sharp pain shoot through her shoulder. Using only her legs, she managed to move it a bit. Elation at not being completely entombed mixed with terror that she wouldn't be able to get out.

Suddenly, the distinct sound of rustling met her eager ears, and she squeaked as a small face appeared in the crypt space, dark brown, wide eyes in a tanned face peering back at her. *A child... oh, thank God!* "Help me... saeadani. Please... uh... min fadlik."

The face disappeared, and her heart lurched as she lost sight of the child. Battling the desire to cry, she sucked in a deep breath and pressed her lips together.

25

"Fuck! We've lost her!"

Of all the things Rick did not want to hear, the words that left Hop's mouth were at the top of his list. "What the fuck do you mean?"

"The signal has suddenly disappeared," Hop growled.

He looked over at the screen in front of Hop, willing the indicator to show where Abbie was located, praying that Hop had just gone temporarily blind and stupid. But no, he didn't see it either.

It didn't matter that Baniti was whizzing in and around other vehicles to get them as quickly as they could to Abbie. The snarl of traffic that had allowed her captor to get farther away had Rick's mind racing and his gut tied up in knots.

Looking over, Hop reassured, "But Jeb says she's been at the same location for the past fifteen minutes. So that's where we'll head."

Rick closed his eyes, trying to block out the images

flying past the van windows, but all he could see in his mind was Abbie's face.

"You've got to stay focused," Dolby said.

Rick jerked his head around as he opened his eyes, ready to slam his friend.

"I know, I know, it's shit advice," Dolby continued, lifting his hand in a placating manner. "But you know it's true. Listen, if she's been in the same place for fifteen minutes, that means they've got her someplace steady. They're no longer traveling."

"Then why can't we get a signal? It's not like she just had a necklace. She had a fucking tracer put in her arm."

"I don't know, but in the City of the Dead, maybe there are places where a signal is just not getting out."

He didn't want to think about the kind of place that Abbie might be where a signal wouldn't get out. His stomach clenched again as his hands tightened into fists in his lap.

Baniti called out, "It's close! It's close! Give me the last location. I will get us close to her!"

With Jeb on the radio, Hop leaned forward and gave Baniti the directions necessary.

Looking out the window, Rick stared in stunned silence. He'd been all over the world, and third-world poverty was nothing new to him. He'd seen parents raising their children in caves dug into the side of hills. He'd seen families sleeping in bombed-out buildings, mud huts, wooden shacks, and tents. He'd seen kids playing with a ball made of bits of string and rubber, kicking it in the dirt underneath a brutal sun. He'd always been amazed at the resiliency of the human spirit.

But seeing the families eking out their entire lives amongst the crypts, mausoleums, crumbling buildings, and garbage piles made it hard to breathe. And the idea that Abbie was being held somewhere nearby… *Focus. Fucking focus!*

As soon as Baniti brought the van to a stop, Rick threw open the side panel door. He was almost out when Dolby's hand gripped his arm. Jerking around, he was faced with two Keepers staring him down.

"You know if you go racing in, you could get her killed," Hop said, grabbing his weapon.

"Dig deep, brother," Dolby said, his gaze never wavering. "We go in strategically. We go in fast, but we go in smart."

Rick hesitated for only a second before he sucked in a deep breath and let it out slowly. Nodding, he secured his weapon and said, "Got it. I'm good. Now let's go find her."

Racing through the maze of the crypts, many now just concrete rubble or turned into houses, he ignored the startled faces of those coming to see what was happening.

Baniti began to shout in Arabic to the ones nearby, "Did you see something? A man carrying a white woman? Or maybe a big blanket or rug?"

Several people went back inside their makeshift houses, concern on their faces. Rick could only imagine that outsiders were looked on as a source of money from begging or someone to fear. Jerking his head around, he barked, "Offer them money."

Baniti raced over and held his gaze. "If I do, then most will claim to know something just to get paid, but it will lead us nowhere, and we'll waste time."

"Fuck!" he growled.

"This way!" Hop called out, his gaze staring at the screen on his watch. "Her last location."

Now, ignoring the curious faces, the four men raced along the narrow pathways between mausoleums. A small child ran around a corner, skidding to a stop, his dark eyes impossibly wide as he stared. He called out to Baniti, but as the Keepers swung their attention to him, he clammed up and turned as though to run.

Ready to ignore him, Rick started forward, then looked back. Something about the child's expression made him halt. "Baniti! Talk to him."

Baniti hustled over, kneeling on the dirty sidewalk in front of the little boy. He'd barely greeted him when the child began pointing behind him. After a few sentences, Baniti looked over his shoulder. "He says a woman is trapped in a place of burial."

"Tell him to show us!" Rick ordered, his heart pounding with a surge of adrenaline.

Baniti spoke to the boy, who turned and began to run. Hop nodded, his gaze shooting toward Rick. "Her tracer just picked up again. The kid is heading in the right direction!"

Instantly, three large Keepers raced after the child.

Oh God, he's gone!

Not knowing if the child ran away from fright, Abbie heaved upward again, ignoring the pain in her shoulder. *I can do this... I can do this.* A cry from deep inside roared out as she shifted the slab another half inch. Emboldened, she began to shout between gasps of air. "Help! Help!"

A moment later, hasty footsteps were heard approaching, and her heart slammed against her rib cage. Her life was balancing on the razor's edge between fear and hope.

Rapidly spoken Arabic from a child met her ears, and then another dark-eyed, tanned face peered down at her.

"Oh, help me, please!"

Other adult voices speaking in Arabic filled the air, and she spied several Egyptian men peering down at her. She gasped in more oxygen as hands began to lift the slab away.

"Abbie!"

Jolting, she cried, "Rick!" She struggled to help the Egyptians to move the stone, but her hands halted when she looked up into the ravaged face of the man she loved. "Rick! Oh God, it was Paul. He's the one who took me!"

His arms encircled her, and she was lifted from her stone coffin. Wincing, she shifted to ease the pain in her shoulder.

"Where are you hurt, babe?" he asked, his gaze searching hers before moving to Dolby. Jerking his head toward her, he held her as Dolby pulled out a knife and sliced through the tape around her ankles and wrists.

"I'm fine."

"You don't look fine—"

"No, really. I just strained my shoulder trying to lift the slab off me."

"Fuck, Abbie," he groaned, holding her close.

She buried her face in his neck for a moment, breathing in the scent of him, giving her heart a chance to beat to something else besides fear. All she wanted to do was stay in his arms, letting the safety chase away all remnants of the nightmare. Sucking in a deep breath, she lifted her head again, and repeated, "It was Paul who did this, but we've got to get to the embassy. I've got to talk to Tom. Paul was working with Michael! He set up Sam, as well!"

Baniti stepped closer, his sharp gaze on her. "Mr. Olsen will meet you. But not at the embassy. Come. Come."

"What the fuck?" Rick bit out.

"You know he will do things his way," Baniti said, shifting his gaze back and forth between the Keepers and Abbie. "You know how it works."

She hesitated, pressing her lips together. Sucking in another deep breath, she nodded, then looked up at Rick. "Okay… let's go wherever Baniti says to go."

"It is not far," Baniti promised.

Rick set her feet on the ground, and she dropped to a squat in front of the child. Realizing she didn't have her purse with her, she cast a searching glance toward

RICK

Baniti as she held out her hand to the little boy who'd heard her calls and ran to get help. "Shukran."

Baniti hustled over, thrusting numerous Egyptian pound notes to the adults who'd helped push the stone away before reaching his hand into the pocket of his galabeya and pulling out a small bag of candy.

She took it gratefully and handed it to the wide-eyed boy whose face broke into a smile as he accepted it slowly. She waited until he opened it and took a big bite, marveling as his smile widened even more.

Standing, she moved with Rick toward Baniti who whispered, "The money would mean less to the child and would possibly be taken by one of the adults, and he would never get anything for his help. But the candy is a treat he'll enjoy now and remember forever."

By now, crowds of Egyptians were pressing in, curiosity seekers and those who'd seen money exchange hands and hoped to get some for themselves. Abbie had to admit that if she had been by herself, she would've felt afraid, but with Baniti leading the way and three massive men encircling her, they made their way back to the street where the dark van was parked next to the old white one.

Once again, she climbed inside and saw Tom sitting alone. Rick, Dolby, and Hop entered behind her, and Baniti closed the door just as Tom's driver pulled out of the area and back onto a road.

"Are you okay, Abbie?" Tom asked, his voice rough. The lines in his face were deeper, more pronounced. The unflappable man appeared rattled.

She nodded, wanting to offer assurances to her boss

while at the same time uncertain of his role and everything that had played out.

"Baniti called me," he said, swallowing. "I had my suspicions about Michael."

"You could've fucking told us," Rick growled.

Tom's jaw tightened as he looked toward Rick but slowly nodded. "It was only recently. There was something about Sam's death... that was why I only met with you when you came into the embassy. It was why I was willing to turn so much over to LSI."

"But it wasn't until today that you knew for sure?" She managed to choke out, wanting clarification. *Needing clarification.* The idea that Michael knew she was being buried alive clawed at her throat.

Tom shook his head. "No. Not until I heard you were taken today and discovered Michael had talked to Paul."

"So where is Michael now?" she asked.

"He's under arrest. I had the order in place as soon as I had the evidence."

"And Paul?" she pushed, clasping her hands together to keep them from shaking.

"We'll get him," Tom said.

"Fuck," Hop cut in. "You don't know where he is, do you?"

"I—"

"No," Rick growled. "We'll get him."

Abbie waited to see if Tom would disagree or argue. But instead, she watched as he held Rick's gaze and then slowly nodded. That was it. No words. Just a nod.

26

Paul bypassed the private lounge, making his way directly to the hangar where his escape plan would take its next step on his journey out of Egypt. As he'd always found, money could buy him anything. Stepping inside the small hangar, he spied the private plane he'd hired, allowing him to bypass normal airport security. It wouldn't be long before he'd arrive in Greece. Once safely ensconced in his rented white villa by the sea, he planned a stay as he finished the sales of the outstanding artifacts they'd uncovered.

There was still plenty to sell, and what had been a three-way split between him, Cora, and Jason would now all come to him. He was grateful those two had brought him on board with their plans, but they'd outlived their usefulness. They couldn't have completed anything without him, and he was more than fine with being the one to walk away with the money now.

He looked up as a beautiful blonde in a skintight skirt and low-cut top with sky-high heels waved him over to the plane. *Looks like my flight just got more interesting.* He walked toward her, and the closer he got, the more his gaze dropped to her luscious tits. *Oh yeah, this will be a flight to celebrate.*

"Welcome aboard, Mr. Smith," she said, her voice dripping with promise. "Please follow me, and we'll soon be ready for take-off."

She climbed the steps in front of him, the curve and sway of her ass drawing him in. Once inside, she waved toward the well-appointed interior. It wasn't opulent, but it was a cut above anything he'd flown when arriving in Egypt. *My days of commercial flights are over!*

Turning, he smiled down at her. "Will I be lucky enough for your company on the flight?"

Ruby-red lips curled upward, and she grinned, showing perfectly white teeth. "It will be my pleasure to take care of you."

The door closed behind her, and she waved her hand toward the plush leather seats. "Choose whatever seat you'd like, Mr. Smith. The pilot is ready, and we'll leave shortly. Can I get you something to drink?"

He walked by, his hand sliding over her ass. "I think I found the seat I'd like to have."

She laughed and tossed her hair over her shoulder. "I'm sure something can be arranged, sir." She walked away to the hostess station, and he watched as she checked her supplies and poured a drink.

Pulling out his phone, he scanned his emails. He had two buyers lined up for some of the smaller items. With Khalil out of the picture since his arrest yesterday, he was looking for new interest in the largest sarcophagus.

Seeing the interest already, he chuckled. *This will be easy.* Of course, yesterday's raid on the cruise boat caused him to make hasty decisions and move artifacts around. He'd quickly called upon a few men who'd worked for him in the past to retrieve the artifacts they'd stored in the City of the Dead and bring them to him as he hid in a small hotel. Now, they were currently on board with his luggage. The sarcophagus had been hidden in a new place amongst the crypts, waiting for him to make a sale.

He fastened his seat belt, shifting in his seat as his gaze landed back on the flight attendant's ass while she bent over to retrieve something from the bottom cabinet. He was definitely interested and wondered if she would be amenable to spending a few days in Greece with him, preferable with her luscious red lips wrapped around his cock.

The plane began to roll out of the hangar, and he leaned back, a smile playing about his lips. Suddenly, the plane braked, and his body jolted with the hard stop.

"What the hell?" he barked out, eyes narrowing as he looked up toward the attendant whose wide eyes gave away her surprise.

"I don't know, sir. I'll see what the captain says."

Before he had a chance to unbuckle or the attendant could knock on the cockpit door, it opened, and a tall man walked out, his airline uniform indicating he was the captain.

"What's going on?" Paul's hands went to his seat belt, refusing to feel so small next to the captain. The buckle wouldn't unlatch, and he looked up, brow furrowed, and growled, "Get me out of this! I want to know what's going on!"

"Well, now, you see," the captain drawled in an ungodly American accent, "that's the problem. We don't want you to get out of the seat."

Paul jerked, his eyes narrowing. "Do you know who you're talking to?"

"I do," the co-pilot said, coming out of the cockpit. "But do you?"

A trickle of unease ran over Paul as he stared at the two large men, both with bulging muscles that were barely contained in their crisp white shirts.

The attendant reached to her face and pulled her false eyelashes off before gliding her hands to her forehead and underneath the blond bangs to slide the wig off, letting it drop behind her. She held his gaze, but all pretense of coy flirtatiousness was gone. "Hi, Paul. Remember me?"

The air flooded from his lungs as he stared at Abbie's face. His eyes widened as his mouth dropped open. "But... but... you..." And then his gaze moved to the unsmiling man who came from the back and walked next to Abbie. And his stomach dropped.

Faced with the man who'd tried to kill the woman he loved, Rick's fingers curled into fists, flexing them at his sides. The desire to let Paul out of his restraining seat belt and beat on him was overpowering. A low, animalistic growl erupted from deep inside his chest, and he took a step forward.

Then a soft hand landed on his arm, and his entire body locked into place. And so did his heart. He dropped his chin and looked down at Abbie, seeing her staring up at him. He waited. As much as he wanted to drop Paul into a sarcophagus and close the lid, he knew this was Abbie's call.

"I've got this," she said, her voice soft.

He chuckled, knowing her resolve was anything but soft.

Paul blustered, "I have money. Lots of money. I can make this worth your while. I can—"

"Oh, shut up, man," Dolby groaned, his expression showing disgust. "You talk too fuckin' much."

"We're not going to kill you," Abbie said, stepping closer.

Rick, not willing to have her too close, moved up with her.

Paul licked his lips, his breathing erratic.

"But then you did try to kill me—"

"No, no!" Paul cried out, his hands lifting.

Rick growled again, and Paul immediately dropped his hands.

"No?" she asked, one brow lifted.

"No. I was just frightening you. I was going to come back. I would never—"

"You're not a good liar, Paul," she said, shaking her head. "But while I'd like to do the same to you and leave you to rot, that's not what I'm going to do." She inclined her head toward Paul.

Hop stepped forward, a gleam in his eyes as he pulled out a long knife. Paul reared back, fear oozing from his pores. Hop slipped the knife under the front of the seat belt, dangerously close to Paul's cock, and sliced the belt. "Aw, you weren't scared I might cut off your dick, were you? I wouldn't do that. Hell, you might need the pecker in prison."

As soon as Hop stepped back, Paul jumped to his feet, tripping to scramble backward, but Abbie was faster.

Grinning, she pulled away from the wall of Keepers and walked straight up to Paul. "Looks like your attempt to bury me in a sarcophagus didn't work. You didn't count on my strength and the courage of a little child." Before he had a chance to react, she cocked her arm and swung, hitting him in the nose. His head snapped back, and as much as her hand hurt, the satisfying crunch of his nose breaking more than made up for the pain. Turning, she walked straight into Rick's arms.

He held her close, his heart pounding a rhythm of love just for her. Kissing the top of her head, he looked over at a grinning Hop and Dolby. "That's my girl," he said, prouder than he'd ever been in his life.

27

The glistening water in front of Abbie sparkled with diamonds as she stared out from the lighthouse. A breeze lifted her hair, blowing it away from her face. Closing her eyes, she lifted her chin as the sun warmed her skin and remembered the Egyptian sun as it did the same. But the coast of Maine offered the cool, damp spray of water as it crashed against the rocks below.

"I love it here," she said, inhaling deeply, filling her lungs with the crisp fresh air.

"Are you sure you're doing the right thing?"

She opened her eyes and smiled at the man standing next to her. "Yes, Mace, I am. I turned in my notice to the CIA and arranged to have my belongings shipped back to the States." Shaking her head, she said, "I had a good Army career. I had a good CIA career. But I want something for myself. I want to work for people who support, not take advantage. I want to work for a team."

Twisting her head, she smiled at the man on her

other side and accepted his arm around her shoulders as he pulled her in close.

"And when baby Blake arrives…"

She winked at her brother and said, "I'll be ready to show him who's the most kick-ass auntie around."

"Then welcome aboard to LSI," Mace said, a smile crossing his normally stoic face.

She shook his hand and then watched as he and her brother headed back down the stairs of the lighthouse to join the others gathered below. Looking over the water, she allowed herself a few minutes alone to let it sink in that she was finally back in the States for good.

Her last weeks in Cairo had been hectic. As soon as the boat had docked, Shakir's special police hauled away Giselle, Cora, Jason, and Khalil. She had no idea what their fate would be but could truthfully say she didn't care.

She'd said goodbye to Hop and Dolby, grateful for their assistance and now their friendship. She'd had a last night with Rick in her villa, filled with kisses and promises and all-night sex before waving goodbye to the three Keepers as they left Egypt. Then she'd gone into the embassy to talk to Tom. If he'd thought she wasn't serious when she'd said that had been her last assignment with the CIA, he didn't act surprised. Turning over all her open cases, she'd formally resigned and spent a couple of weeks getting ready to move back to the States.

She'd paid Sabah and Mustafa handsomely, pleased to discover that another embassy couple would be moving into her villa and wanted to keep them on staff.

She'd had no desire to engage in any more sightseeing, glad for what she'd been able to see and do in the beautiful country but ready to leave that part of her life behind.

Then she'd watched as her belongings were packed and spent one last night sitting in the lounge chair next to the jasmine in her garden oasis, sipping wine, memories flowing like the waters of the Nile through her mind.

And looking out the window of the plane, she'd peered down to say goodbye to the pyramids and watched as the green along the Nile faded into the beige of the desert. Then leaning back in her seat, she'd closed her eyes and dreamed of the next stage of her life. And smiled.

Rick held his niece in his arms, nuzzling her hair, his senses filled with her sweet scent. She looked up at him with a gummy grin, and he chuckled.

"Are you sure?"

Squeezing Eleanor a little tighter, he lifted his gaze toward his brother and nodded. "Yeah, I'm sure. I love being here with you, Helena, and Eleanor. I'm a kick-ass uncle and plan on continuing that role no matter where I am. But California calls, and I'm closing on a house soon there. It feels right for me to stick with that choice."

Rank lifted his gaze toward the top of the lighthouse and then turned back to Rick. His brother didn't have to say anything. Rick knew what was coming and answered the unasked question. "Sometimes, we have to make the decisions that work for us as individuals. And she understands. We have to do what's right for us."

Three weeks later, he laughed as Jeb, Bennett, Poole, and Dolby cheered as they played water polo in the backyard pool of the house he'd just closed on. The sellers needed a quick sale, and he was ready to put down his California roots. Having his first party there, he'd invited them all. Leo was on a lounge chair, grinning as Nat walked over and plopped down onto his lap. Carson manned the grill next to him with Rachel, Teddy, Chris, and Stella sitting at a nearby picnic table. Hop was next to Leo and Nat in a lounge, typing furiously on his phone.

"Who are you texting?" Nat asked, staring at Hop.

He looked up, his distracted expression darting around, piquing Rick's curiosity.

"Oh, just dealing with a situation that... that..." Hop's words fell away as he continued to text again.

Hearing the sliding door open behind him, Rick turned and grinned as Jeanie carried a platter of meat over to the grill, handing it to Carson. His gaze moved beyond her to land on Abbie walking out with a platter of vegetables. Hustling over, he took it from her, bending to kiss her. He kept the kiss light, but it was full of promise, something he could tell she understood as her eyes sparkled in return.

"Hey, Abbie," Nat called out. "Did you get the new images from Mace this morning?"

"Yeah, but I told him I'd look at them tomorrow since we were partying today." She laughed.

Nat offered a chin lift along with a grin, muttering, "Damn straight."

Carson looked over and said, "You can put that job ahead of the one I'd just given you yesterday. Mine isn't time sensitive."

Abbie acknowledged with a nod, and Rick could see her shoulders relax at their boss's easy decision. With Mace and Carson in a partnership, LSI and LSI-WC worked together and not in competition. That was why it was easy for Abbie to decide to move to California to be with Rick. It also worked in his favor that while Blake was in Maine, their parents were in California. So she worked for Carson and Mace, setting up her secure computer programs at LSI-WC. The model worked so well that Nat began using her logistics and analytics prowess for Mace as well.

"You guys have such a gorgeous house," Stella said as she moved to help set out more of the food before wrapping her arms around Chris's waist.

"Housing is expensive around here, but when we decided to move in together, it made sense to get the one we both liked," Rick said. He'd finally shown Abbie the house he was considering, and she'd loved it. And decided that waiting to move in together didn't make sense. They were glad the sale went through so quickly, and by the time she arrived last week, they could direct the movers straight to the new house.

Everyone soon plated the meal, and the tables were filled with Keepers and loved ones. Laughter and fun-filled jokes abounded, and Rick cast his gaze over the group of friends. He'd thought his SEAL buddies were the best team he'd ever worked with. And then, with Mace and the Maine Keepers, he knew he'd found a new career that suited him perfectly. But now, out here with LSI-WC and with Abbie at his side, he'd come home.

"I may need to leave early," Hop announced, his phone still in his hand. "There's flooding in my parents' hometown, and the Red Cross is calling for volunteers."

"Whatever you need," Carson replied.

Hop offered a chin lift as he moved to Rick and Abbie to offer his goodbyes. "I'll see you when I get back. Should just be gone a couple of days."

By the time the last of the Keepers had left for the evening, he was ready for time with just her. He stepped out onto the patio, his gaze landing on the beautiful woman swimming in their pool. Her long, dark hair was pulled back in a braid, the length floating behind her as her strong, sure strokes pushed her body through the water.

He walked to the edge and dove in, pushing to the surface near her. She laughed as she swiped the water from her face, then wrapped her arms around his neck. He pulled her close until her bikini-clad body was pressed tightly to his front and her legs wrapped around his waist.

Kissing her lightly, he nibbled and teased as he maneuvered them around the pool. "Happy, babe?"

"The answer to that question should be obvious, but I'll give it anyway. Yes… I'm deliriously happy. My days of living overseas are over. I'm working for the Keepers. Mace and Carson easily agreed for me to analyze images for both of them. We'll go back to Maine and visit William and Sara." She leaned forward and let her tongue trail along his lips before continuing. Just when he was about to take the kiss deeper, she separated and grinned. "But I get to live with the man I fell in love with. Since I got everything I could have wanted, I guess I should ask you the same question. Are you happy?"

"Abbie girl, I thought I had a good life. But being with you makes life truly worth living."

"Oh, good answer," she said, kissing him again.

They continued to make out in the pool until the urge to take her body was more than he could resist. With his arms securely around her, he climbed the steps of the pool and carried her inside their home to their bed. Just where they belonged.

Don't miss the next Keeper!
Find out what adventure awaits Hop!
Hop

Lighthouse Security Investigations West Coast

Carson

Leo

Rick

Hop

Hope City (romantic suspense series co-developed with Kris Michaels

Brock book 1

Sean book 2

Carter book 3

Brody book 4

Kyle book 5

Ryker book 6

Rory book 7

Killian book 8

Torin book 9

Blayze book 10

Griffin book 11

Saints Protection & Investigations

(an elite group, assigned to the cases no one else wants…or can solve)

Serial Love

Healing Love

Revealing Love

Seeing Love

Honor Love

Sacrifice Love

Protecting Love

Remember Love

Discover Love

Surviving Love

Celebrating Love

Searching Love

Follow the exciting spin-off series:

Alvarez Security (military romantic suspense)

Gabe

Tony

Vinny

Jobe

SEALs

Thin Ice (Sleeper SEAL)

SEAL Together (Silver SEAL)

Undercover Groom (Hot SEAL)

Also for a Hope City Crossover Novel / Hot SEAL…

A Forever Dad

Long Road Home

Military Romantic Suspense

Home to Stay (a Lighthouse Security Investigation crossover novel)

Home Port (an LSI West Coast crossover novel)

Letters From Home (military romance)

Class of Love

Freedom of Love

Bond of Love

The Love's Series (detectives)

Love's Taming

Love's Tempting

Love's Trusting

The Fairfield Series (small town detectives)

Emma's Home

Laurie's Time

Carol's Image

Fireworks Over Fairfield

Please take the time to leave a review of this book. Feel free to contact me, especially if you enjoyed my book. I love to hear from readers!

Facebook

Email

Website

ABOUT THE AUTHOR

I am an avid reader of romance novels, often joking that I cut my teeth on the historical romances. I have been reading and reviewing for years. In 2013, I finally gave into the characters in my head, screaming for their story to be told. From these musings, my first novel, Emma's Home, The Fairfield Series was born.

I was a high school counselor having worked in education for thirty years. I live in Virginia, having also lived in four states and two foreign countries. I have been married to a wonderfully patient man for forty-one years. When writing, my dog or one of my four cats can generally be found in the same room if not on my lap.

Please take the time to leave a review of this book. Feel free to contact me, especially if you enjoyed my book. I love to hear from readers!

Facebook
Email
Website